Wrestling the Bear

Wrestling the Bear

Short Stories

Jeanne Sirotkin

Stephen F. Austin State University Press
Nacogdoches ★ Texas

Book Design: Laura Davis
Cover Art: "Circus Bear" Susan Newman Friedman

LIBRARY OF CONGRESS IN PUBLICATION DATA
Sirotkin, Jeanne
Wrestling the Bear / Jeanne Sirotkin
ISBN: 978-1-62288-006-5

1. Title.

Manufactured in the United States of America

Stephen F. Austin State University Press
P.O. Box 13007 SFA Station
Nacogdoches, TX 75962
sfasu.edu/sfapress
sfapress@sfasu.edu

Distributed by Texas A&M University Consortium
www.tamupress.com Stephen F. Austin State University Press

Acknowledgments

Cimarron Review: "Wrestling the Bear"
Chattahoochee Review: "Ten Mile Road"
Northville Review: "Kill!! Sudoku!!!"

Contents

Wrestling the Bear 11

The Only Woman Visible 23

Motor City Caper 33

Kill!! Sudoku!!! 54

Renegade 56

Thomas Edison's Last Breath 65

Lot 23 71

Carnavale 81

Martini's Bar & Grill 88

Ten Mile Road 93

The Manual 103

Spikes O'Death 117

Fish hunting in Vermont 121

What You Don't Know 130

Weather 132

Feline Domesticus 140

I Slept with Monica Lewinsky 146

The Emperor of New York City 157

Leisure World 165

Thanks to my family, my friends, strangers and stray dogs and most of all to Michael, mi casa es tu casa, always.

Wrestling the Bear

Bert entered the Bear's Den, a bar on a main street in a small Detroit suburb. A stuffed yellowing polar bear sat in a glass box and greeted customers at the front door. Bert nodded to the bear then stopped and blinked. For a moment he thought the bear nodded back, but the bear's glassy eyes stayed focused straight ahead. It was almost spring but the air still felt Arctic.

The Friday night regulars perched on stools off to one side of the bar, doing shots with their beer.

"Hey, Bert's back!" Heads turned.

"Nice tan, my man."

Every winter, when construction work slowed, Bert drove his grandparents down to McAllen, Texas in the Rio Grande Valley. He helped them set up their winter camp, parking their Winnebago with several hundred other metal RVs in a circle like modern age covered wagons.

Bert drew himself up to his full height, all six foot four inches of solid muscle and walked towards the bar, adjusting his new stiff white Stetson. He felt Texan as he leaned on the countertop, placing a boot on the metal rail below it.

"Give me a Hair of the Bear," he said, ordering his favorite drink.

He was Butch Cassidy or Jesse James, living on the fringe. He liked being thought of as a primitive man living a survivalist life and cultivated that look with almost addictive workouts at the gym. Thirty years old, he was in his prime.

"Did ya get any of that fine Texas nookie?" Mikey grinned at him, flashing his gold tooth. The tooth attracted women, he told Bert, but it could only be seen when he grinned - which he did a lot.

"Naw, not this year," Bert replied. "Got me some mighty fine Mexican ass. I just learned to make love in Spanish," he drawled affecting a Texas accent, letting them think that he had broken hearts from north to south and back again. He unbuttoned the pearl button on his shirt cuff and rolled up his sleeve.

"Take a look at this souvenir." There, tattooed on his huge forearm, was a cactus with a giant rattler winding its way around it - fangs bared. This was as wild as his winter sojourn had gotten. He had drunk too much tequila and woke up as the needles were pricking away at his arm in a low brick building next to the bus station in Brownsville. The tattoo artist was a Mexican midget with long black hair held back in a ponytail who stood on a stool as he worked.

"Gringo, your girlfriend, she gonna love this," he said. "Takes real cojones to sit through this job. You doing great. Rodrigo's a great artist. Very famous. You tell her that."

Bert didn't tell Rodrigo that there was no girlfriend, that he steered clear of those kinds of entanglements. When he'd looked the midget in the eyes, he saw the beautiful gringa that the midget was imagining. Her small hand linked through Bert's beefy arm. Her fingers stroking the tattoo. Bert could even feel her warm salty breath. So he'd just nodded at the midget.

"Yeah, man. She'll love it," he'd said.

Now, he showed off the tattoo at The Bear's Den. Mikey flashed his gold tooth smile and the rest of the crew nodded in approval at the artwork.

"Must of really hurt," Molly, one of the young waitress, said as she reached out to touch it.

Bert pulled his arm back and shook his head, rolling down his sleeve. That's when someone handed him the flier. He almost tossed it, thinking it was just an ad for the circus. It had a drawing of a bear standing on two feet towering over some men in spandex. But in bold black the letters said: ***WANTED. WRESTLERS!!*** *$500 to the man who can pin Victor, the world champion wrestling bear. Call and register for your three minutes of fame. Saturday, March 22 at the Light Guard Armory Hunting and Fishing Show between 1-3:00 p.m. Hosted by the one! The only! Fabulous Hulk Hogan. No fee. Hurry, number of entrants limited!*

The Hunting and Fishing Show was an event he knew well. It was one of the formal father and son outings he'd participated in years ago. It was an annual event, along with the annual Let's Try Bonding Hunting Trip up north. Both activities relieved his father from having to make eye contact.

His father, Ralph, had remarried so many times that Bert confused the wives – Vivian, Jane and Suzanne, maybe others. They were as blurry to him as they seemed to be to his father. Here one day and gone the next. Bert and his father preferred to pretend that the women didn't exist. He doubted that his father knew or cared that Bert had never married. It pleased his father that Bert took care of himself, held a steady job, and could dead lift 600 pounds.

They'd go out hunting each November, opening day of the season, an almost holiday in Michigan. Classrooms emptied and thousands of men phoned in sick. The last time they went was years ago. Bert and his father had loaded the pickup and headed north on I-75 with Bert in charge of navigating. They arrived just before daybreak. That year there was no snow for tracking. The frost made it hard to walk quietly through the woods. No matter how carefully they'd tried to step, each footfall sounded like bones crunching. They headed for a blind that Ralph had set up the week before and crouched in it waiting, eyes fixed on the brush and on the horizon. "Remember, don't drop your shoulder when you shoot," his father reminded him, feeling like he was fulfilling his role as a proper parent. They leaned back on an old mattress. A pocket of air remained thick between the two men as they crouched in the blind without touching. Nothing was required of Bert. Just squeeze the trigger at the correct time. Except that day Bert peeked into his father's eyes for the first and only time, and was almost swept away. The sadness felt heavier than any of the weights he'd ever lifted. It sucked at him until he shook his head and closed his eyes.

Bert tucked the flier in his pocket. The bar was steaming up. The only window in the place, up front, was completely fogged over. The band, "The Wailing Borrachos" played an extra loud raunchy Southwest Detroit Boogie Beat. Dancers crammed the small square that passed as a dance floor. Lucinda, one of the regular Friday night crew, tried to get him to dance.

"C'mon Bert. It's a rockin' Friday night and it'll be gone before you know it!" She tugged at his arm. "What are you waiting for, come on!"

He didn't feel like it. That's what he was waiting for, to feel like it. To feel something. "Naw," he said sitting tight on the barstool. "Just got into town and I'm sort of out of it. You know what I mean. Maybe later, honey."

At closing time, she was waiting for him, sweaty from dancing and looking for a walk home or something more. She lived in the neighborhood, around the block from Bert's apartment. Once a year they'd get together – her tiny frame and his bulky mass made for a strange coupling.

Bert could smell her desire. He knew all he had to do was reach out and pull her to his chest. The veins in his temples ached. His hands felt thick. He couldn't make the leap from desire to action, from want to connection.

"Lucinda, darlin'," he said. "Tonight's not the night. You look so great, I wish it were but it's just not." He nuzzled her and then bit, a little too hard, on the back of her neck.

She punched him and rubbed at her neck. "Geez, hope you didn't leave marks. Just for that, you've got to walk me home."

They walked to her bungalow but he went home to sleep alone. As he lay in his bed, he imagined a whole troupe of dancing bears stomping from foot to foot. The bears were singing with deep growling voices. He couldn't make out any of the words. They moved in unison. One, two, three, Stomp. One, two three. He could feel the bed shaking with the rhythm of their feet.

The next morning, he woke around noon and phoned the number on the flyer.

"Jones and Jones Entertainment" a voice barked.

I want to register to wrestle the bear," Bert said.

"We can squeeze you in and I do mean squeeze, har-har-har," Jones and Jones chortled. "First I need the basics – name, rank, serial number and next of kin."

Before Bert could respond the voice went on.

"Har-har-har. Just kidding. How's about we get your name, height and weight for starters. And let me tell ya a bit about Victor the bear, in case ya wanna change your mind. This here's a Kowabunga Grizzly. He's a monster of a bear. Maybe 700, maybe 800 pounds. Solid. This is one of those, you know, ultimate challenge things. Any repairs or medical bills are yours too. Jones and Jones don't bear no responsibility, get it?" Jones and Jones cackled away on the other end of the receiver.

"All I've got to do is pin this critter, right?" Bert asked.

"That's it – a three count. No holds barred."

Bert pictured himself lifting the massive body for a take down. The biggest one of his life. He could hear the thud and imagine himself riding on top of something resembling a dusty rug.

"Alright, sign me up. I'll put on a good show. Bert Jenkins. 6 feet 4 inches, 275 pounds." He flexed his muscles as he talked on, exaggerating his expertise. "I've wrestled alligators and wild boars. A Kowabunga Grizzly shouldn't give me a hard time. And I get to meet Hulk Hogan, right?"

Years ago he'd gone to the Pontiac Silverdome to see Hogan wrestle Andre the Giant in front of 93,000 manic fans. Hogan, the much smaller wrestler, body slammed the 7 foot 4 inch 500 pound giant and the stadium went berserk. It was just before his parents' divorce. It had been good to escape their house, which had felt electrified. He'd yelled so loudly that night cheering the Hulkster that he'd lost his voice. He remembered losing it for the rest of that year. But maybe no one else had noticed that he didn't speak. His voice was changing at the time and it felt good to just let it be, give it a rest. He took up wrestling and weightlifting shortly afterwards.

"Yeah, yeah, sure. No problem. You can meet the Hulkster. In fact, if ya pin the bear we'll have Hogan deliver pizza to your house. Right to your door."

"OK. I'm on board then. What else do you need? Do I need to bring anything with me?"

Jones and Jones snorted. "Ya might wanna bring along your Last Will and Testament, and a designated driver. He can double as the designated mourner if Victor goes on a rampage. Just be at Entrance C of the Armory by 12:30. Free admission, too."

He decided to stop by his mom's place as the day warmed up. She was a hairdresser who once worked at Antoine's Style Salon on Woodward Avenue trying to save enough money to open her own shop. She had established a cult following of suburban women with hair emergencies but had never managed to save enough to open her own business.

Then a couple of years ago, a customer, Mrs. Fitzgerald had rescued Betty from the endless supply of matrons in crisis. She was the wife of William Fitzgerald, who owned and operated a line of funeral parlors, and Betty's new customers became silent patrons of her art. Mr. Fitzgerald would hand her a picture of the deceased and Betty would replicate the hairstyle on the corpse. She traveled from parlor to parlor throughout the metropolitan area whenever her services were needed. It left her with plenty of time for crossword puzzles, soap operas, and WWF wrestling on TV.

Bert drove into the Flamingo Trailer Court. A dozen flamingos that once were pink but now were a faded gray lined the drive. They leaned every which way, in odd directions, like a disheveled hairdo. Betty's home was along the back row. Bert drove slowly, trying to decide whether or not to tell her about the bear. His mother was a true wrestling fan. It transformed her into a dragon lady, into a wild screaming banshee. At one of his high school meets, she had attacked another mom who she had overheard criticizing Bert's wrestling style. She had to be pulled off the woman by two strong men in the audience and carried outside, cursing all the while. Bert remembered feeling trapped somewhere midway between amusement and embarrassment. Betty was banned for the rest of that year from attending meets.

Bert should have been a state champion his senior year. He'd had a perfect record going into that last meet of the regular season. Then he'd lost his first match. The hair on the back of his neck had stood up when he realized that the ref had intentionally made the bad calls that caused him to lose. An ever so slight leer appeared in the ref's face as he raised Bert's opponent's arm in victory. Bert walked out of the gym and into the hall. He punched the first thing he saw - the door, with its window of glass and embedded mesh. It ripped his hand, just missing the tendons but tearing it up badly. So ended his high school career.

He opened and closed his hand, thinking of it. Then he squeezed his hand and made a tight fist as he walked up the dusty path to his mom's mobile home, kicking up little clouds of dirt. He released it to pick up the crushed cigarette packages that were tossed all about.

Betty answered the door with an unlit cigarette dangling from her lips. Her platinum hair was highlighted with a cranberry tinge. The color changed from week to week. Blue and cranberry were her favorites. Bert was relieved that today was a cranberry day. He could handle that color. The occasional lime green days made her appear ghoulish. And made him slightly seasick.

"Bert, baby, how are you?" She stood on tiptoes, removing the cigarette to kiss him, as he bent down. She planted a red lipstick mark on his cheek, which he rubbed at, smearing it like blood across his face. "You look good, sweetie. Welcome back home. Aren't you early this year?"

"Norman called down to grandpa's. He's got work for me starting next week, so here I am. Money was getting tight anyway. Time to be back home, I figured. You been OK?"

"Lots of work on the dead heads. Kept me out of trouble. Been real quiet around here this winter otherwise. C'mon on in – don't stand out there like some stranger."

"Listen Ma. I can't stay today. But I wanted to tell you something." Bert thought for a moment. "I'm going to wrestle again, two weeks from today. At the Light Guard Amory." He could see that her face looked puzzled. "It's the Hunting and Fishing Show and I'm going to wrestle Victor the Bear." He waited for a response. Her face, which had hardly aged except for a few fine lines around her eyes and mouth, took on the same tone as her hair.

"Bertie! Honey. You can't wrestle a bear. You're teasing me, aren't you."

She stepped past him, outside for a smoke. The little bit of wind blew her flimsy bathrobe, flapping it against her body, which looked wispy and frail standing next to Bert. Betty cupped her hands around the cigarette to light it. She crossed her arms over her chest, and blew smoke up into the air. It hovered over her head like a nuclear cloud.

"No, Ma, I'm not. You can watch if you like. On the twenty-second, sometime between one and three, at the show. Hulk Hogan is the referee. You like him, right?"

He felt her softening, the smoke settling around her head. She took another puff, then smiled.

"O.K. Sweetie pie – if Hogan's there I wouldn't miss it for the world. What a man! And my darlin' son wrestling too! Just so's you know, I think you're crazy, wrestling a bear. What's this world coming to anyway? Next thing you know, it'll be alligators." She tossed the partially smoked cigarette into the yard and ground it into the dirt with the heel of her brocade slipper. "Just remember, you didn't get the crazies from me. That's your daddy's fault." She gave his arm a squeeze. "Lord, feel those biceps. You did get those big strong muscles from me, don't forget that!"

Bert gave her a peck on the top of her head and made a quick exit to spare himself any rant about his father. He knew that if she got started, he'd never get her to stop. She'd spin her tires, which had gone bald long ago, with that old speech about what a cold fish his father had been. Bert knew when to exit.

During the next two weeks, Bert increased his gym time and, with construction work starting, he was pumped up. He cut and pinned photos of bears to his bedroom walls and to the ceiling so it would be the last thing he saw as he fell asleep. He taped a photo of a large grizzly standing on its back legs with its mouth opened to the bathroom mirror. A huge solitary creature. Hibernating in winter. Mating in spring. It watched him shave every morning. He stared it down.

On the morning of the meet, Randall, a carpenter on Bert's crew pulled up in his blue Dodge pickup alongside Bert's apartment. He was a pimply-faced kid with oily blond hair partway down his back who had volunteered to chaperone the expedition, to be the corner man.

"Look what I got, Bert!" Randall said as Bert climbed into the truck. "I fixed me up a real repair kit." He leaned over the seat and hoisted a beat-up brown leather bag into the front seat between them. "Got me tape and gauze. A sling and bandages. Some of them butterfly strips to hold you together. And I got some smelling salts too. Found 'em in my ma's medicine cabinet. Think they'll work, though' they might be older than Granny Jones. If you don't need this stuff, maybe the bear will!"

Randall bounced around on his seat as he drove, his eyes popping. He lit up a cigarette.

"Hey! Mind waiting on that?" Bert rolled down a window. "I'm gonna need my lungs working on all cylinders today."

"Sorry man. No problem. You call the shots today. You the man. Yessir. I'm working for you today. I'm right here. Woo! Woo! One squeeze from you and that old hairball's gonna make for the north woods. You'll be rich and famous. On all those talk shows. The he-man who beat the bear." He stubbed out his cigarette in the dirty ashtray.

Bert stared out the window after rolling it part way back up. He opened and closed his hand, which throbbed in the peculiar way it always did when he thought about wrestling. He clenched it and the throbbing traveled up his arm, squeezing at his chest.

The truck jiggled and skidded its way down Baseline Road, jumping sideways as it hit numerous potholes. Road repairs were either a non-priority issue or else the potholes formed at such a speed that the crews could not keep up. Bert wistfully thought of the miles and miles of smooth Texas blacktop he drove across each winter. Spring back home was the worst time for the roads. He expected, one day, a pothole to yawn open and devour him, leaving no trace. Anything seemed possible.

Above the emptiness of the potholes, dozens of billboards shouted messages:

Stay on the right track, to Nine Mile and Mack. Invest in Your Future. Phone 1-800-I Sue Big for big results. God is Watching You. Talk Line – Connect with Sexy Women. Merry Maids to Clean your home.

The final message was some graffiti scrawled on an overpass as Baseline Road dipped below one of the octopus arms of the Detroit freeway system. The blue pickup slipped under the overpass in slow motion; at least that's how it seemed to Bert. The words painted on the overpass read *walk backwards.*

"What the hell's that supposed to mean?" Bert thought, as they approached the LightGuard Armory. "Maybe it's the name of a local garage band. Walk backwards – what for? From where?"

Randall swung the truck into a space in the crowded lot. They spotted

Entrance C and walked towards it. A security guard sat in front of the entryway, armed with a box of donuts and coffee. "Can I help you?" he asked.

"The bear, we're here to wrestle the bear," Bert replied.

The guard grinned. "Sure thing, mister. You look like one of those crazy guys. Big enough anyway. Right that way." He pointed with his thumb down a dingy hall. The hallway mixed the smell of popcorn with ammonia and sawdust. It led behind the grandstand and out into the center of the arena where a stage had been set up. The rest of the Armory was divided down the middle. Fishing gear on the right, and Hunting supplies on the left. A strip of food concessions ringed it all.

Bert and Randall walked up to a man in an ill-fitting grey suit, possibly Jones and Jones, who held a clipboard.

"Bert Jenkins." He reached out with one of his big paws to shake hands. Jones and Jones pushed the clipboard at him.

"You're number three on the card. Final bout. Just sign this here waiver so's the front office knows you're a volunteer. Like that I didn't hold no gun to your head and make you do this." Jones and Jones was a short, scrawny man with a neck like a chicken. "If you like, why don't ya watch the action from out front? I'll let ya know when you're up. Victor should have a good warm-up with the first two wrestlers. Just don't go flying the coop on me if it gets too wild," he said, scribbling some note to himself as he talked.

Bert and Randall stood in the back of the crowd, which let out a cheer as Victor, a massive brown bear with a slight hump on his back, lumbered onto the stage. He wore a loose muzzle which allowed him to open his mouth part way and appeared to lack front claws. He walked out on all fours, then stood up. And up. Maybe seven feet up, maybe eight. The crowd went whooped and hollered. Victor seemed unfazed.

Hulk Hogan, dressed in gold spandex, walked over to the mic. His oiled pecs reflected the lights pointing from the exposed rafters above towards the stage. Hogan was almost as broad as the bear.

"All you wrestlin' fans, turn your eyes this way! In the far corner is the undefeated champion of the world – Victor the Bear! Four-footed and undefeeeeted!" He turned towards a nervous squat man in blue wrestling tights who puffed and blew out his cheeks as he waved his arms over his head. "And in this corner the first challenger of the day – Matt Newman. Down and dirty in Motown! Let the blood battle begin!" He stepped aside as the challenger charged into the ring.

Bert studied the bear as the barrel-chested wrestler attacked it. Victor stood up on two feet and looked offstage wistfully. He looked bored as the first challenger streaked at him and grabbed an arm. The wrestler clung to Victor and tried to kick out one of the bear's legs for a takedown. Sweat poured down his body as he flailed about. Victor didn't budge. Finally, tired of the event, the bear swung his arm and whacked the wrestler sending him flying off the stage. And out of action. The crowd hooted and jeered. The work crew tossed pieces of raw chicken to the bear to placate him during the short break between bouts.

"Ladies and Gentlemen," the Hulkster's voice boomed over the speakers. "The next challenger, from Paw Paw, Michigan!! Thom Brown is here, ready to rumble. Let's hear it for Mister Brown. This action is going to be fast and furious. Man vs. beast. No holds barred!!"

Thom Brown jumped into the ring and danced from foot to foot. He shook his shoulders to loosen up as he danced. Victor watched him and shifted his weight ever so slightly, foot to foot, trying to match Brown's footwork. Bert thought he saw the bear grin. Maybe just a little bit of a smile. Brown was quite tall and must have thought that would give him leverage. He went at Victor lowering a shoulder. Nothing budged. Brown lost his footing on the ground, which was slippery from the raw chicken. As he fell, he grabbed at the bear. The match ended as Victor, obviously trained in the art of wrestling, pinned Brown with one arm – releasing him on the count of three and dancing around the stage to the delight of the crowd. "Victor, Victor!" They chanted as the bear paced back and forth.

Jones and Jones scurried up to the stage and handed the Hulkster a brown paper bag. He kept a wary distance between himself and Victor. Hogan extracted a two-liter bottle of Coke from the bag and handed it to the bear. Victor clasped it between his paws and lifted it to his lips. The muzzle was fitted loose enough to allow him to drink. He chugged the entire bottle with his head thrown back. When he finished, he tossed the bottle and licked his lips with a thick, black tongue. He shuffled, restlessly, from foot to foot and Bert again glimpsed what he thought was a smile.

Once again, the Hulkster approached the mic, pitching the show.

"Give me a roar!" And the crowd responded. Hogan strode back and forth across the stage, posing and flexing his muscles, which stood out on his body like a relief map. The crowd encouraged him and he pumped both arms over his head.

"Now it's time for our finale - the match of the century," he bellowed. "Victor the wild bear dragged to the Midwest from Montana is ready to take on friend or foe. And our challenger, from Berkley, Michigan, Wild Bert Jenkins, the King of Alligator Wrestling!"

Bert removed his warm-ups and handed them to Randall. He saw the gold flash of Mikey's tooth and heard the voices of the Friday night bar crew cheering as he moved toward the stage. He stepped onto the platform as the crowd whooped it up.

If I could get my arms around him, maybe he'll lean over and I can take him off balance, he thought. As he approached the bear, Victor smiled. This time Bert was sure of it. And Victor's breath smelled like a dog's. Just like the drooly old yellow lab he had grown up with. Bert rested his head against Victor's chest and put his arms around him. "Good boy," he said softly, patting the bear's back. The fur felt like swamp grass.

Then he lifted. Only the bear's skin moved, sliding loosely over muscle. He could hear the bear's heart and smell his musty breath. An odd sensation overcame him. He felt himself inside the bear's skin. He felt the bear's skin slide over his own bones; he felt the heartbeat and the pulse. The weight of the heavy body. The sensation of claws. For a moment Bert was roaming the mountains, foraging, scanning the lay of the land. He felt a cool rain run off the hollow reeds of his pelt. He looked out through beady black eyes and knew he wasn't alone. The nostrils of his nose opened and closed, sorting the smells. The rain, a raccoon, deer, pine trees, a marsh. He belonged here. His ears twitched and swiveled from side to side. Bert focused. He squeezed and lifted one more time. Nothing moved except the bearskin. A voice in Bert's head said "walk backwards" and he did. The bear followed him. Bert looked him straight in the eye and got down on all fours, feeling the weight of the fur still draped over him. Victor followed as if hypnotized, dropping to the ground. Bert recalled one of his favorite moves from competition, a pull through, and he ever so slowly reached out towards Victor. Victor eyed him curiously as Bert quickly pulled the bear's arm under his belly, which lowered one of the massive shoulders. Victor rolled over, finishing the motion for him, and Bert rubbed his belly as the bear lay there on his back, both shoulders down while Hogan hollered: "And a ONE, And a TWO, And a TWO AND A HALF..." a long pause before "And a THREEEEEE." Hogan's face was red and Mr. Jones and Jones looked anything but pleased.

Bert turned and looked at the crowd. He spotted a middle-aged woman with green tinted hair. Betty moved towards the stage as Bert sprang off of it and grabbed her. He wrapped his arms around her tightly and gave her a hug. A squeeze that made her catch her breath. Randall thumped him on the back. He hugged Randall. The crowd chanted "Bert beat the bear! Bert beat the bear!" Bert moved through the crowd, hugging them all, man and woman, friends and strangers, lifting them off their feet and pulling them to his chest.

The Only Woman Visible

I hand Manny a glass of chocolate egg cream. Just like I always do every afternoon precisely at 1:00. He takes a gulp of the seltzer water, thickened with chocolate syrup, and belches.

"You trying to give me a heart attack, Edie!" he roars. "Or maybe cancer? I think cancer. I got it already. I feel it, right there" He jabs at his rotund midsection.

I take the glass from him and put it down on the TV tray next to his comfy chair. "Manny, the doctors say there's nothing..."

"Doctors! Whatta they know? Quacks, Charlatans! The whole lot of 'em. I know what I know."

The last doctor had called us into his office and asked us to sit across the mahogany desk from him. He shuffled papers, cleared his throat several times then peered out at Manny over the top of his reading glasses. "Mr. Snyder," he said. "Your orbits are out of whack. They need realignment." He gave him some pills. Sugar, I bet. Manny took *those* pills, orbits out of whack sounded just right to him, but once the pills were gone he felt a lump somewhere else inside him, growing. "Heavy like a bowling ball," he said. "I want a new doc. No more wasting money on fakers and phonies."

I've always been frugal. I minded the store once Jeffrey, our only child, became old enough to go to school. I've got my routines, thirty-two years worth. In our apartment on the second floor, above the store, there's a giant plastic Hennessy display bottle next to the front door. We put pennies and spare change in it whenever we go in or out. It took fourteen years to fill the first time. In the old days, Manny would leave the apartment without coaxing. We saved enough for a Florida vacation where I stayed on the beach each day until dark. I thought that the sun might burn everything away; that

I'd peel like a lizard, sprout wings and fly away. Manny never liked the sun, so he stayed indoors. Now that bottle sits, half full. Or half empty. Some days I see it one way, some days the other. No one deposits coins.

Our last regular night at home, ten years ago, felt normal for us. Jeffrey had just graduated from college. A package arrived with his admittance slip to the School of Optometry. Manny couldn't bear it. He constantly lambasted educated folks and professionals, reminding us all that he is a "self made" man.

"You think you're hot stuff now mister, right? Better than your old man."

"Dad, cut it out. Come on, Dad. I'm not a kid."

"Shuddup your mouth when I talk, Mr. Know-it-All." He grabbed Jeffrey's arm with his paw and squeezed until Jeffrey jerked it away.

"I'm out of here. I don't have to take this crap anymore. You won't see me again. I mean it."

I averted my eyes, pursed my lips and headed into the kitchen. I banged the pots and pans around. It was raining that night. The sound of the pots and the tattooing of the rain on the kitchen window drowned out their angry voices. Jeffrey left, slamming the front door. I heard that.

Early in the morning the phone rang. Manny answered. He turned to me. His face melted. It dripped down one shoulder. Puddled and then stuck forever around his waist. He held the phone out to me, pushed it away. It hissed. Static. Buzzed. Wings beating like a black crow flying over our roof or an owl in the daylight. I did not want to hear it. Our only child dead in a car accident on the Williamsburg Bridge. Something deep inside shriveled up.

It was that bridge that started all this. Manny refused to cross another bridge after the call.

"Brooklyn's good enough for me. Whatta I need to go over there for?" he said not long after the funeral. A year or two later it became the apartment; he wouldn't cross the threshold. Soon he couldn't tolerate the closing of doors. He took the bedroom and the bathroom doors off their hinges. I can only coax him out of the apartment for doctor visits. They give him pills. He spits out most of them. Especially when he's told they're for his mind. Mental pills, he calls them. "Nothing's wrong up there," he claims, jabbing a fat finger against his forehead. "I got the cancer hiding, somewhere. I feel it growing."

Every morning dressed in a white V-neck T-shirt and boxer shorts, grey hairs sprouting from his chest, he shuffles to his old recliner, his comfy chair, pulling a red threadbare robe around his fleshy white body. He tugs at the ends that don't quite meet. The recliner is threadbare too. The green cloth has worn to shiny silver where he rests his immobile body. When he stands up, a ghostly image of him remains on the seat.

And the socks. He always wears socks, even to bed. "It's because of the cancer," he says. "My feet are always cold." So I turn up the heat until our windows sweat, but it's useless.

I leave the egg cream on the TV tray, knowing that he'll drink it sooner or later. He turns the television up to blot out other sounds. Our upstairs neighbor, Mr. Mayo, pounds on the floor. "Pipe down," he hollers. He can't get too angry though, because we let him buy from our store on credit. I leave the apartment tiptoeing on bare feet, careful to close the door silently. Even the click of the knob disturbs Manny. I climb to the roof to water the couple of scraggly tomato plants that I grow on the sunny blacktop where I hang my wash to dry. A plastic lawn chair sits underneath the clothesline. This is my refuge. I come up and hang clothes. I hide things up here, away from Manny's prying eyes.

I place my feet on the black tar edge of the roof. Carefully. The little toes grasping on, hunched over like old men saying their prayers. I study my feet. They aren't a matched pair. They look like they belong to two different people. A mother and child perhaps. Two strangers meeting, while out for a walk.

My feet are not my feet. Once they were hooves and galloped across a dry earth path, a cloud of dust billowing in their wake. Once they were webbed and paddled the seven seas. Once I had claws instead of toes.

I hold a small book with a broken clasp. An old schoolgirl's journal. Blue plastic with white cursive letters that say *"My Diary"*. I am slowly tearing out the pages, like the pages of a calendar reversing time. A day or two of memories at a time.

"Eeenie-meenie minee-mo," I chant. "My-mother-told-me-to choose-the-very best-one and you-are-not-it." I open to a page and tear it out.

Dear Diary, the next page begins and I read on. *My sisters don't understand. Well, I'm not surprised. They were always wanted. But I'm the last of seven. My mother, speaking in Russian and Yiddish, walked the neighborhood knocking on doors, trying to find the woman she'd heard about - the one with medicine to get rid of babies. Some concoction she brewed on a kitchen stove. My pregnant mother couldn't bear the thought of me coming into this world. Especially not after losing her only boy, three years old, to the fever. She tells me this. Again and again. I think she supposes it makes me feel special. Like someone chosen. Meant to walk on this earth. Unlike the other baby. He had a name, but nobody ever says it. I will tell you his name, Martin. It's as if he'd never even been born. She didn't want me, but the woman couldn't be found so she had no choice. I want to grow up to be wanted.*

I lean over the roof and peer at the ground. There's a small patch of earth between the sidewalk and the apartment building. I grip the edge of the roof with my toes and let the page fall. It falls to the spot of dirt between the sidewalk and the door. I imagine it growing roots and sprouting, becoming a twisted tree, gnarled branches rising from the little plot of ground. Another page, a blank one, I bunch up tightly in my fist. It flutters, performs a dance and flies off. I don't see it touch down.

"Edie!" Manny shouts. "The TV Guide, Edie!" And then a pause, "God damn it, woman! Right now!" His voice is loud and strong, drifting up from two floors below. I close the rooftop door and latch it in place as I back down the narrow stairwell, careful of my bare feet. The stairwell is dark until I reach the third floor, where I'm hoping that Mr. Mayo isn't at home. I tiptoe past his door.

In the apartment, Manny sits in front of the ancient black and white screen, agitated. "My feet hurt," he complains. "Maybe they're gonna give out on me. Rub 'em, sweetie. Make me feel better. Such pain, you wouldn't believe." He waves his feet at me like giant hands covered by mittens. The TV Guide is sitting just beyond his reach, upside down on the sofa where he tossed it last night as he lumbered to bed. I tuck it next to his huge body, inside the arm of his chair, and then I pull a footstool across the floral carpet, placing it next to him. I sit and stroke his feet until he falls asleep. His head drops to his chest, propped up by his extra chins. His mouth opens and I hear heavy breathing. A snort, a shiver, a puff, and repeat. When a bit of drool forms at the corner of his mouth I know it's safe to leave.

I take *My Diary* into the kitchen and I drag a wooden kitchen chair across the linoleum. A leg catches where one of the yellowed squares of tile is missing a corner. I give the chair a shove and stop to sit on it beside the small white stove. I light a match and hold it to the front burner. The gas catches and flickers of orange and blue prance like little demons teasing and taunting me. Just for a moment I turn the plastic knob low enough for the flame to go out. The smell of the gas makes me nauseous. I don't remember when I've eaten last. Too busy fixing Manny his meals. Opening and closing the store each day. Balancing the books. The smell causes my head to whirl. I think of Mr. Mayo up above and lose my nerve.

And then there's Manny, the gigantic Mt. Manny, needing this and that. What if I were to go and leave him here alone? So, first things first. I turn off the gas and wait a moment for it to disperse. Then I relight the burner and open the diary. Each page must be accounted for, before I can move on and do what must be done.

He kissed me in the Tunnel O'Love. And I let him touch my breasts. Let him run his hot sweaty fingers over them. "Edie," he moaned, his lips on my neck. Good thing that ride didn't last longer! I don't know what I would have let him do! I won't tell my sisters. They're prissy prudes. It was a perfectly lovely night at Coney Island. The boardwalk was so crowded that I didn't see anyone else from Bensonhurst. I let Manny buy me cotton candy. Blue spun sugar clotting my mouth and lips, and my hands all sticky, too. Between that and the hot dog from Nathan's, I almost puked on the Cyclone. The way that coaster drops so steep and rattles on the wooden tracks and jerks your head to and fro, I didn't know which way was up when I got off. My legs were flopping. Me, staggering like an old drunk. Good thing I didn't puke! I don't get many dates these days with most of the men off to war. Puking might have wrecked my prospects. Manny was let go early; honorable discharge, he says, his back acting up like nobody's business. Cramps and pains. He's got papers to prove it. My sisters don't believe him. I told them I won't be an old maid. Manny could be my only chance! War or no war. I'll give up nylons but I'll not give up on marrying. They should keep their advice to themselves. My sisters glare at Manny as if he were a thief, a robber, a butcher or some rag picker each time he walks into our apartment to call. But I know that Manny really truly wants me.

I hold the page with kitchen tongs and watch it burn, trying to make out the last few words before it becomes ash. The ash floats down onto the linoleum floor that I scrub and scrub but it never shines. The finish has worn off. I hear the ocean far away at Coney Island and taste salt in my mouth. Salt and sweet and something bitter. I tear out another page and burn the young foolish woman. Page after page, I'm so tired of reading them. Tired of tossing them off the rooftop like a ticker tape parade in Manhattan, watching them vanish piece by piece. I tear out a fistful and cremate my past. The pages of the book that recorded my life, my only life, before my marriage to Manny.

I hear "Told you so, told you so," like a jump rope chant in the schoolyard. I see my sisters' faces cocked to one side, heads shaking. "Tsk-tsk," they tell me in unison. For a moment I think they're here and I stand up straight, smooth my apron and re-pin my hair at the temples where it's just begun to gray. My hands don't recognize the body they touch. The tricks that gravity is playing on my belly and my breasts. I look around the kitchen.

The clock on the wall stares at me with its turquoise plastic face. Its fingers jump like someone with one of those twitching diseases, one of those street people herking and jerking as they talk to themselves. "Saved and damned," they say with their heads shaking and arms waving. "Saved and damned." The clock reminds me it's time to go down to the store. I stuff the plastic cover, all that's left of the diary, into the trash. The young girl that was me is gone and I'm free to move on.

Dewayne is behind the cash register. He shoves a magazine under the counter as I enter. I pretend not to notice. Help isn't easy to find. Reliable help. Dewayne is young and strong and doesn't miss work. He likes this part of Brooklyn. No gangs shaking him down. Only one patrol officer who requires a cup of coffee and a piece of the apple strudel I bake each Thursday. It amuses me that Manny has no idea who works for us. It's probably just as well that he never goes downstairs. He'd take one look at Dewayne and shoot him, mistaking him for a burglar. Which is how he sees all young black men.

"Hey, Miz Edie, how's it goin'?" Dewayne greets me. "Been a slow one here. Except for that Arlene from across the street; she gone coco loco. She come in here and buy every one of them girlie magazines you got. Every one. She say she gonna make herself a bonfire and toast marshmallows with them. Hell fire and brimstone talk - all of that. I bet! More like she's a lezzie and don't want to say. Hiding in the closet. Was a slow day 'til that. Now we're sittin' pretty." He pats the cash register. I want to ask him if it's a girlie magazine he's got tucked in his lap, but I bite my tongue.

The wooden floorboards creak as I walk across the store and behind the counter to take over. I like that the boards make noise. That makes it hard for even the littlest thief to sneak around palming candy bars. The boards seem loudest when someone tries to tiptoe, as if they're calling out for us to pay attention. I meant to get some brighter lights put in here too, some of those newer fluorescent ones. Too late now. The dim light and the worn dark wood floor make the store look like a movie set or a historical museum. Tom Sawyer and Becky Thatcher could walk in the door any moment, bare footed and wearing straw hats, and ask for penny candy.

I do have a big glass jar of nickel candies on the counter. Gum. Jawbreakers. Lollipops. For kids, whether or not they've got their nickels, as long as they aren't thieving. This is a new policy, implemented since Manny retired. 'Nothing for free' was his motto. Extending credit meant collecting interest, money making money. I've been able to manage just fine without it. In fact, I tell Manny that I *am* collecting interest because I like that word, 'interest'. I'm 'interested' in what my customers do with their lives, what they buy and what it might mean. Mylanta or aspirin. Ramen noodles or a bottle of wine. I'm 'interested' when they tell me what their husbands, wives, children, bosses, landlords, bus drivers did or said. I'm 'interested' in their shoes, their make-up, their piercings, or tattoos or necklaces or rings.

I have an hour before closing and send Dewayne home. It's time for the last call at Edie's Grocery Store. While I wait for latecomers, I take a basket and load it with items I need upstairs.

The screen door slams as I place a red and black cardboard box of E-Rat-icate in my basket. A skull and crossbones warning posted the box top. I look up at the young woman standing there. A familiar face. Her soft wavy brown hair falls to her shoulders, poofed a little on top, pinned back on one side with a barrette. She's wearing a cotton housedress belted at the waist and a her sweater is fastened with tiny pearl buttons that look like baby teeth. On her feet are saddle shoes and bobby socks. There's a look of puzzlement on her face. She puts one hand up in front of her mouth, covering her cupid red lips. Her nails are painted the same color as the lipstick. Neither of us moves. My heart is exploding in my chest. She turns and floats out the door without opening it. Wait, I want to call, but don't, and then she's gone. I understand. I know that she's come to hurry me on. The diary is gone. Ashes to ashes.

Upstairs, Mt. Manny is erupting. Belching. Gurgling. "Hunger, Edie. I got hunger. I need supper now! Maybe it's my last supper. You never know. Everything on the news is bad. Stock market's falling. They got schmucks running the world. Idiots who don't know nothing about nothing."

Until death do us part, I remind myself as I prepare dinner. No spices. Meat and potatoes. Comfort food that never delivers its promise. I unload the basket. Dry goods in the pantry. Eggs in the fridge. The red and black box goes below the sink with the emergency supplies - a plunger, a rusted pipe wrench, steel wool and Drano. I touch my lips like the young girl in the store did. I cover my mouth as I exhale forcibly, so my soul can't escape. I press my hot palm against my mouth. I need my soul a bit longer. When my parents died we covered all the mirrors in the house so their souls would not be trapped inside the glass, so they could rise and float away and leave this world behind at the proper time.

That night the girl comes again and stands next to my bed, watching me. Quietly. Manny and I have had twin beds since Jeffrey died. Manny says he's afraid to sleep in the same bed with me anymore, what with all his tossing and turning, his legs kicking and thrashing about. He says he might roll over one night and suffocate me or break my tiny bones. It's for my own good, he tells me, to sleep alone.

The young woman opens a pocketbook, takes out a handful of subway tokens, and places them on the nightstand between the two beds. She arches one eyebrow as she bobs her head. Up and down like one of those plastic dolls. Side to side and up and down. Her head bobs, looking this way and then that. She takes it all in. Her long slender neck has a gold necklace around it. Inside the ivory heart shaped locket, I know, is a tiny scroll with the Ten Commandments written on it. Her head continues to bob until I sit up in bed. I look through her in the dim glow of the nightlight and see the mirror. I see a long corridor of empty rooms, one leading to the other. There is no one in any of the rooms and no one in the mirror. I sit on the edge of the bed and look around. I am the only woman visible, although a tidy little pile of subway tokens sits on the nightstand.

Manny snores in the other bed. A scurrying sound tells me that mice are afoot. Mice and silverfish and roaches that annoy and won't quit. Traps and poison are all that work. The cardboard box under the sink. Manny's fingers twitch as he jerks the covers over the mound of his body. One foot encased in a sock sticks out over the bottom of the bed.

I'm wide-awake and slip out of bed. In my top dresser drawer I keep a pack of Newport Lights, for secret night time smokes. I extract the crinkly pack from among the handkerchiefs and hairpins. I pull on my chenille robe and a pair of fuzzy slippers and pad softly out to the living room. No critters are skulking about in the apartment now. At least I don't hear their rummaging and scratching any more. I open the window and crawl onto the fire escape. I have a black and silver-tipped cigarette holder for my cigarette. It makes me feel like a movie star. Casablanca. Bogey forcing Ingrid Bergman at gunpoint back onto the plane. All black and white and hazy, like my life.

I sit back against the brick of the building as I light up, imagining that the tip of my cigarette is a star, a part of a constellation rising high above Brooklyn and arcing east toward the horizon. Every pore of my body sucks in the night air. The tobacco makes my skin tingle. The metalwork of the fire escape surrounds me. I'm a parakeet in one of those Victorian birdcages. I study the blue veins on my legs, which I can see even in the dim light. They look like the lines on a map. A street map. A subway map. Manhattan on the right leg, the boroughs on the left. The rest of the world is off the map, on someone else's legs sitting on another fire escape or on a front stoop. I look around at other buildings and think I see the faint glows from their cigarettes as they sit, smoking, waiting for dawn, too.

I actually hear the click of the new day, of the calendar turning. It is the sound of an egg cracking. A yellowish wash pours over the apartment buildings. An apricot coloring appears on the edges. Little wisps of ocean fog puff up the streets. I dump my ashtray over the side, into the alleyway below as daybreak drifts downward. Two cats are fighting below. Hissing and yowling at one another. I'm tempted to howl back at them. But don't.

Instead, I walk into the kitchen and flick on the light. It's as if a trumpet has sounded and a mad flurry of activity ensues. A silverfish, its millions legs twitching, vanishes down the drain. In the pantry the mice make noises as if they are running frantically, bumping into one another to get away. A large brown roach squeezes its shiny armored body under the cupboard into an invisible crack. I imagine their dirty little footprints and droppings everywhere. I have to kill them. Otherwise they'll come back over and over. Every day. They'll gorge themselves on my food. I'll get no rest, no peace. Poison is the only resort. The cardboard box is under the sink. I take it out and I'm ready.

I hand Manny a special chocolate egg cream. It's just like I always do each afternoon precisely at 1:00. I feel as detached as a page of the journal. I don't recognize this man, my husband, anymore. He grunts at me with his eyes glued to the TV. The day is warm and damp yellow sweat stains are forming on the armpits of his white T-shirt that I bleach and bleach but they never come clean. His feet are bundled up for winter.

They say it happens ever so slowly. The blood vessels constrict and spasm. The bleeding starts and the organs shut down. Maybe he'll feel warm at last.

I move as if walking underwater into the bedroom. From the bottom dresser drawer I take out a soft sweater with pearl buttons and scoop the tokens from the nightstand into my pocketbook. I'll ride the subway to Bedford Avenue and walk across the Williamsburg Bridge. Somewhere in the middle, the girl will be waiting for me. I know this. She'll hold my hand and I'll never be alone again. The apartment door closes, noiselessly, behind me.

The Motor City Caper

I hadn't been back in Detroit for a decade. So when Bruce, my agent, called and pleaded, " Karen, we need you to make one more stop on your book tour. Just this time and I'll never mess up your schedule again," I bit the bait and agreed to a twenty-four hour stop in Detroit. Detroit's the kind of place that makes you feel like running away even with a hook in your mouth.

I got away from Detroit when I was young. Ran to the West Coast but ended up on the East, living in Boston with frequent runs to New York, "The City". Somewhere on my winding path I discovered my formula. I am a writer. A writer with an attitude. A writer of pulp mysteries. It's a living, and a pretty decent one at that.

It was Bogie's fault that I became a mystery writer. I fell in love at the movies. Not with Bogart exactly, but with the character he portrayed, Philip Marlowe. And that led to Raymond Chandler. And that led to my attitude, which gave birth to the hard-boiled babe detective, Sue Christy. Housewives love her because she's everything they are not. Men love her too because, frankly, she is sexy as hell. If masturbation damns you for eternity, I'm responsible for a whole generation of men sent below with blisters on their fingers.

Book tours are an unfortunate requirement for the maintenance of my career. Twice a year, out comes the valise. I dress in a man's suit - 1940s wide lapel tailored to fit - and smoke cigars even though I despise them. No one sees the real me, a Back Bay Boston single mother who raised a son and tends an overgrown kitchen garden. Costume equates identity. So I agreed with Bruce and scheduled Detroit as my first stop, booking a room at a non-descript Holiday Inn in a north suburb of the city near the bookstore where I would be signing my books, about as incognito as I could be on familiar turf.

On the day in question, I was scanning the Detroit News and having my morning coffee in the hotel restaurant. The paper was filled with crime stories: Two teen-age carjackers killed during a high-speed chase, relatives of a councilwoman who had died mysteriously last year; a woman leaving baby in dumpster who was the child of her twin sister – that sort of twisted story. It's odd, but often fiction seems more believable than truth. People send me all kinds of tales and swear up and down that they're true and couldn't I put them in one of my books. No way. They'd be voted hands down ridiculous. They might be true but truth that sounds silly or just unbelievable.

A woman approached my table. Familiar, yet I couldn't place her. She wore an expensively tailored Liz Claiborne dress and an elaborate Midwest hairdo that sat on her head like a blond wig. "Karen?" She said, extending her manicured hand, multiple bracelet jingling. Somewhere in the recess of my mind, her voice echoed. Teen-age girls in fast cars chasing boys. Drive-in movies. Parties. Time ran backwards for a moment.

It was Lynn, one of the old gang transformed into a suburban matron. Or maybe she had become a spy or a high-class stripper. I shouldn't make assumptions because of the outfit, I told myself as I smoothed down the collar on my mannish tailored suit and ran a hand through my long tangled dark curls. I was glad to see her, in spite of my aversion to the Motor City. She brought back good times. She sat down and told me her true story. She was, indeed, a suburban matron, a doctor's wife but one with an odd nonsuburban-like tale.

First we exchanged the usual it's been ages chitchat: our children (three already grown; she was an early bloomer), what everyone was up to (degrees, locations, occupations), do you remember this and that. She'd been following my career, she said. And then she cut to the quick.

"My husband, Mark Johnson, is an orthopedic surgeon" she began, "and this really happened." Here we go, I thought, this really happened. She said that a lot of unusual things had happened in their lives before this. Her husband treated the infamous and supposedly non-existent woman who microwaved her poodle to dry it. He worked in an emergency room in Tennessee when a woman came in with hysterics sobbing "I only put it on low for thirty seconds." They get a good laugh when this is cited as an example of an Urban Myth. But that wasn't the reason she'd searched me out. This time the story that was eating away at her, which she needed to unload, was one of the oddest "This Really Happened" tales I've ever been told.

Lynn kept glancing around the restaurant. No one was within earshot and I doubted that the fake flowers in the vase on the table contained any bug or listening device. "Go on" I reassured her. I owed her more than one favor for old times, for covering up for me when my mother would search for her wayward daughter. And besides that, I'm a good listener. It's a professional requirement. "Go on," I urged her.

She had been with her husband at a medical conference. It was a shoulder course that used cadaver specimens for dissection. They'd attended other similar courses around the country at various times in his career. The shoulder specimens made it possible to simulate actual patients. Many courses supplied these and other sorts of body parts for surgeons to practice on. Probably not heads for the neurosurgeons, I thought, or hoped.

The night before the official start of the conference they attended a theatre production, an avant-garde community theatre producing some sort of European dream cycle play. The theme had to do with real life vs. dream life, so the discussion at intermission seemed part of the play. A physician friend was supposed to meet them before the show. As it often occurs in the medical field, he was running late. He appeared at the break. The conference was in turmoil, he said. They were concerned about the procurement of the shoulder specimens. Their supplier was a local anatomist. A reliable guy. Always able to come through with the numbers and types of specimens needed. But not this time or any time in the future, it would appear.

There'd been a fire at St. John's Episcopal Church deliberately set with gasoline. The fire started in the church office and destroyed all the records causing extensive damage to the chapel and the rectory. The anatomist was the bookkeeper for that church and was nowhere to be found. Money was missing from the church accounts.

The police went to the anatomist's lab. They wanted to talk with his assistant, Manuel Rodriguez, a pleasant young man and a recent immigrant. The lab appeared deserted but the police entered and found Manuel dead on the embalming table. Not dead from natural causes. And the worse was (Lynn could barely talk at this point), he was partially dismembered. An all-points bulletin went out for the anatomist. He was easily identifiable by a rather large port-wine stain on the right side of his face.

A waitress approached for our order. "Excuse me, ladies," she said. "This isn't a lounge. Ya wanna sit, ya gotta order."

This seemed absurd considering that the place was practically deserted. Eating large quantities of food is a favorite Midwest pastime, I reminded myself. Super-size that breakfast, please. If it tasted good the first round, then seconds and thirds will be better. People in Michigan are seven pounds over the national average. It's work to maintain that. It was too early in the morning for me to be a good sport about being back in my hometown.

After we ordered gratuitous food, Lynn returned to her telling of the tale. It was obvious to the organizers of the course that they would have to look elsewhere for specimens. They searched for the anatomist's paperwork. As you might imagine, triplicate and quadruplicate forms are needed to obtain body parts. There were no forms in the files. There appeared never to have been forms. No records. Anywhere. Just a constant supply of body parts. The conference had to scramble for parts – importing them from Canada at quite the cost. Unlike any cost they'd ever paid. And body parts were, apparently, unavailable at this moment in the States. It seemed that a lot of educators all over the country had used the same anatomist as a supplier.

She stopped. I couldn't help it. I was hooked. Intrigued. My writer's antenna was twitching. "So, where's the anatomist now?" I asked. Lynn looked at me and shrugged. "That's it. That's all I know." Chapter One, I thought. Bring on Sue Christy.

Sue sat back at her desk and swung her long legs fitted with black biker boots onto the desktop. Dr. Malcolm Boyd, Chief of Surgery at St. Marcus Hospital, sat across from her uncertain where to focus his eyes. He was the type of man that Sue made quite nervous. Middle-aged, debonair, well dressed, and self-possessed. He wanted to avoid focusing his eyes on her low-cut blouse at any cost. But his eyes kept straying to the swell of her breasts above the beige silk. His hands were sweaty as he slid his business card across the desk in her general direction. He was obviously here on important business.

You understand" he began "this has to be very discreet. No leaking rumors to the press. The medical profession has its friends and its enemies. Unfortunately, the press has not been kind to us lately so we must count it amongst the latter."

Sue smiled. "I have a tattoo that says 'discreet' in Old English letters. Would you like to see it?"

She started to unbutton the top pearl button of her blouse. Dr. Boyd blushed and put up a hand in protest. "Don't worry" Sue laughed "a silly joke, but surely you know my reputation". Actually, she did have a tattoo but it was a small black spider on the far edge of her shoulder blade.

Years ago, Sue had worked for the hospital solving the mystery of the missing monkeys for their research lab. Animal protectionists had infiltrated their staff and one by one the experimental subject animals were vanishing. Sue had used the assistance of two of her brothers as undercover employees to break up the racket, while dating a young research assistant herself to be on the inside. She had fond memories of their dinners together – too bad he was involved in the animal heists. It was handled quite smoothly with severance pay and restitution and no police involvement. So, once again, the hospital was turning to her for the kind of service that she was able to provide.

Dr. Boyd had a number of newspaper articles with him. One told of the damage at a local church from a fire that Sue vaguely recalled. The police wanted the church bookkeeper for questioning. Dr. Boyd explained to Sue that the bookkeeper was their medical school anatomist – a man with a port-wine stain on his face. They were able to trace his background – a native of Brownsville, Texas, a Ph.D. from University of Texas at Austin. What the paper did not reveal was the complicating story. His assistant found dead in the lab, embalmed and partially dismembered. And a trail of body parts, the source of which no one had been able to determine. That was it. The body parts. The piece that they wished to keep out of the hands of both police and press. Both the newspapers and the television news had become quite sensational over the last decade, as if they needed to keep up with the movies and talk shows. Any twist in reporting was ok as long as it entertained, titillated, or horrified. The potential for all three was quite strong here.

Sue stood up and paced the floor for several minutes; oblivious to Dr. Boyd who sat still with the palms of his hands pressed together, knees locked.

"O.K." she said. "I'll take it. Give me three months, maybe more with travel time and all the information you have on the port-wine anatomist. Any thing on the assistant. Lists of all lab personnel employed at your facility. You are, I assume, my contact person?" Dr. Boyd nodded. Sue continued "You'll meet with me weekly – dinner at the Whitney. Hopefully we can wind this up quickly. You're recently divorced?"

Dr. Boyd looked uncomfortable again. "How did you know that" he asked.

"I wouldn't have, except that it's summer and you have the white band tan of a missing wedding ring" she pointed out to him.

He looked at his hand and made a mental note to take care of that with Coppertone as soon as he could. "I'll get all the paperwork over to you. Dinner at the Whitney on Wednesday at seven?" he replied.

"Better make that eight," she said, jockeying for control. He jotted a note to himself on his palm pilot as he rose to leave. She could tell the effect she was having on him as he shook her hand and left, a bit unsteady on his feet.

She dialed Amy's number without thinking. Amy had been her consultant for years. Her phone number was as familiar as a nursery rhyme: Hickory-dickory-

dock or Broadway 34129. When they were teenagers they'd played Girl Detective, creating scenarios for each other to solve. Sue had never quit playing and turned sleuthing into a career, while Amy had become a housewife raising three children. Whenever Sue was in the unraveling process of a sticky case, Amy was willing to try her hand, in between diapers and dishwashing. This was an unusual case and one to share with Amy.

Sue phoned her and grabbed a sweater. Amy's husband was a cop and they lived in the city on the far west side, in a neighborhood of firemen, policemen and other civil servants commanded by law to remain within the city limits. The girls had grown up a few blocks away from where Amy now lived. The years had not been kind to the neighborhood and it made Sue both angry and sad to visit Amy. She gunned her classic pink Mustang convertible as she pulled out of the garage, glad that it was summer in the Midwest and she could drive with the top down. The car never failed to turn heads. Sue loved cars, a result of growing up in a household of seven boys. They had each taught her something about the mean machines and how to keep them running. Cars were just like the mysteries that she solved. She was like a mechanic fiddling with life's tricky problems. Dr. Boyd had dropped a tricky one in her lap with this assignment. She might need her brothers as well as Amy, even though she liked best to keep the cases between the two of them – the chick detective thing. Nancy Drew and George, Zena and Gabrielle, WonderWomen slinging around town on vines of steel. But sometimes she had to call out the posse.

She ran her hand through her short-cropped blond hair. The wind felt good as she sped down the freeway trying to keep within the honorable five miles over the limit. She didn't often get tickets although she was often stopped by testosterone laded cops. She didn't like to date cops though and, in spite of her toying with Dr. Boyd; she didn't like to date clients. Work and pleasure, separate like church and state. Sue hoped this new assignment wouldn't interfere with her current beau. Jason had been patient and understanding so far with her lifestyle, lack of regular hours, unavailability and preoccupation while on a case. He was a cultivator of bonsai trees.

Sue pulled up in front of Amy's bungalow. The bars on the windows and doors always unnerved her. As children, the houses were not only unbarred but also most often unlocked. This neighborhood was relatively safe. Only the really dumb, brain-damaged criminal types would mess with homes filled with cops and firemen. Amazing thing was that there were some of those types, so protection was required. Before going into the house, Sue set the kill switch on her car. She was not letting any joy rider swipe it easily.

A young boy sauntered up to her. Too young to cause her concern. He swaggered towards her, pants sagging, chains hanging from belt loops. Maybe eight, she thought. No more than nine for sure. Cute kid. Broad smile. Friendly. "Hi there" she said. "Hey Lady! How 'bout some pussy?" he responded. He strutted like he meant it. "Shit" she thought, blindsided and momentarily stunned. She wished she had a different tattoo than the tiny spider on her shoulder, a big one – neon, maybe – that said 'NO WAY'. A useful message for this baby prowler. "Go home" she tried.

"Ain't nobody there" he said. "Locked out 'til five but I got me some good sugar if you got spice".

This reminded her of the magazine in the dentist's office "Highlights for Children" with the illustrations called "What's Wrong with This Picture?" Subtle things quite topsy-turvy if you looked carefully. The sun with a moon face. A tree with a shoe on a root. Someone with their pants on backwards. Two right arms. Two left legs. A baby in a wolf suit.

Well, she could be bad-assed too. "Scram, right now". She pointed her finger like a gun at the center of his forehead. "You tuck that tail between your legs and hurry off. I'm old enough to be your mama"

"I like that" he grinned. She stomped up Amy's steps, turning her back on the boy. "Shit! Shit! Shit!" she said out loud as she pounded on the door. Amy let her in and noticed the boy standing in front of the house, legs spread, arms crossed in a gangsta style pose. "Antwan" she called "you better get out of here or you'll get a lickin' when your mama gets home and finds out that you've been bothering my friends." The pose melted. A sullen look crossed his face, eradicating any sign of cuteness. He slunk away, flipping her off and mumbling under his breath.

"Love this city" Sue said, as she flung herself into an overstuffed chair dangling her legs over its arms. The crowded kitchen – control central for the Krasny household – functioned as a living room also.

"What can we do about it? An accident of birth for us. Sometimes you have to wear blinders, make the best of a bad situation" Amy replied. It was quiet in the house. Naptime. A good time to do business.

Sue filled Amy in on the details of Dr. Malcolm Boyd's visit to her office. "This one has to be kept quiet. We're being paid to keep it from the press. They want to locate not just the anatomist but his suppliers. I may have to do a bit of travel – it'll get me out of this damn city anyway".

I closed the notebook I'd been scribbling in. Time to meet the press. Sign the books. Expound on literature and detective lore. And the inevitable auto questions. I straightened my tie in the mirror. Nice thing about this persona is that I never have to consider what to wear. It's proscribed.

The bookstore was in walking distance. Something I always request when selecting the hotels I stay in on tour. No matter how much I know about cars, I resent them. Every time I fill a gas tank I imagine a small mouth lined with teeth, like the plants in "Little Shop of Horrors", whining "Feed me. Feed me." And the gasoline becomes dollar bills that I pour and stuff into its mouth. A metal monster demanding obedience. I don't say this at book signings. Especially here in Detroit, home of the auto. And Sue would not agree with me either. She's an honest to goodness Motor City Mama.

There was already a crowd lined up at the desk that the store had put off to one side for me. My mind was preoccupied with Sue, which was probably just as well so that I could sign the books in her language with my signature -- "Keep spinning those wheels, Best wishes, Karen Hogan" "It's not lost until it's found, Good Luck, Karen Hogan" and so on. They always want me to mention their names. That day's included "To Mrs. Randall, To Steve and Diane for their anniversary, To George, To Sally" etc. I looked up and found myself out of character when a handsome man asked me to sign his book " To Dr. Boyd". He looked more like an actor than a doctor.

"Wait a minute" I said to him " You're a character in my next book, not this one."

He was amused but the row of patrons behind him started to fidget. They danced from foot to foot and peered around the person in front them, offended that I stalled the line to speak with this guy who looked like a young Paul Newman. I have this thing for eyes. I believe that you can communicate by eye contact alone. It was certainly happening then. This was someone I wanted to know.

Dr. 'Paul Newman' Boyd handed me his card, quickly adding a home number. "I'd love to have a preview of my role, if you're willing to divulge classified material." He glanced over his shoulder. "The natives are restless. Do call me though." I looked down at the card. Thank goodness he wasn't Malcolm Boyd. "Ted Boyd" he said as he shook my hand and left. Department of Neuropsychiatry, Detroit Receiving Hospital. I picked up my pen and adjusted my attitude. Looked like I might have to cancel Cleveland, I thought with satisfaction.

I sat down to work on the next installment that evening. Ted Boyd's eyes floated above the notebook, the intense blue very distracting. I dug deep inside myself to inhabit Sue as the next chapter rolled out onto the white page.

"You don't have to prove it to me." Sue's fingers clenched the handle of the Saturday Night Special. The hot Brownsville, Texas sun made her shade her eyes with her free hand. "We're all innocent. I've been there." She stepped backwards keeping the gun level; aimed right at the area that she had learned long ago threatened a man. Don't aim at the heart. They don't care about the organ. Aim between the legs and they'll stand still.

"Hey, babe. Easy now. I was just kidding. No harm meant." He was sweating. Ready to beg. The woman she found him crouched over was sobbing in the corner of the alley. Her dress torn. This was no one's idea of a joke. The alleys in this part of south Texas functioned the same as streets. Sort of like the 'A' side or the 'B' side of a record. The 'B' side, the alley side, is life on another planet – different rules applied. Sue wasn't sure that she wanted to blow him away in spite of the urge to pull the trigger.

"You going tell me the straight answers I want?" She asked, then repeated the words in Spanish. "And cut the crap. I know you're no altar boy. First, you tell me what's going on here." She gestured at the woman huddled in the corner.

She watched his nervous eyes look for help and settle on the gun pointing steadily at his crotch. "O.K. O.K. Listen. We all gotta make a living somehow. I got a green card. I live here but I work over there." He pointed towards the river. "You know what a coyote is, gringa?" She nodded. He went on. "I'm the ferryman. I cross the illegals. First they pay the coyote, their guide. Then they pay me to transport them. I do what I'm told. It's dangerous. This bitch here. She tried to cheat me. She had it coming." He spit in her direction. More like a curse. Looked like she didn't need a curse. Bad luck was following her like a stray dog.

I'll have to find a shelter to take her to after I get what I can from this scum, Sue thought, and a bruja to remove the curse. "So, you do what I tell you, answer some questions and I let you go. I'm looking for someone, a man. A man with a port wine stain across his face. You know who I mean?"

His eyes changed. The hooded extra lid slid down to cover them. Snake-like. His face became flat. "No senora, I've never seen such a man."

"You want to live or die, right here, right now?" Sue spit over his spit to make her point and leveled the gun once more. Funny how easy it was to be calm and steady. An old trick where you detach yourself and your arm has a life of its own. Cool and collected. Her heart was, in fact, racing. She was a long way from the Motor City. "You tell me where to find this man."

"This man, he is from up north senora? But born down here. One of us."

"That's the one"

"We hadn't seen him in many years. The coyotes know him well. This year he

is back to claim his territory. You must look for Jose Branco. Up in Hidalgo. Jose is his cousin. And, senorita, you are very beautiful. I would be careful if I were you."

"OK, Charon. Back to your raft." She noticed the look on his face, first angry then puzzled. She started to laugh as she realized that he'd thought she called him 'cabron', bastard. Her laughter made him nervous and he kept his eyes on her trigger finger now instead of her breasts.

She waved the gun off to her left. "Go on – get the hell out of here."

I tore the page out of the typewriter. Sue was certainly blundering into a mess. I looked out the window at the ocean – the Gulf of Mexico. My trip to Detroit seemed centuries instead of months ago. The house I'd rented on South Padre Island stood on stilts to protect it from storm surge. It had withstood the last two hurricanes the owner, Judge Evans, had bragged as he showed me the shutters stashed in the musty garage should a storm approach and I need to board up and evacuate.

"I hope ya don't mind" he'd drawled "but on occasion I need to put up one of my ranch hands in the garage below." He had seen the look on my face. It was a dirt and sand room beneath the house inhabited by palmetto bugs, a nice Texan way of saying 'cockroach'.

"It's better conditions than what they got back home, cross the border. They don't mind. Don't ya worry little miss. They won't bother you none now. Why if they need to use the john, they got that field out there which suits them just fine." He stared at me, tucking his thumbs into his belt loops, challenging me to speak up like the liberal Yankee know-it-all bitch he had me marked for. I just looked blankly at him. I felt like a third grader trying to understand something the teacher was asking me to memorize like the Pledge of Allegiance. In third grade I'd been sure that the words said "And to the republic for Richard Stands." For years I tried to imagine who this Richard was. Was he Richard the Lion-Hearted, or Richard the Third, or maybe Richard Nixon? School had been like that – fixating on words and what they might be and what they could mean, trouble understanding the lesson at hand. But I understood the Judge. He could keep migrant slaves in his garage and no Yankee bitch could tell him otherwise.

The Judge squinted his beady eyes, although the broad brim of his Stetson protected them from the sun. "This here is my card. You just call if you have any problems, ya hear?" The embossed card had the same symbol – a fancy "E" in a circle – that formed the buckle on his belt.

I sit and stare through the porch screen towards the water. The Gulf changes constantly like the inside of my head. A pinwheel of colors, moving from foam to calm, occasionally kicking up monster waves. The weather is suddenly cool and the waves are coming sideways down the beach. Agitated. Wind's out of the north. A reminder that I'm still indeed in the United States and it is December. It's an easy disconnect down here. Business is transacted in Spanish. Eighty percent of the people appear Hispanic. The gringos are a motley group, a handful are local people who've been here for generations having drifted south from Houston or Louisiana or Arkansas. The rest are people who've deliberately selected the edge of the country as far south as they could get. They are running from something though, not towards anything. They have secrets and they have stories. A good place to come to write, I thought.

The Judge had read my books I noticed. They are constant best sellers in Texas. I can tell when introduced to someone, especially a male, if they've read my books. Their eyes give it away. They look me up and down and compare me to Sue. My dark, bushy hair is their first shock. And my age, decades older than Sue. And I don't wear leather clothing. Finally their eyes linger on my breasts. Small. Ample enough I think, but nothing like the voluptuous Sue with her hypnotic cleavage. If Sue wanted, she could pack a gun or carry anything she wanted hidden inside her lacy black bra.

I hear the crunch on gravel of tires pulling into the driveway and look down below. The Judge is getting out of his dusty pickup. A shotgun rides in the back window like most of the trucks around here. He stands next to the truck for a while kicking at the tires and looking off in the distance at nothing. Apparently, I'm supposed to go to the door and inquire as to the reason for his visit. He doesn't have any ranch hands with him this trip. I turn off the computer and go to investigate.

He's dressed in his usual manner. Stetson. White shirt with string tie fixed with a silver and turquoise slide. Neatly pressed black pants with his special silver "E" belt buckle. And boots, finely stenciled and pointed toed. This time he removes his hat and rubs his almost bald head with a dusty hand.

"Little lady" he begins "seems like you are getting yourself into a bit of trouble down here. We don't much like Yankees hereabouts. And nosy ones even less."

I draw myself up to my full height, which is half a head taller than his. "I'm sorry sir. I don't quite know what you're referring to." I try not to blink. I'm good at that, having practiced it as a game with my son when he was little.

Last one to blink is the winner.

The Judge pokes at the dirt with his boots. "Now listen to me, miss. You've been asking after a feller around here. A man with a port-wine stain. I don't think you ought to be jumping into water when you can't see what's waiting for you below. Them sharks have a mighty nasty bite. You tend your business. That typing thing you do. And we'll tend to ours. I'm hoping, ma'am, that you catch my drift." He shifts from foot to foot.

I shrug. "O.K. whatever." I can promise anything if I cross my fingers behind my back. He knows this and clears the phlegm from his throat. "And if I were you, ma'am, I'd lock them doors at night too." He hoists himself up into his pickup and pops open a beer. He takes a long sip, and nods as he started the engine. "You be careful, little miss."

I go inside, banging the door intentionally and grab a sweater. I think that a walk on the beach will clear my head. The beach is almost deserted with the north wind blowing its cold Yankee breath. A few hearty vacationers huddle in the dunes building sandcastles. An elderly couple that I see each morning on the beach walks by me. Regardless of the weather they walk several miles with a metal detecting wand, scanning for treasure. Rumors abound about lost pirate treasure washing up onshore but what they usually find are coins or jewelry shaken loose from ordinary tourists and travelers. They claim that they make their living this way – supplementing their pensions. They nod to me as I approach.

"Why Miss Hogan, what a day for you to be out! This here's weather that'd pickle a pepper. Makes both the gander and the goose get all bumpy." They wear identical slickers and rain hats every day regardless of the weather. Until they speak it is hard to tell which is the goose and which is the gander, Gladys or Bernard.

I smile and ask them if they had any luck today.

"Look at this watch" Gladys says and fishes around in a large sack extracting a watch that is either a Rolex or a knock-off. "It's a lucky day. Well, at least for us. Not for the gentleman missing this one. It weren't out here long. Still running. And we found lots of colored glass today too." Artists in the area prize the glass, already polished by the wind and weather. The rounded bottoms are especially nice hung in windows, multi-coloring the day with their reflected light.

I feel my anger at the Judge vanishing as I walk. The tide is heading out. The beach unrolls at my feet. All sorts of deposits left by the north wind are revealed – shells, rocks, sand dollars, jelly fish, bits and pieces. I keep my eyes on the ground noticing the crabs scurrying sideways for cover. That's why I don't notice the two men approaching me from the dunes. That and the wind. The north wind is fairly noisy and I'm preoccupied with my story. What would Sue do now to obtain information? Maybe it was time for her to call in her brothers from Detroit to deal with the net of crime that she is skirting around. Seemed like nothing good would happen to her alone in Texas.

Sue gunned the engine of her rental car as she pulled onto the highway heading from Brownsville to McAllen. She had her pick of the Tejano music stations as she drove with the music and the air conditioning both on full volume. The cold air under her short skirt felt good on her thighs. "Te quiero. Te perdi. Soy el rey llorando," I am the crying king, the radio sang as she rode along.

Hidalgo is a small town on the border, just across the Rio Grande from Reynosa, Mexico. Someone in Hidalgo would talk to her, she felt sure. Some man always comes across with the information she needs while a fantasy movie plays in his head: Help the girl and she'll hop into my bed, he thinks. Sue had learned from experience that the underlings rarely know what their bosses are actually involved in. No one here would imagine that the illegals they were ferrying could end up in an anatomy laboratory up North carved into pieces. She would have to convince someone to lead her to the man with the port-wine stain.

An article in the morning paper was connected to her case, she is certain. A train car had been found in Iowa that had sat in a rail yard over the summer with its door locked from the outside. The decomposed remains of a dozen or so suspected illegals inside. No water or food. No exit. Dehydration and suffocation as far as anyone could determine. The surprise is that this didn't happen more often. Or that the press didn't report it more often. Easy to see how the smuggler's tracking system could break down. She punched Amy's phone number into her cell phone as she headed west, the road ahead of her flat and empty.

While I am pondering Sue's next step, the sand keeps shifting at my feet as if someone is swirling it with their hand. I could see Sue; her sweat soaked blouse clinging to her skin. A thin rivulet of sweat rolling down her neck. Hand on the radio dial. And the road, with its constant oasis of water floating on it. The light a curtain of heat. A teetering on the edge of the moment. A voice rising from the sand chides me "Get the picture, girl, get the picture." I guess if the ocean can talk, why not the sand. Two men materialize out of nowhere, one on either side of me gripping my arm way too tight. "Senora, you will come with us." The shorter one speaks in broken English. They are both Mexican. Indian. Aztec, with high cheekbones and deep brown skin. They're dressed in Salvation Army high fashion.

Unlike Sue, my Spanish is lousy and they speak to each other rapidly with a staccato accent that I can't follow. "You do what we say. Our boss wants to talk to you. You do exactly like we ask and we don't hurt you. This way." They turn me around and we head back down the beach. Gladys and Bernard have vanished. No tourists in sight. Yelling would only excite the shorebirds. Great, I think, this is just what I need. I should have taken Ted Boyd's offer to wait a few weeks and have him accompany me down here. My publisher isn't speaking to me right now after I abandoned the book tour. My sweater is coming unraveled. This appears to have been a foolish path to choose to follow. Extraction is one of my great skills; a matter of finding just the right words, and this time it does not look easy. The two lackeys grip my arms tightly, pressing their dirty fingers into my skin.

When we reach the path across the dunes to my rental home, they turn. They know where I live. They walk me up the wooden stairs of the little house on stilts and let go of my arms only when we are in the door.

"You're to pack a bag, now." They gesture to the bedroom. The shorter one holds open the door. I watched him carefully and decide that they are harmless as long as I obey. I get out an overnight bag and throw in some clothes, along with a copy of the Sue Christy story of the moment, several pens, toiletries – spray deodorant that might function as a simple weapon - and my phone book. The fat one grabs the bag and rummages through it but doesn't remove anything.

"I left my gun in my pickup" I try for humor. They look blankly at me, and the fat one steps to the window to check the drive below. No truck.

"Write a note. Now!" He said. "Write – 'Gone to Mexico, back at later date' write that now and sign your name."

I do as commanded and sign the note, "Sue Christy". I don't know if that will count as a clue if I don't return. I hope so.

Sue woke up with her head hurting. She sat up but the room appeared unstable. It floated into focus, then faded. As she fell backwards onto the bed, she caught a glimpse of a large wooden wardrobe in the corner. Blue and white tiles covered with black peacocks came into focus. She could hear them screaming in her head. Texas has a lot of peacocks that are kept for protection against snakes.

They have voices like crones possessed by demons.

Other sounds penetrated her cocoon. Street sounds. It did NOT sound like Texas, especially not like the dusty town of Hidalgo that she last remembered pulling into. Drugged, she thought. A sophisticated trick that she hadn't been prepared for in a small town. She could see the face leering at her. A port-wine stain and a gold tooth. "Yankee gringa, go home. This isn't your turf. You don't understand how we live. Once warned. Twice burned. And Third time, a ticket to another world." Something hot. She remembered. Her breast felt sore to touch. It was red and blistered. She could discern a shape in the wound. A small circle with an 'E' in the center.

Looks like I may have to stick it out with Jason, she thought. He can pretend that the E stands for 'Envy' – that he's the envy of all the men around. Better get my head clear first and figure out where I am. Better yet, figure out how to get out of here.

Everything is out of focus. The blue tile on the floors and walls. An old wooden wardrobe in the corner. The tiles come into focus first, milky blue with black peacocks and black onyx. A tall room. Tall, narrow. A dark wooden bed. I feel like I have the flu. I'm a big plate of pasta. This isn't a prison and it's certainly not heaven. It has an old colonial beauty about it. Get up, my mind tells my body. You may be tough but you're lucky to be alive. I grab my bag, which is sitting on the floor and lurch out into the corridor.

It appears to be an old hotel, where - I have no idea. A stone stairway with a carved wood banister leads to the main floor. I approach the front desk. "Where am I?" I ask. The clerk just stares at me. I realize that I'm a mess and that he doesn't speak English. "Donde?" I gesture around me.

A little smile appears. "Hotel Pennsylvania" he replies.

"Que ciudad?" I ask and the smile fades. I'm making him nervous. The ridiculous nature of my question is apparent but I don't have the vocabulary to explain.

"Districo Federale. El Centro. Cerca El Monumento de la Revolucion," he replies avoiding eye contact.

That's Mexico City, I think. I know as much about it as I do Bozeman, Montana. No, that's not accurate. I know less. I've done Bozeman on a book tour. I sit down in the lobby to clear my head and take this in. I rummage through my bags. No identification except for the story I've been writing. No money either – no dollars or pesos.

Outside the hotel I find some young American backpackers heading towards the bus terminal up the street. They know where the American Embassy is located, they say. On Reforma, the main boulevard. Right turn on Reforma and it's hard to miss once you make it to the park. Good thing I have a sense of direction and that the air, in spite of the smog, clears my head as I walk in what appears to be the right direction. I spot the American flag on a colonial building alongside the park. The little breeze making it flap is a relief, like a hand waving welcome to me. I climb up the steps, feeling absolutely ancient, and open the heavy door. I explain my predicament to the sweet young clerk at the desk.

"I'm Karen Hanson, the mystery writer. I've been kidnapped." Her smile is fading. I can tell that she wishes that I was not a problem. I'm creating more work for her. I'm whisked into another office and the door is shut.

When the door finally opens an hour later a pale thin man dressed in a black suit enters. I can tell that he recognizes my name as he looks me up and down and appears disappointed.

"Ms. Hanson? Robert Bronson, at your service. I'm a fan of yours, a Sue Christy fan." He extends a clean manicured hand. His cuff links are gold and his shirt is a freshly pressed white linen. "I've already checked with our Texas bureau and they were able to corroborate your story. At least as far as your presence in Texas the last few weeks, writing on the island. An elegant writer like you ought to be able to fill in the blanks quite easily for the State Department. Both governments involved in this affair have an interest in keeping the media at bay."

It seems to me, I think, that everyone wants the press out of everything.

"Let's just say, for the record, that you were the victim of mistaken identity? Perhaps a mistaken identity in a drug deal? I don't think, in that case, that we would need to involve either the police or the federales. A mistake is a mistake and translates well."

I usually think quickly in tight spots. Not quite as fast as Sue, but I am able to see the big picture. The last few days have blurred my thought processes. I need time to think. Mr. Bronson apparently takes my silence for non-compliance.

"If you do care to pursue this, we can contact your family and perhaps some legal representation can be arranged. Kidnapping is quite an accusation. Especially if two countries and their officials, a respected judge, are involved."

I don't recall mentioning the Texan Judge Evans to anyone, but Mr. Bronson somehow seems privy to this piece of the story. At least I assume that's what he means.

He continues, "You do understand that here, in Mexico, you may have to go to prison until this is resolved, especially if they suspect that drugs might be involved. You'll need a local go-between to supply you with food, toiletries, all the little usuals. Things that Americans take for granted. The prison system here is quite primitive. You'll need a local person just to mail or receive a letter. Time is a factor and at your age I don't advise this."

I am not *that* dense. I get the drift, the message, the warning. Mistaken identity is my ticket home. I don't think that Mr. Bronson will care for my portrayal of his character in the forthcoming Sue Christy book. He sits behind his desk pressing the tips of his fingers together and holding them to his lips while waiting my answer. I am a writer. I have other ways of seeing that justice is served.

As Sue's head cleared she remembered partial moments from the night before. Or from however many days before Hidalgo had been. A dark cantina with a name something like "El Ratoncito". A drawing of a mouse, or a rat, with huge fanged teeth on the window. Two men at the bar. A 'Dos Equis" to drink. And the port-wine stained man with his leer. The knockout drops must have been in the beer. She thought she had carefully kept her eyes on it. Not careful enough. She stood up groggily and searched the room for her belongings. Her gun had vanished which made her feel naked and vulnerable. Her bag was on the floor. Empty, or nearly empty. No dollars. No pesos. They'd left her Tampax alone and a roll of lifesavers. She popped a lifesaver into her mouth. It helped rid it of a sour taste. Her breast throbbed, as she was sure they had intended, as a reminder. A receipt, in Spanish, from a bus was in the bottom of her bag. It said: "The Tampico Express." No name. No identification. Much to her surprise, she was able to open the door to the room. She slipped out of the hotel relieved that she wasn't followed. The street was crowded with people –men and women in sleek trendy clothing mixed with barefooted peasants in an array of colorful rebozos and huipils. Taxis and collectivos criss-crossed in and out of bumper-to-bumper traffic. Walking helped her organize her thoughts. The embassy, she thought. That's the first order of business. She turned a corner onto the Paseo de la Reforma, obviously a main boulevard. She asked the first street vendor, a tiny withered woman selling corn on the cob sprinkled with chili powder, where the American Embassy was located.

"A la derecho," the woman gestured barely looking up. That way, up the street, towards the park. Sue tried not to look too hungrily at the corn.

"Cinqo pesos," the woman held out a tiny brown hand creased with so many lines that it looked like a map of the world.

"No lo tengo" Sue replied, but she could tell that the woman did not believe her. How could a gringa not have five pesos! She popped another lifesaver in her mouth and headed up Reforma in the general direction that the woman had gestured. Mixed in with all the traffic were many incredible classic American cars from the 60s and 70s. All chrome and shiny. A lowrider Chevy Impala with big fuzzy dice on the rear view mirror drove by with several young men hanging out the windows. The occupants honked their horn, although the sound was lost in all the commotion. They shouted "Rubia! Rubia! Hey baby, you come with me?" Sue guessed that she couldn't look all that bad, not as bad as her head felt anyway. She grinned and kept walking towards Chapultepec. The cars attracted her but the horny men did not. She saw the Embassy as she approached the park. The red, white and blue waving from the flagpole was a relief. A welcome home invitation.

She told her story to three different underlings, the same simple story. She'd been on vacation in Texas, gone into a bar to have a drink, and woke up in Mexico City. No identification. No money. She could tell that not one of them believed her. They must have figured that she was another scamming American looking for a free trip home. A clerk brought her a cup of coffee as she waited to speak with an official, with someone who might actually be able to help her.

"If you are lucky, Mr. Gonzalez will help you," the clerk said with a Mona Lisa-like smirk.

A door opened. A large man beckoned to her. His belly hung over his fancy leather tooled belt. Sweat stains appeared, like yellow moons, on his white shirt under each of his arms. He stroked his greasy hair with a fat hand as he listened to her story then walked over to the chair on which she'd collapsed. His chubby hand lingered on her shoulder. His stubby fingers made little circles on her collarbone.

"Senorita, you have no identification so I am the only man in Mexico City that can help you." He walked over to the office door and bolted it. "But first you must help me. Do you understand?" He ran his hand down her arm, fingers brushing her sore breast.

"Damn it," thought Sue. "I'm too hungry, tired and broke to fight this off and besides, I'd have to beg or sell my body on the street to get home. This will cost Dr. Malcolm Boyd triple overtime, at least." She turned toward "the only man in Mexico City" and smelled his garlicky hot breath on her neck.

He thrust his hand under her skirt, pulled her up towards him and began to unbutton her blouse. He's panting and practically drooling, she noticed with disgust, as he pressed her backwards onto his desk. But he stopped as quickly as he had started and stared at her chest as her blouse fell over her shoulders.

The red welted "E" in a circle is visible. He let go as if he had been branded.

His eye twitched noticeably and he retreated behind his desk. Sue felt only relief as she eased her body back into the chair.

"Permit me a phone call or two and we'll come to an understanding", I say to Mr. Bronson. He unlocks a desk and hands me a phone with a direct line to the States. I dial Ted's number. At least it's the number I believe I've dialed before. A Detroit Area Code. "Farmer's Insurance" the phone on the other ends responds. A mistake. Perhaps. My fingers have the jitters as well as my mind. I try again and apologize to the receptionist. Maybe I've confused it with Malcolm Boyd's number. I try my agent who answers right away with apparent relief.

"Where the hell are you?" he asks.

"Not in Texas" I reply "and it certainly isn't Kansas either. It seems I've ended up in Old Mexico. Took a wrong turn, or something like that. And Bruce, I've got a big problem. No money, no papers. I'm stranded at the embassy now." Bruce is well connected. Any glitch in my tours and in my publishing career, he corrects it. I hand the phone to Bronson who gives his spin, his little creative story on the situation to Bruce. They talk a bit and shortly I'm handed a paper, a transit pass and temporary ID. A driver arrives and I'm escorted to the airport where a ticket waits for a flight to Boston via Dallas. The driver stays close to my side, translating and perhaps protecting me, until I am at the gate. He hands me an envelope. I thrust it unopened into the bag with my Sue Christy story as I board the plane.

Everyone on the plane looks suspect. I imagine that the odd glances in my direction have to do with my outfit and disheveled appearance, but I can't be sure. Everywhere I look I see men with port wine stains obliterating half their face. My seat is toward the rear of the aircraft so I run the gauntlet and collapse in 33-E, a fortunate aisle seat in case I need to make a quick getaway. I pull out my notebook to write and to conjure up some relief for Sue, but the envelope falls out and I open it.

A photo of my son, Jason, is tucked inside. His smiling face with dimples and wavy hair looking up at me. So much like his dad, who was a musician, a blip on my radar, entering my life and exiting just as quick. And he'd never even read one of my books. But Jason is solid, my flesh and blood. I stare at the photo and turn it over. Our address is on the backside.

My hands shake. A wave of nausea. Either it's the turbulence or I've been drugged again. And I'm not sure how to extricate Sue from the story.

Sue boarded the aircraft with a temporary passport that Gonzalez had grudgingly issued. He'd spit twice as he handed it to her and told her to wait on the steps for a taxi. She was sure he mumbled an Aztec curse as she left. When she reached the airport it was apparent that someone had paid for her ticket. Someone with a sense of humor had booked her through to Toledo, Ohio. She'd have to call one of her brothers to drive down from Detroit and retrieve her. Toledo was the entryway into a state that Michiganders like to engage in demographic battles. One that they wished to avoid crossing, touching or landing in. However, it was their unavoidable connection to the rest of the country. Toledo was the home of Tony Packo Pickles – hot and spicy - and the Toledo Zoo with its underwater hippo display. The Toledo Mudhens, a farm club, played ball there. Just the name, Toledo, made Sue think of The Inquisition. She touched the sore spot beneath her blouse, then realized that a dozen pair of drooling male eyes were watching her every move and removed her fingers.

A sealed envelope accompanied the ticket. She waited to open it until she'd boarded and sank into her seat, glad that the one next to her was empty. It was on hospital stationary. She recognized the curlicue handwriting of the elegant Dr. Boyd.

"We thank you for your service and regret that we no longer require your investigation. Our sources have confirmed that we will no longer be a party to any indictments resulting from the incidents you have been exploring. At the request of the hospital board, your service is terminated and a check that we think you will find highly compensatory awaits you, upon your return. I trust that your usual discreet manner will prevail in this instance. Best wishes, Dr. Malcolm Boyd" and a postscript –" The pleasure of your company at dinner this Tuesday 8:00 p.m. at the Whitney is requested."

Visions of the woman in the Brownsville alley filled Sue's head and the leer of the port-wine stained man. Amputated limbs floated behind her closed eyelids. She did not like anyone messing with her mind. And she hated leaving an unsolved case to fester. The powers that be were obviously stronger than any she had imagined, were connected right up to the top of the political ladder and would remain there. Her hands shook as she opened her eyes and tore the letter into shreds. Across the aisle a man smiled deeply at her and offered to buy her a drink. She accepted.

I close the notebook and turn to the voice across the aisle. "Permit me to buy you a drink. I'm a fan of yours and you look like you could use a drink about now." I look at my hands and smooth my flyaway hair. How could he have recognized me? No costume. No lingerie style clothing. No leather. He reaches into the pocket of the seat in front of him and pulls out a copy of "Sue Christy and the Afghan Opium Fields" – an early volume, a special Latin American edition with a younger picture of myself on the back cover.

I notice his eyes, a beautiful hazel/gold color with just a few creases in the corners. He does not have a port wine stain to my relief. He smiles deeply when I accept and presses the call button for the stewardess.

Kill! Sudoku!!

Sudoku made me snap. Up to that moment I was fine with everything. Even the knowledge that Eminem planned the assassination of JFK. Or that the Crips or Bloods could knock at my door any second and blow me away. I was safe humming along the road in my souped up Corvette, drag racing late at night and early Sunday mornings. Mostly I behaved. Occasionally I shot rats out back in the alley. Pushed a garden hose down their burrow hole, watched them pop up then WHAM! They splattered all about. I've got a good eye and steady hand. Sometimes a neighbor peeked out between their blinds with panicked beady eyes. I've got a great cover for that one. I'd ring their doorbell and flash this Halloween tin badge.

"FBI, Ma'm. I'm undercover, " I say in my deepest voice. "Just practicing. Pay no attention to anything you hear. It's part of Homeland Security. We work for you. Protecting land, sea and shore. Top secret." I wink. It works every time.

My wife is patient. She's a good woman, a real looker. Bakes. Cleans. Humors my every whim. My mother phones regularly asking, "John, when are we going to meet this girl, this wifey of yours?" She implies in her little snippy voice that she thinks Angela is imaginary. My Angela! I am not going to let my mother get within a half mile of her. The humiliation my mother is capable of inflicting is legendary.

My Sudoku habit started from delivering the morning paper. Every morning before dawn I rolled and stuffed the papers into plastic bags before heading out on my route. I leaned out the car window, tossed them onto porches with the accuracy of Sandy Koufax. Afterwards I stopped at Dunkin' Doughnuts for a chocolate old fashioned and a cuppa joe while Angela slept in late. She likes to get her beauty rest.

One day at the doughnut shop I opened the paper to read the comics and Sudoku caught my eye. Lots of rows like a crossword but all numbers, the assignment being to fill in the missing blanks. Now I like that! None of those messy words that might mean this or that. Numbers I understand - their role, their position, the tidy way they sidle up one next to the other. It took a couple of days to figure out the patterns. It's there though. It's like decoding secret messages from Mars. I carry the puzzles with me everywhere I go. I don't speak to anyone anymore unless it's 911. Got to ponder each new mystery.

Angela is the poor Sudoku widow. She wears black, even to bed now. Black lace, black leather. I don't care. They have this new Sudoku puzzle with sixteen numbers to a row instead of nine. You have to be a master to solve it. Focus all your energy. I'm transcending sleep and meals and I feel the power flowing.

The phone has been ringing for days. Probably a bunch of customers who don't understand. Or maybe it's *The Detroit News*. My garage is full of their papers.

Just as I near completion of my first sixteen-numbered Sudoku, Angela tosses a glass of water over me. Snap, crackle, pop! I whip the pistol out of the drawer and drill her. Twice. Like I said, I'm a good shot. She's standing next to the bed, bare-naked with a Bible in her hands. That old Holy Book looked exactly like a gun –a clear case of self-defense.

But she only staggers. No blood. More like a burning smell. She drops the Bible and vanishes. I open it and find the bullets lodged in Revelations, just above and below Chapter 2:10 *"Do not be afraid of anything that you are going to suffer. Indeed, the devil will throw some of you into prison, that you may be tested, and you will face an ordeal for ten days. Remain faithful until death, and I will give you the crown of life."*

Sirens wail in the distance, pulsing closer to my street. I know sirens; my mother has called them before. They'll arrive with needles and questions, with jacket and straps. They'll take away pencils and sharp things. Oh ye of little faith, I am the Master of All Things Great and Small. I will wear the crown of life. I push the sofa against the front door and cover the window with blankets. I tip the dining room table on its side and crouch behind it, yellow pencil and sixteen-numbered Sudoku in hand, hoping to reach the final solution before they burst open the door.

Renegade

ꟹ

I kiss Sheila's lips and find myself in a pattern I can't control. My hand trails along the curve of her ivory body and I feel what all humans feel. At least I think so. My memory seems intact. Sheila's red hair draws in light through the chinks of the crypt door; her hair sparks and crackles. I press my body down tight on hers. Someday soon our lovemaking will start and finish at the exact same point in a pre-recorded loop. But not yet. We are not fully formed holographic images. Our souls are unable to crossover to what lies beyond the Earth or inside of it. We have yet to fulfill our debt to society. I haven't accumulated the body count required by my sentencing, neither has Sheila. She's not telling me her remaining number and I'm not telling her mine.

It was Heroes' Day when I met her, my love and my nemesis. *They* constantly remind us that the day honors harvested organ donors so that we never forget their sacrifices. As if I ever could!

I arrived at the National Heroes Cemetery T-line stop, unlatched my wheels from the line and coasted over to a bench. The line whirred and hummed impatiently as most of the riders disengaged, rolling away in multiple directions. Several families dismounted from group transit platforms. They took their time, clutching young ones and picnic baskets, steadying the elderly, all dressed up as if they were attending an opera or a wedding.

My wheels retracted into the soles of my shoes and I tucked my transit gloves into my backpack alongside a bottle of Blue Agave that I'd brought to share with Cousin Joe. I straightened my black eye patch, which denotes that I am a partial organ donor. My fingers skimmed across my intact eye hidden underneath it. It seemed so easy to do and so invisible to the organ police on patrol. Then I stood up and stretched, brushing travel dust off of my flex jeans. Nothing ever stuck to them. I liked that, everything including dust rolled off me. Easy. Free. No ties that bind. A man on his own. This was my one obligatory duty, National Heroes Day.

With a limp that I'd perfected, I headed towards the cemetery gate. Above the cemetery a multitude of flags caught the breeze and flapped like a flow of crows displaying their wings. A few white clouds formed a lake on the horizon. The rising sun was a hazy yellow, winter barely done. As the new day opened, the sky turned purple and blue. Voices, guitars and flutes played, their sounds drifted out of the cemetery. *Glory, glory, hallelujah.* The celebration was in high gear. We'd learned from our friends in Mexico how to party in graveyards.

The gates dissolved as I approached and reformed behind me. I followed the walkway to Crypt Building #2. The path was lined with flowers: Tulips, Four-lips, and For-get-me-nots, both real and virtual. The heroes made their own final videos, which were enshrined in memorial crypts scattered throughout the cemetery. The videos were old tech holographic but incorporated the new sensory systems so the viewers smelled, heard and partially felt the images. They didn't feel quite human – more like cotton or lambs wool in spite of their transparency. Yet a kiss was almost a kiss. Their tears tasted salty.

I reached the wall of Building #2 and pressed the release button on Crypt 20079. Cousin Joe Floated out. He smelled like old tennis shoes, smoke and tequila. I poured him a shot of the Blue Agave and tippled it out on the ground.

"Here's to you, mi compadre!" I poured myself a shot, saluted him and swallowed. The clear liquid zapped my brain. He followed me over to a grassy spot, hovering two feet above the ground. I set up my antique George Foreman grill. Joe had always loved the picture of George on its box, George's big black shiny muscles and his toothy grin. Joe flexed his muscles; they bulged and hardened. He turned this way and that, posing.

"Steak for breakfast, cuz," I told him. Joe continued to flex his muscles and pose while I cooked it charred on the outside, blood red in the middle, just the way he had liked it.

"Hey, man" his video called out to me. "Don't let the bastards wear you down. I've got your back covered." He hooked his thumbs into the loops on his pants, then lit a Mint Bomber. He exhaled. The smell intoxicated me. I could barely bring myself to look at him. The smoke made him appear as if he were a gangster or a biker in an old-time movie. I glanced at him again.

Through his body I saw two small Providence Elms and a Bonanza bush thick with early white berries.

On the lawn around us, families lounged on blankets and reclined on gel seats. Their loved ones hovered, shimmering in the bright sunlight, some of them posing like Joe. The Heroes were both male and female, although judging from the images floating nearby it appeared that more males had been donors. The Heroes were all around forty years old, the mandatory age at which they had to ante up unless they chose to postpone the inevitable by agreeing to a early partial harvesting of their duplicate organs – one kidney, one lung, one eye. The reprieve allowed those donors to retain a solid presence on Earth until they turned forty-nine when the rest of their harvesting would be complete. This group was easily spotted because of their patched eye. That little piece of black cloth brought major perks. Not everyone cooperated though, necessitating the Organ Police.

A tawny cat with a white stripe like the Milky Way down her back, sat a few feet away and licked its paws. The sky was so blue that I knew the Cloud Posse had been out clearing the heavens for the holidays, their patrol fleet shooting Phaseout at marauding wisps passing by. The color blue made me wish for wings. My shoulder blades ached from the desire to escape. I reached up and touched my eye patch.

Joe took another puff. His video loop repeated itself, "Don't let the bastards wear you down." He posed and flexed again. Faintly through his body I watched the cat lick its paws once more. Its repetitive motions, the bending of head, the nuzzling of the paw, the purr and stretch made me realize that it was virtual.

I looked up at Joe. He had been two years older than me and I emulated him – the clothes, the gestures, and the pick-up lines. I even wore my hair like his, a waterfall in front and a D.A. behind, something we'd spotted in an old movie. We looked like outlaws. Renegades. It made people stare. We always traveled together - he led and I followed. Only now I didn't want to follow him. Joe flexed his muscles again and grinned.

We signed up at eighteen – Joe leading the way, heading raucously for a short life. A promissory note for one hundred thou seemed like a bottomless pot of gold, especially after the devaluation of the dollar and the collapse of the global economy. And the return payment, due twenty-two years later, was a joke. I assumed then that if I lived to forty I'd be an old man. My pecker wouldn't work so I'd be willing to lie down and die. Signing as an organ donor seemed like the only option other than enlisting in the All Volunteer

Army. The AVA was a rental unit and the volunteers risked losing more than organs at a much earlier age. *They*'d send you anywhere to fight for anyone willing to pay the price.

The National Heroes solved a big problem for *Them* - the lack of bona fide organ donors. Before legal harvesting began, the black market raged. Tourists woke up in Asia in bathtubs of ice, missing a kidney. Morgues were raided for bones and skin. Illegal aliens who entered the country with the wrong coyote disappeared. No one talked about where the unwanted babies went. Street kids and derelicts vanished.

I touched my eye patch once more. My eye rolled underneath it. It felt round and viscous. What the patch covered was the fact that I wasn't going to let them harvest me, no way, not now, not ever. My ID card, listing me as a partial donor, was a forgery. They said you were given you a dram of ecstasy at the induction center, when you presented with your video for encrypting. It was blissful we were told. We'd be respected and honored. Then they'd take your body parts and implant them in the deserving and the undeserving, especially in those at the top of the queue, the rich and the famous. I flexed my muscles back at Joe, made a wicked face, lips curling down. He winked.

If I had to run I wouldn't be the first. The pack of outlaws in the hills has grown. But that isn't the lifestyle for me. I had a little basement apartment where I kept a bag packed in case someone turned me in to the Organ Police. Then I'd have to take off but I wouldn't join one of those Hill packs, I'd go it as a loner. I wouldn't want to fight with the other Alpha dogs up there where there are no rules. I didn't know how long my act would last before I'd have to run, but the patch had gotten me lots of perks and my guilt had been minimal.

A hand touched my should and brought me back to the here and now. "Mind if I sit with you, with you and your friend?" she asked.

She was backlit by the sun. Flaming red everywhere. Red hair billowed about her head, red chiffon dress with black shoes like a flamenco dancer, layers of petticoats underneath. And a black eye patch. Her hand was pale, almost translucent. When she bent down, I saw a splattering of freckles across her chest, between her lovely breasts. She wasn't holographic, I thought. I felt a pressure from her hand on my shoulder that I didn't think the videos could produce. And a heat coursed through my body. I was amused that I'd ever thought that lust would dry up and blow away. At forty-one my body was alive and well.

Our eyes connected, at least my one good eye did. My right eye locked onto her left unpatched eye. My hidden eye throbbed and I felt as if they'd already harvested my tongue. I could only stare at the glorious red-hot vision.

"Sheila," she said extending a hand attached to a sinewy arm.

"Roy Bacon," I replied taking her hand. It felt smooth and cool, like ivory or something exotic. "And this here is Cousin Joe. Or was. I'm not sure how it works with these images. They don't seem much like a 'was, or an 'is' – more like something in between."

At that moment Joe lit up another Mint Bomber. Sheila sniffed the air and sat down next to me on the grass, which was a special blend of year round Rock-and-Rye mixed with some California drought resistant blend. Evergreen and hardy. Before my fortieth most esteemed birthday I was a landscaper specializing in new hybrid technologies. I knew these things. Sheila stroked the grass and watched Joe exhale. He winked at her and she laughed. She leaned back on her arms, shifting her weight. An imprint of her long slender palm lingered on the ground until one by one the little blades stood back up, shaking off her touch.

I plunged a fork into the steak, juices bubbled round the puncture marks. I sliced off a piece and offered it to Sheila, all the while feeling my heart pound in my ears. Ridiculous, I thought. Juvenile.

"Are you it?" she asked. "His whole family?" She brushed back a strand of long red hair that the wind was wrapping around her angular face.

I watched as the chunk of meat vanished between her bright red lips. She licked her lips with the tip of her tongue and tilted her head to one side. Her hair refracted the sunlight as if she had some sort of glitter in it.

"I'm all that's left around here. He's got a brother in Singapore. His parents are still waiting in Cryo-Holding for a donor. His organs weren't a match. At least that was what *They* said."

She smirked. "They never are, unless you're an Obama, or a Rockefeller, or a Konichiwa." She studied my face but I gave nothing away. Perhaps a little flare of a nostril as I sucked in air. I didn't feel threatened.

I looked over at Joe. Maybe it was my imagination but it looked like he had a hard-on. "Let's put Joe back and go for a walk," I suggested. I'd never seen an erection in a hologram before. They're a reliable, well-worked technology. Something was disrupting its energy or its magnetic field. It can't react, I told myself. Maybe it was some sort of mirror trick.

Sheila smiled and her cheeks reddened, matching the rest of her outfit. She'd noticed Joe's alteration too. "I'll wait here," she said.

Joe followed me, docile, floating back into his crypt. I pressed the lock button. With my fist, I thumped my chest. "See you next year, old buddy." The air bolts engaged and he was gone. I tried to feel faithful. I tried to feel like a true blood brother, compadres forever. I wondered if the holograms had any consciousness at all. Did he know I was a traitor? I think he would have wanted me to rebel, to fight back, to cling to Earth and life. I felt an aura of regret in his presence.

When I returned to the picnic spot, the Foreman was still hot. The breeze had died down and the air felt thick. Some of the families had moved on, others dozed in the heat of the day on the lawn. Not so far off in the distance I could see low purplish hills. *They* told us it was dangerous in those hills, that the urban center was here for our protection but I didn't believe *Them.* The urban centers had full time surveillance for their own use. Someone was recording me right at that moment. I had to be careful and not look at the hills too long.

I forced my eyes to the ground. I didn't want to run right then anyway. Behind my patched eye I imagined Sheila stretched out on my cot, her ivory body turning this way and that. I removed her shoes one at a time, and then pulled off the black petticoats from underneath her red dress.

My good eye wandered until it settled on Sheila, in the flesh, leaning against a tree - one of the real elm trees and not a holographic holiday decoration - up a little hillock. Every muscle in her supple body reclined at repose, almost asleep. A magnetic impulse drew me closer.

As I approached, she rose almost like vapor. In one serpentine gesture her whole being lifted off the ground and moved toward me. I could barely swallow. She was the incarnation of everything I'd ever wanted in a woman. I suspected she could read my mind so mentally I put her clothes back on. My mother, bless her long departed heart, had always said that I was a gentleman and a scholar (in spite of evidence otherwise). I wished Mom had lived long enough to reach the new era of transplantation. I would have willingly given her my organs although *They* would have made some excuse to deny it. Bad blood. No match found.

Sheila hooked her arm in mine. She ran her fingers down my arms, stroking the blonde hairs. A shiver lodged itself in the bottom of my spine as we walked, following the smooth pebbled path away from the grounds of Building 2. Each colorless pebble on the path was exactly the same size. The path formed a large circle in front of twelve building like the face of a clock. A large rolling grassy meadow, dotted with trees and a little brook, stood in the center. The brook played a babbling tune that sounded pre-recorded.

I smelled Mint Bombers as we walked. I told myself that visiting Joe was like partying in a smoky club so his smell was lingering about me in that way. I sniffed my jacket but the only odor I smelled was my own, hormonal and musky, yet the air remained heavy with Mint. I looked across the meadow and noticed a woman sitting beneath a tree. A Hero lay with his head in her lap and she appeared to be stroking his hair. Every so often his body floated up and she grabbed at the image, her hand slipping right through him. She'd touch her face as if transferring the caress from his body to her own.

Along the edges of the meadow stood bluebird houses on posts. Narrow wooden boxes with mouth-like holes. The birds flitted about, sometimes perching on the roofs of the boxes and singing. They tipped their heads back and warbled. Their voices sounded real but I wasn't sure.

We strolled along, backwards, past the picnickers in front of Building 1, the recent arrivals. Families spread elaborate meals out on blankets on the grassy picnic spots. Ling-ling berry pie. Quail fricassee. Their Heroes hovered around them. Some dressed in fancy costumes, others in silk pajamas. All repeating their motions endlessly.

One Hero strummed a guitar, a tall lanky man with a bad complexion. His wispy thin voice, floated across to us. "There are heroes in the rivers, heroes in the sky, heroes in the day that's a'breakin so Mama don't you cry." He sounded as if *he* were about to cry. The song repeated with exactly the same intonations. His guitar didn't have any visible strings yet music came out from it. Sheila pressed on my arm and we kept walking.

"The music's only as sad as you let it be," she said. "If you don't like the lyrics, change the words. If you don't like the rhythm change the beat. Here, come on and dance with me." She started to hum, a slow dance, and I took her in my arms. A one-two-three, one-two-three, pause and dip. I swear the sun dimmed and one by one the stars came out, twinkling everywhere. As if the tune conjured up the atmosphere. Moonlight, and a flaming redhead leaning against my chest. She was quicksilver in my arms, both hot and cold, as we twirled across the grass.

She stopped singing and the day reverted as she led me on.

A bridge, a moving aereo-suspension model encased in a clear tube, joined buildings 11 and 12. A waterfall poured down around the sides of the tube. We heard hands clap and feet stomp. Whoops and hollering. Loud accordion music played, a Judeo-Hispanic Klezmer band. As we walked the path we saw a wedding party carrying a bride on a chair above their heads. They circled over and over as the bride waved, then clutched the seat of the wooden chair as it bounced. "Ooopa-oopa," they shouted. Two times in one direction, reverse and repeat.

We paused in front of Building 10. Sheila turned to me and pressed her lips against mine. It wasn't anything like a kiss. For a moment I struggled to breathe. Once I saw a snail in an aquarium sucking on the body of a newt. It floated in the water like it was dead. I pulled back in a panic. She touched the side of my face, calming me. "Go ahead, peak inside this one. It's different," she said, gesturing at Building 10.

This must be the lonely Heroes' tomb, I thought as I walked under the arcs of the portico. Its white marble and limestone glowed, scrubbed clean for the holiday, but it was devoid of mourners, deserted. The crypt wall numbers were made of imbedded silver filigree, more ornate than the ones on Joe's vault. A light flashed on the front of #41165. As if hypnotized I pressed the button. A rush of perfume that smelled of lilacs and nectarines greeted me. I couldn't move. I stood like an idiot as a crystalline web floated out, and lingered like a canopy above my head.

"Roy, I'm so sorry," a sweet voice behind me spoke, her voice. "This is the only way. You'll see. They'll alter you, only slightly. We can be a team." I tried to turn but couldn't. Nothing worked. The smell increased as my legs collapsed and the web descended.

I woke in a laboratory. A huge operating theater stood in the center. Video screens lined three walls. The intoxicating smell was gone. The only smell was antiseptic. I was fixed to a reclining gel chair by strapping from a material I couldn't see or feel, but it was there. I wiggled my fingers and they felt alive.

A person, covered in an operating suit from head to toe, approached the chair. Over his chest was a government insignia with the initials OPP, Organ Police Patrol. I could see only his eyes but his height and bulk made me assume he was a male.

"Mr. Bacon, cooperation is the basis of society. Cooperation comes in many forms – voluntary or exacted. But in the end, cooperation is your only salvation." His voice sounded pre-recorded. He droned on. "We don't make deals with criminals, only demands. You'll make your final video, with our classified reality technique, and be exiled to Building 10 after the harvesting. This will be your final integration. Your remains will be neither here nor there until you've captured the number of renegades that a judge deems redemptive."

He injected my arm. A warm feeling of bliss climbed up toward my shoulder and entered my chest. Sheila's face bent over me with a kiss. Short breaths, panting, a tightening in the groin and a release beyond anything I have ever felt. "So sorry," she murmured over and over, "so sorry." Her voice rose and fell, each word floating out in a bubble sounding like notes from a flute.

Now we linger behind the silver filigree numbers inside Building Ten. The crypt is dark and so small that we must sleep entwined, tangled up in a lover's knot. I can exit the tomb whenever I like and go to work. I know that I'm different from the enshrined Heroes because I don't hover or float, my feet move one by one across the ground. Even though I feel no pain and fail to bleed when cut, I have a simulated physical presence. I sense my pulse, my breath starts and stops in a curious rhythm. However, my yearning for life is gone. They removed that.

I watch the cemetery carefully scrutinizing all who enter, especially those wearing black eye patches. I know their tricks just like Sheila knew mine. It's slow work except for once a year in spring when Hero's Day comes around. Then the renegades flood in and my body count rises. I toast my small victories with Cousin Joe. "Don't let the bastards wear you down," he counsels me. Afterwards, I return to our crypt to curl up and sleep in my lovely Sheila's white arms.

Thomas Edison's Last Breath

He materialized one day in the corner of the room, my private room where I work at home. At first he was a vague dark shape that I tried to ignore. I smelled his cigar before I could get him in focus. He slowly took form - short, squat, hairy, with a five o'clock shadow. He looked electrified with extra wide eyes and shocked hair. His cigar reminded me of my nasty old uncles. Men who wore their pants up high with suspenders and liked little girls to sit on their laps. This isn't real, I told myself.

"Don't bet your last dollar on that, babe" he answered me. By that time I could see him clearly. He wore a too small Lone Star Beer t-shirt and Santa Claus boxer shorts. That's all. His paunchy belly hung over the stretched elastic of the boxers. His feet were dirty and callused and sprouts of hair clustered on each toe.

"Who are you?" I asked.

"Whatta dumb broad!" he said, "Don't ya recognize me --- I'm your Muse."

I blinked my eyes but he was still there. I stood up and walked away from my desk with my eyes closed. "I'm leaving now. You can leave however you got here. Just don't be here when I get back." I tried to sound tough. In fact, I *am* tough but he wasn't buying it.

"It's a one-way ticket, sweetie pie," he snorted. "I'm here to stay."

I hate it when people snort instead of laugh. I expect them to grow a tail, a snout, floppy ears and change into a little beast like in a Disney cartoon.

I grabbed my car keys off the filing cabinet and left The Muse alone with his cigar. Even though it was summer, I wrapped a blue cotton sweater around my bony body for warmth. I thought about calling my neighbors who are exterminators, or a shrink, but decided instead on a trip to the ice cream store. My husband, Ralph, would be home in a couple of hours and he'd help with the eviction. Ralph is an accountant and, in spite of that, is very supportive of my creative work. He keeps me going through heat waves, snowstorms and writers' blocks.

It was quiet when I returned. I didn't want to go upstairs and open the door to my study so I flailed around in the kitchen throwing Ramen noodles and canned mushroom soup into a pot for dinner. Unfortunately, they congealed and burned on the bottom of the pot.

"I'm home!" Ralph called. He opened the closet door, shaking the wrinkles out of his London Fog overcoat as he hung it up.

I ran to him and blubbered on about this man and the mess he'd made of my day and how he'd contaminated my study with his cigar. Ralph stared at me as I described this guy's outfit (or lack thereof). "Jesus, Deena. Are you sure you didn't imagine this? It's been a long week." He kissed the top of my head and walked over to his desk in the living room, carefully placing a stack of papers in the "to be filed later" box and loosened his tie.

I worked hard to control myself. Ralph hates it when I engage in histrionics. "No Ralph. I'm just telling you exactly what happened. He's probably up there asleep right now. He refuses to leave. He says he's mine, like it's for keeps."

Ralph got his baseball bat out of the closet and led the way upstairs. He opened the study door quickly and turned on the lights. "Where is he?" Ralph asked. He drew himself up to his full height, well over six feet. The bat rested on his broad shoulders as he looked around, ready to attack. "Come out, come out wherever you are, old buddy."

I shrieked and pointed to the corner. There he was, curled up in a ball, sucking his thumb, mumbling and drooling. "Deena," Ralph tried to speak calmly. "There's nothing there."

The Muse sat up, rubbed his eyes and spoke. "I've been working overtime for ya – got a coupla good ones dreamed up." He pointed to Ralph. "He can't see me. Remember I told you, I'm *your* Muse."

Great, I thought. Just great. Now my husband thinks I'm a looney-toon.

"What's a looney-toon?" The Muse asked. Even better, I thought. This creep reads my mind.

"Get out of here now!" I yelled. Ralph stared at me. "No, not you, Ralph dear. The Muse. I can't work with him here."

"Oh yes you can. Just try me," The Muse answered.

Ralph took my arm and led me back downstairs. He spoke softly about vacations and romantic dinners, a trip to the lake, a weekend in Chicago perhaps. He was really trying. But the problem was Mr. Scumbag Muse in the study.

The next morning was Saturday. I decided to try the cold shoulder treatment, to work and ignore the bastard. I started writing early while Ralph was still asleep. When I entered my study I didn't even look at the corner. I sat myself in front of the computer and clicked on Word. I'd been writing a story for *Outdoorsy Magazine* about a woman lost in the Boundary Waters of Northern Minnesota. My intrepid woman canoeist was about to extricate herself from the woods at night by orienting herself to the stars. A wolf pack was nearby, having made a fresh deer kill.

I went online to research. Research is an addiction of mine. I like it as much as I like writing. I've become an infomaniac, I thought. Then I felt him grab me. He toppled me out of my chair and tore at my skirt with his hairy paw. 'Oh babe, you'll love this" he growled as he thrust himself on top of me and penetrated me with his stubby little penis. He held me by my hair and pumped wildly howling "Yes, yes, yes!" He bit my breast as he came and fell off of me before I could catch my breath.

Ralph stumbled bleary eyed into the room in his neatly buttoned pajamas. "What's the matter. What is this?" He looked down on me as I lay on the floor.

"Ralph, oh Ralph" I sobbed. He put his arms around me. Ralph's big arms were reassuring. They're smooth and the little blond hairs are practically invisible.

"You're a mess. What happened?"

"Ralph, The Muse, he... he raped me" I said.

The Muse was having his after sex cigar, reclining in my favorite chair.

"Honey, it was just a bad dream. There's no one here."

The Muse winked at me. I didn't respond. I knew there and then that this would have to be my secret. I'd have to figure out a way to control this beast – maybe with obedience training. Lesson One: How to train your muse to follow your commands. I would not let The Muse take charge in my study. I shut my eyes and blotted him out.

"Deena," Ralph said. "You must have had a fall and hit your head. I'll get you an ice pack and some coffee." He stumbled downstairs shaking his head.

I washed up and returned to my study. The Muse had his pudgy hairy body draped across my comfy chair.

"All right, you little creep. Why did you do that, why?" I asked.

"Hey!" The Muse said. "You were the one that said you were a nymphomaniac. I'm here to satisfy." He shrugged his shoulders and picked at the dirt under his nails.

"You idiot" I shrieked. I figured that while Ralph abhorred my histrionics I could really let The Muse have it. "You moron. You simpleton. You ignorant pig. I said I was an *info*maniac not a nymphomaniac!" This felt good. The Muse hung his head, shuffled his feet and retreated to a corner to suck his thumb. I turned back to my story. I wanted this one to be the Really Good One. A break through. The prizewinner as well as the ultimate tale of outdoor survival.

"Excuse me," The Muse piped in. "I've got a Really Good One for ya. Great story. About a bunch of terrorists that plot to steal Thomas Edison's Last Breath. You know it's kept in a jar at the Henry Ford Museum, just down the road. Old Henry got it from Edison's son."

I stuck my fingers in my ears. "La La La La," I chanted. "I can't hear you." I felt like a ten-year-old but it worked temporarily.

Over the next few days The Muse badgered me about Thomas Edison's Last Breath. I tried to explain to him that just because it's real doesn't mean that it would work in a story. And terrorists? I'd been assigned a mental case for a muse. Rotten luck. I put ashtrays all over the room. That was the only accommodation I was willing to make.

Ralph puzzled a bit over the bruise that appeared on my breast. He tried to explain it by saying that it must have been from the fall in my study when I imagined that I had been raped.

"Deena," he said. "All artists have overactive imaginations."

He was extra kind and solicitous the next few weeks. A bouquet of flowers freshly picked from his perfectly tended garden appeared every day. Snapdragons and babies breath. Day lilies and forget-me-nots. Coffee was brewed and waiting for me each morning, when I woke. I tiptoed into my study and tried to work without waking The Muse. My story was not progressing and I was sick of listening to The Muse prattle on about Thomas Edison and the terrorist cell in Dearborn, Michigan with their insane plot. It had infiltrated my brainwaves. I couldn't even think of the serenity of the Boundary Waters.

One morning, tired of my stalled story, I stomped in and shook The Muse awake. "Coffee," he croaked.

"You don't drink coffee, idiot. I do." I replied.

"Oh yeah." He rubbed his eyes. "I forgot. Hey! How 'bout my story today?"

I looked at his paunchy slovenly self and wondered why I was doing this. "Okay" I said. "Let's make a deal. I do your story and you leave me alone. No nothing. No harassing. And you put on a pair of pants. And you get a haircut."

He stroked the stubble on his chin and made his counter proposal. "And if it's a success and gets published, I get a promotion. I'm in charge. Clean underwear every week. Walks on Sundays. Fresh cigars whenever I please. Then ya gotta deal. Three weeks of nothing – boy scout's honor."

It seemed O.K. to me. No harm in it anyway. Pigs would fly before this guy would get me published.

"Let's hit it, babe" he said. He rolled up his sleeves and put his hands on my temples. I wrote as if I were possessed, rattling and banging away on the keyboard. It was like taking dictation. These were some terrorists he had me create. They wore masks like Zorro to keep their identity a secret. The leaders were two men shaped like a pear and a turnip. The Pear used women as sex slaves. The women appeared gratuitously in the story to perform sex acts. Whenever the law closed in on their secret enclave in Chicago, the Pear and the Turnip escaped using the women as human shields to avoid apprehension. They maintained a gang in Dearborn, Michigan close to the Henry Ford Museum for surveillance purposes. Thomas Edison's last breath, captured in a vial by his son and on display at the Museum, was purported to contain Ultimate Potency with spirtiual transforming powers. It could be the supreme weapon in terrorists' hands. This was a national secret and of great concern to homeland security. The FBI tried to infiltrate the gang but wound up busting a counter gang of inept terrorists who were plotting to steal Edison's brain instead.

On the day of The Big Heist, once inside the Henry Ford Museum, the terrorists seized the vial containing Edison's Last Breath properly labeled as such. The National Guard was called out to retake this great American treasure. A final shoot out occurred – bloody as hell. The terrorists are unmasked and we discover (gasp!) that Jimmy Hoffa, a.k.a. the Turnip, isn't dead. At least, he hadn't been dead, but is now. He'd been holed up with Elvis a.k.a. the Pear, in Chicago biding his time. Elvis's bullet-ridden body lay in a pool of blood on the museum floor. Unfortunately, a stray bullet broke the glass vial, releasing Edison's last breath, which turned out to be incredibly toxic and floated out over the City of Detroit rendering everyone below totally deaf. That was the demise of the Motown music scene. Even in death The King triumphs.

Three thousand words later I laid my head on the desk. "The end," said Mr. Muse as he lit his cigar.

Disgusted, I printed out a copy and mailed it to the toniest glossy I could think of at the moment. At the last minute I remembered to enclose a white S.A.S.E. I returned to work on the canoe story.

I've enjoyed the couple of weeks of silence so far. Even my coffee tastes extra fine in the mornings. Today it's a cup of New Orleans French Market Chicory. My Minnesota wilderness adventure tale is about to be finished, although the main character seems a bit bland to me now. The mail arrives early with its usual stack of bills and politely worded rejection letters. I tape rejection notes up on the walls in the bathroom. They form an unusual sort of wallpaper. It's a perverse sort of encouragement. Then I notice that Mr. Muse's story has come back rather quickly. When I open it, a check for $500 falls into my lap - enough to cover a supply of cigars and several pairs of proper boxer shorts.

Lot 23

Donald woke, his cheek pressed into the sand. It was early morning and he'd been on the beach all night. He scooped up a handful of warm sand and let the grains drizzle out between his fingers. The rising sun had already heated the ground. Salt stung the little bites and cuts on his hands. Welts rose on his legs from the fleas. Sand filled all his crevices. He itched everywhere. A small crab did a two-step sideways on spindly legs and disappeared into a hole.

As he sat up, a slight breeze rose. It made him giddy, intoxicated, and once again full of possibilities.

The tide was going out. Remnants of the latest oil spill left a wavy black line the length of the beach. Donald looked up and down the deserted beach. Far north on the beach a little figure wandered, moving like an ant. A man or a woman? Or an illusion? He shook off the sand and headed into the dunes to relieve himself.

He'd found his way down here by bus to the mainland across the lagoon. It was a place where a man could lose himself – an edge of the known world where you are forced to stop because you can't easily move on. A locker at the bus station across the bay now held most of his possessions. He'd traveled light, fleeing from charges of arson to which he had no defense other than ignorance. He'd thought that he could obliterate his mistakes. He was almost forty years old and on the verge of falling off the globe, clinging by his toes to the equator.

Yesterday, for one US dollar, a fisherman ferried him across the bay to the island. Donald carried only a small backpack with a canteen, some food, a stash of pesos and dollars. And his cards, his special decks slightly shaved across the top in a way that only his trained fingers could perceive. Deep in the pocket of his khaki pants was the deed to Lot 23.

"No problema, senor," the fisherman said. "If you want to wade back, at low tide is not so deep. The shark, he no take too big bite. Each year maybe only one or two gringos he eat." He chuckled as he nosed the boat into one of the island's coves and idled the engine while Donald clambered overboard, pants rolled up his lanky legs, pack held above his head. "Adios, amigo. I come back in one day or maybe two. See if you need ride then. If you want the cantina for the cerveza or agua, maybe three kilometers walk north. You find 'El Alacaran'. Tell them Juan Rosario sent you."

As soon as Donald was clear of the boat, Juan roared away dousing Donald in saltwater. He wiped his eyes with his arm and peered ahead. The island spread before him. A white snake twisting and turning and appearing to vanish to the north. To the south, it ended abruptly opened to the sea.

He waded to shore, keeping a wary eye on the water, shuffling his feet to avoid the stingrays so they'd move off when bumped, rather than whip him with their barbed tails if he were to step down on them something he learned from a book. Before leaving the States, he'd read all the data he could find on this place; an archipelago of two dozen inhabited islands forming a hundred-mile long chain. But inhabited was obviously a manner of speech. Sand and emptiness floated between sky and water.

Following the details of the map on the back of his deed he walked to the approximation of Lot 23 and climbed the dunes, which formed a ridge above the long line of beach. Using stones he paced out his lot perched above the water. He tried to square it up but sun made his lines waver. An illusion that felt like the summary of his life so far. Divorced. On the run. Everything he had prepared for so meticulously seemed to melt away. Donald sat, eating a lunch of dried meat, in the shelter of a clump of sea grapes that afforded little protection from the noon sun.

Mad dogs and Englishmen go out in the noonday sun. And which one am I? He thought. Mad dog, or maybe just a mad gringo? A cobbler trying to put something together from sand. Repair. Revive. Something to make my life quit spinning. I need to get off the carnival ride or grab the ring, win the prize. A sleight of hand won't do me here!

He watched as the tide ebbed. Dark patches fanned out on the beach and seemed to creep towards him. A thirst, similar to the ravenous thirst he'd experienced in Nam, pushed him to head north up the beach.

He walked several kilometers to the "El Alacaran". Unaccustomed to walking on sand, the backs of his calves ached. He encountered no other buildings until he reached the open-air palm thatched hut on stilts.

Inside the hut a generator powered an overhead fan and an ice chest held beverages. "When the catch is good," a short plump woman with a dark mestizo face standing behind the bar explained, "we cook fish on the beach. We are good fisher people. Plenty of days with fish."

"You," she said "we put some meat on your bones. Maybe darken you a little bit too. Too blanco. Maybe you won't be recognized then. Maybe you won't recognize you."

Donald felt himself drawn towards her. A familiarity, the sort that happens when time collapses and becomes confused. She wasn't young and she wasn't old but when she grinned at him, her mouth revealed crooked teeth and a few gaping holes. A gold tooth right in the front kept his eyes fixed on her. Her cheekbones were high and Indian, her nose wide and splayed, her eyes slanted. Each time she turned her head her face changed. From Indian, to Spaniard, to Carib black, and Eurasian. He imagined that she winked as she handed him a chilled Corona. Not an ordinary wink either. A second gauzy eyelid seemed to drop over her eye.

No one asked him any questions. The half dozen men drinking cervezas and sitting on crates scattered about the room acted as if it were an ordinary occurrence to have an unshaven gringo appear on their doorstep, as if they knew his business.

"Mi casa es tu casa," they cackled after he bought them a round of beer and entertained them with some simple card tricks. They crowded around him as he made cards appear from underneath the collars of their shirts. A King became a Knave, the Knave became a Queen, and then five Aces appeared side by side.

As a kid he had been fascinated with magic tricks. He'd purchased a cardboard box of tricks and a costume when he was thirteen and billed himself as Donald the Mysterioso! performing at birthday parties in the neighborhood. Presto! Chango! He made a scarf appear and disappear. Visual illusions, sleight of hand. Cards were his favorite. A shuffle that was not really a shuffle. He continued to perform tricks as an adult, amusing friends and impressing women. In the army it became a distraction from missions, a way to pass time, to accrue extra rations and cigarettes. Controlling the deck was his specialty. Pick a card, any card, and he could find it.

The men in the cantina whistled and stomped their feet on the planked floor with each trick. Afterwards, Donald bought a supply of water, drank several beers. staggered back to Lot 23 and fell asleep.

Emerging from the dunes now, he considered his options. The land spread in all directions, open to the sea. Building a shelter was his most pressing need. He needed protection from the land, the weather and the sea. The sand was stratified from the dunes to the water edge. As he stepped from the dunes, he left behind all vegetation - the sea grapes that grew behind the dunes, the tufts of grass that sprouted in the armpits of the sand hills. Every few steps the color and texture changed. When he walked, it was as if he were mesmerized. The sand became dark and dense as he approached the water. The closer he walked, the more it felt like the midwestern land he was accustomed to. A solid place to step. But he knew that was an illusion.

When he reached the water the outgoing tide deposited remnants of the ocean along the shore at his feet. Jellyfish, shells, polished pieces of glass, dented cans, broken lures, tobacco tins. Donald bent down and picked up a piece of the cool smooth glass, rubbed the tiny green jewel between his fingers as he slipped it into his pocket. Scavenger birds hopped along the water's edge, picking at the skeletal remains of fish around which hovered swarms of insects. The retreating edge of water left a lip of foam.

The small figure on the beach grew larger, weaving back and forth. Another mad dog, he thought. The figure would stop periodically to poke at the sand with a large walking stick. It was a woman wearing a pork-pie hat with a sack slung over her shoulder. She wore both a skirt and white-grey cotton pants. Her blouse looked pieced together from multiple fabrics. Plaids and stripes merged as she neared Lot 23. She was smoking a pipe. Donald recognized her as the bartender, her gold tooth visible as she grew closer.

The air tasted salty and thick. A breeze made the light sway as if it were a luminous curtain.

Her name? Maria something, he thought. They're all Maria Something. Mother Mary. Hail Mary full of grace. The smell of incense. As if to remind a man of purity and virginity. As if a man could ever soil the virgin mother. A mortal sin to even think about it.

"Yo! Gringo!" She waved her walking stick in the air. "I have what you need. For luck." She sat down cross-legged between the dunes and the water and waited for him.

He crossed the hot sand and joined her. "I need luck, all of it I can get. I ran out of my lifetime supply a few months ago. Good luck, I mean. I'm hoping I shook off bad luck at the border." He stood above her studying the part between her braids. It looked like the map of a trail. The sack she had been carrying was on the ground tied shut with a thick rope. Periodically it would wiggle.

Maria emptied her pipe onto the sand, snuffing out the ashes with a stubby salt cracked brown finger. She patted the sand. "Sit," she said. "Eat these." From her pocket she spread out some mushrooms wrapped in a paper towel. They were brown and pungent. Their undersides were veined purplish-black and dirt clung to them. He looked at her dubiously. She started to rock back and forth chuckling. He felt very white, very gringo and on very uncertain ground.

"Sit and eat, Senor Mysterioso," she said. Donald's eyes narrowed. That name.

Maria continued to rock. "These mushrooms, they let you see back and forth in time. You avoid the noose and the trap. The lizard she tell you how." The sack gave another thump. "Eat now. I eat with you." She broke off a piece of a mushroom, rubbed her lips with her tongue and chewed slowly.

Donald felt as if he were moving underwater. He sat down across from her and tried to cross his legs but lacked the flexibility. Maria handed him a mushroom. He placed a piece of mushroom in his mouth and chewed. He stared at his fingers, coated with brown spores, while he waited. An acrid taste hovered like smoke inside his throat. He struggled hard to swallow. A heaviness rose out of the sand and surged up his feet into his legs. I've become a pillar of salt, he thought. Or a pillar from the temple that Samson brought down. Another bite and he found himself rocking too.

Maria moved toward him, naked, her body reflecting the white light of the sand. His clothes disintegrated and vanished. Maria sat in his lap with her legs locked around him, her body melting into his. With each throb Donald dug his fingers deeper into her coconut colored back. He wasn't sure but it felt as if it had started to rain, rivulets running through his thinning hair.

For a moment his sweat burned and he was inside a building that was on fire. He shook his head, then Maria was back seated across from him, her head cocked to one side smiling. Her smile that grew and stretched beyond the edges of her mouth as she reached for the bag flopping around in the sand beside her. While he watched, one of her eyes became larger and larger. It bulged and became round. Colors floated on the surface of her skin. Blues, pinks, yellows. She untied the bag and an iguana stuck its head out. It too smiled broadly. Donald shut his eyes when the sun bounced off a gold tooth flashing from its leathery lips. It spoke in a voice that creaked and rustled. A thin, barely heard sound.

"You left me there. Maybe you meant to, maybe not. Maybe you never saw me sitting in the backroom playing cards to stay awake. I saw you. I watched as you pulled over the files, doused them, and lit the match. The flames blocked my path. Ash. I became ash. I nipped at your heels and chased you south. I rode on your back, pulled your hair, yanked your ears. You must give me back life."

A rancid smell, oil and sweat, something rotting down the beach, penetrated past Donald's closed eyes. He felt the lizard's head bobbing with the words. Donald rocked back and forth, clutching his legs to his chest. He saw the medical school office where he had been chief anatomist, where he made the rules and altered them. Only a fire could have destroyed the evidence of his crime, his forged record keeping. No choice, he murmured. No choice, as he rocked. He hadn't known about the old night watchman playing solitaire.

Borders, he thought, why are there no borders here. I crossed over. I abandoned the past and left it all behind. Time and place must have boundaries. Sand shifts. Identities shift. But surely there *are* some borders that can be crossed. Borders fixed as the lines on my palm. I thought I had abandoned that place.

The word 'abandoned' echoed in his head. A band. Doomed. Sounds were coming from his mouth. English. Spanish. Aramaic. Swahili. Pray for me, he thought, uncertain to whom he was directing the message. Fluids poured from his body and flowed over him. He felt as if gills on the sides of his neck were breathing for him. The ground evaporated.

When he opened his eyes the right side of his body hurt to touch, burned by the sun. He lay in the shallow water, low breakers rolling over him. He tried to move but his joints pained him. He turned his head to the right and looked towards the dunes, rising above the shore. The dune grass waved at him but no humans were in sight. No iguanas either. He stood up unsteadily, spotted his clothes, folded neatly, laying above the waterline. His sandals made of old tire treads with leather straps attached were perched on top of the pile.

He wobbled his way towards the pile and dressed. The stiff clothing hurt as he pulled up his salt-caked khaki pants and buttoned up a lightweight cotton shirt that now seemed three sizes too large. It flapped in the breeze against his body. The sun setting across the lagoon, was the only clue he had that the day had passed. His lips were blistered so he headed into the dunes for his cache of water.

As he neared his provisions something caught his eye. There, tucked behind the dunes, were four immense pilings driven into the sand on Lot 23, forming a square. Planks that could be used for flooring were stacked alongside them.

He returned to El Alacaran the next day and hired to a crew to help plank the floor. For a fee, Juan Rosario delivered screening material to enclose the walls. Before the week had passed, he was ready to construct a roof.

"No hurry," the work crew said. "Plenty of time, manana." The rainy season was not for another month but Donald wanted something now. Protection from the constant torment of insect bites. He needed to be enclosed. Covered. By day the fleas bit him and, as the sun set, hordes of mosquitoes descended to feast on his body.

Maria listened patiently to him as he bemoaned the lack of a roof. She handed him a can of cerveza and a bowl of dried salted sardines. Their tiny bodies crunched in his mouth.

"The tin for the roof, it is hard to come by. Juan must send his sons to the capital and drive it back to Laguna, then by boat to here. This takes time. Who knows when they go? When the truck is fixed and running. When the babies need medicine. Next time, he bring for your casa. For now, maybe, you want a thatched roof with the palms. This is no problem, except you must have a feast for everyone. The feast, she is important for a roof. The palms must be blessed and everyone fed. Only then will you be safe. Our Lady will protect you and forgive you. Tomorrow, I wait for you. When the sun rises, walk far north, to the cut in the island. We hunt for the meal."

At dawn the sun rose out of the ocean, and he saw everything as if through pink glass. The sparse coco palms barely moved in the simmering heat. It seemed to Donald that the early morning was filled with potential. The world stood on an edge. He didn't see Maria until he arrived at the cut in the island where she was waiting as if she'd been planted there all night. A trick played by the sunrise, he thought.

She handed him a long pole at the tip of which was a noose of rope. "This you need for iguana. We go now while the tide it is low. The water stays at ankles. Other times it cuts off this piece of land from the rest. We go now and return with next tide."

Donald took the pole, rolled up his pants and they waded across the cut at the northernmost portion of the island. With each step the vegetation increased and the island widened until he couldn't see either side of it. The ground hardened and soon they came to a brackish inlet where a flat-bottomed boat with peeling green gray paint was moored. It resembled the wooden rowboats of his youth, except for the completely flat bottom. Maria pulled it from its mooring and pushed it into the swampy inlet.

"Front," she gestured, and Donald complied. She tossed a sack into the boat and climbed in, her thick legs pushing off as she hoisted herself aboard. A pole, longer than an oar, lay on the bottom. Maria stood in the rear and poled the boat through the swampy inlets. Withered trees surrounded them on all sides. Some stunted, some dead. The dead branches were bleached almost white by the sun.

"Look up," she ordered as she poled through the sluggish water. "Iguana."

At first Donald saw nothing but the branches, limbs knotted and broken. He shaded his eyes and then he could make out the shapes. Iguanas, lots of them. Stretched out long and lank, draped on the branches, hooded eyes shut. Their size surprised him. Some appeared to be two to three feet long. Their dorsal crests lay flat to their heads as they basked in the sun.

"Pick one that speaks to you. Then move slowly slowly. Slip the noose over its head. Not so hard to do. Granddaddy Lizard sleep. Slip the rope right to the neck and jerk hard. Snap! Then we cook la cena over the fire." She cackled. "Maybe la ultima cena." The hair on the back of Donald's neck prickled. Maybe from the sudden wind, he wasn't sure. Being sure seemed less important now.

The lizards looked like peeling scaly branches of the trees. Immobilized. The sun had risen to a mid morning intensity. If he looked to the east, shards of glass interfered with his vision. Heat mirages rose from the water. Donald shaded his eyes, looking for an easy prey.

"Here." He felt Maria's hand on his arm. She stood next to him guiding the noose. She was so short that she stood below his shoulder and as she guided his hand, he felt her shrink even smaller and her arm extend and lengthen. It stretched out of the boat, reaching across the murky water towards the sunning creatures in the trees. Donald held the pole steady as the noose slipped over the head of a large lizard on one of the lower branches. He slipped it quickly down, passed the hooded eyes. When the rope encircled the dewlap that hung from the lizard's neck like a beard, he jerked it hard. The iguana swung in the air, its clawed feet splayed, toes extending like long human fingers. It startled for a brief second and then went limp.

At the back of the boat Maria held opened a gray burlap sack. She freed the limp iguana when Donald swung the pole towards her and dropped it into the sack. They hunted until late afternoon, filling the sack, then walked back to the cut and waded through the receding water, south onto the island.

That night, on the beach in front of Lot 23, Maria built a fire. She fed it until it was a hot bed of coals. Dozens of people appeared, as if formal invitations had been sent. Juan Rosario brought his wife and five sons. Several other fishermen who had worked on Lot 23 arrived with their families. Their families knew him as The Gringo Magician. They all carried large palm fronds for thatching the roof, which they placed in a pile that grew higher as the night grew long. They also brought breads, papayas, mangoes and chicharrones. The iguanas were skewered and roasted like birds, pieces dipped in hot sauce.

Donald kept his long sleeve shirt buttoned at the wrists to deter the insects from their blood quest. The smoke of the fire kept them at bay so he stood on the downwind side. He marveled at the obliviousness of the islander to the tiny biting creatures. Unlike him, they seemed untormented.

The smells of the grill reached his nose mixed with the salt air, and the fruit. The constrictions in his chest felt lessened by the generosity of the people. He looked up at the smear of intense white light across the sky. As if all the pinpoints of stars had melted and run together. As if someone had smudged their hand across the sky.

"For you, I save the Granddaddy." Maria winked at Donald as she shoved a sharpened stick through the iguana's mouth and out its backside. She placed it between two notched sticks over the fire. "This one is especial."

Donald rolled up the sleeves of his cotton shirt as the heat from the fire warmed him. He lay on his back staring at the milky stars. The black had a depth to it that he had never noticed before. Little children chased each other, shrieked and jumped over his prone body.

"Donaldo, we want a trick," a little girl with long tangled hair tugged on his arm. Donald sat up and drew a pack of cards out from his pocket. A crowd formed. "Magico! Magico!" the children hollered.

He stood up, reached into his pocket, pulled out a deck and fanned the cards. "Pick a card but don't let me see." He covered his eyes. One at a time the children picked a card and reinserted it into the deck. Donald's fingers controlled the placement. He pretended to shuffle, then showed them their cards. They howled and danced around the fire.

His usual finale was to have someone pick a card, put it back into the deck, and then he'd toss the deck into the air. It would appear to be helter-skelter, a confetti shower of cards and he would catch the chosen card by controlling the card rather than the deck.

Antonio, a barefoot boy wearing only shorts and a torn blue cotton shirt, pushed forward and chose the Ten of Spades. Donald kept his eyes closed as he replaced it in the deck.

I can't do this, he thought suddenly. A letting go was tugging at him like the tide. He threw the cards into the air. He saw the stars through the lids of his closed eyes. A flutter like little birds' wings hovered around his head as he grabbed a card. It was the ten of spades that Antonio had picked. The little kids whooped and hollered again "Magnifico! Magico!" Donald scooped up the cards and replaced them in his pocket amazed by his luck.

Maria brought him chunks of his iguana on a banana leaf. She reached into her pocket, unrolled a small packet and sprinkled the meat with a spice mixture. Then she walked over to the stack of palm leaves and sprinkled them also. "Life should be spicy. The roof should be strong and dry. May the eye of heaven watch over you."

He swept a piece to his mouth with a chunk of bread. A burning crept from his lips to his tongue and throat. It wasn't the burn of the jalapeno. It's the body of the old watchman, he thought. I'm taking it inside of me. He ate as if he were ravenous, extracting all the meat from the fine bones. He felt the firmness of the island. It had lost all tenuousness. The water around it encircled him, protecting him with its arms. Voices of the night birds wading in the lagoon behind the dunes reached his ears. We, we, we come home, home, home, he heard them sing in a sort of discordant harmony. Then from deep inside himself another voice rasped. It was old and asthmatic. The voice creaked as if it had been folded up and was now unrolling.

"Burn the cards! Burn the cards!" It directed him. No one else appeared to have heard it. "Burn the cards!" It cried again.

Donald walked towards the fire and emptied his pockets, tossing the cards onto the hot coals. They melted as they burned, turning black around the edges before igniting. Then quickly they became ash. A vortex of wind sucked them out of the fire and swirled them up into the air. Diamonds, hearts, aces and kings. The last card to burn was the Queen of Hearts. The Queen was dark-skinned and smiling. He glimpsed a gold tooth in her mouth as the card dissolved and filled the air with flecks of ash.

Carnavale

The painting on the easel was dark, very dark. One low string of light, a jeweled necklace, appeared on the far horizon. The water phosphoresced with a strange bluish hue instead of green. A small boat bobbed in the foreground, a ghost ship covered by eerie foxfire. Harry squinted at it and frowned. He rubbed the stubble of a gray beard that had sprouted overnight on his chin. Through the open glass balcony doors he peered out across the canal. A pale pink glow rose from the water like the edge of a shell opening. Something inside Harry slipped as he turned back to his painting.

"Water reflects from above and below," he thought. "You float up, sink down and can't tell which is which. Night and day are equal. The sun, the sky, land and sea. I want to paint them, but I can't see them now. There's only a blur. A growing darkness."

The blackness in the paint disturbed him. The painting glowed from invisible light but he feared that the black would overwhelm it. Lately, his vision had dimmed. Not to the point where he'd confessed the loss to his wife, Clarice, or to anyone except his doctor.

"These things often slow in progress, or halt. There's nothing to do now, except wait," the doctor had said. "Patience," but that wasn't a virtue of his. When he stared at the dark canvas its blue brushstrokes stood out like veins. They pulsed and he felt the throbbing in his temples.

The sounds of Carnavale rose from the street below where the night partiers were finding their way home. Venice was decked out in costume for the pre-lenten celebration. The idea was to appear on the streets as something other than what you were, something that your neighbors wouldn't recognize – a man as a woman, a woman as a man; ugly as beautiful; young as old; a plant, an animal, god or the devil.

Harry and Clarice had arrived in Venice from Detroit unannounced.

They came early this year with friends and took lodgings at a pensione where he wasn't known – Harry Gotschalk, the famous middle-aged American painter and his wife. Carnavale in Venice was their excuse to return to Italy. Harry needed Italy to paint. It was the color of the air. It infused his work; it stimulated his senses to the point of intoxication. Nothing could be more stimulating that Carnavale with its mad swirl of color, passion and wine.

This year their friends, Tom and Mimi, had come along also. Tom was a poet who earned his living as a screenwriter. "Kissing ass in Hollywood" he liked to say. He wrote silly movies in which dogs talked and children were heroes and the good guys always won. He was funny and marketed that. Mimi was a pastry chef, trained at the Culinary Institute of America. Twice a year she'd take a group on a chocolate tour of Northern Europe, primarily through Belgium and France. Since their arrival, the couples sampled different pastries every day for breakfast. Custards. Canoles. Lemon tarts. Anise cake.

They brought along costumes for Carnavale, religious costumes for a most unreligious celebration. Harry outfitted himself as St. Jude, the patron saint of hopeless causes while Clarice dressed as St. Francis of Assisi. "Bless the birds and the beasts", she said, waving her elegant hand with a graceful benediction. The beasts and the birds loved Clarice. She was a dancer and moved like one of them. A slender, fluid motion like a wildcat.

Tom chose St Lawrence who was put to death for failing to reveal where the treasure of the church was hidden. When burned at the stake he'd called out to his tormentors "My flesh is well cooked on one side, turn the other over and then eat." What else would the husband of a chef wear, he joked.

Mimi was garbed as the Virgin Mary, her voluptuous breasts bursting out of a low cut robe. Together they made a most unusual party.

The parades last night were magnificent and they'd gotten separated during the wee hours, carried in the huge noisy crowd across bridge after bridge throughout Venice. Unconcerned, Harry had returned alone to paint.

The door at the bottom of the narrow stairway slammed open. Voices drifted up. Disembodied. Ahead of their owners. Harry heard Tom declaim in his deep baritone, "for this I set sail. My mast on your ship, waiting only for a kiss or a gentle breeze".

Mimi and Clarice dissolved in laughter. "Here Tom, look at St. Francis molesting the Virgin Mary." Clarice's voice rose up the stairs.

In his mind's eye Harry could see Clarice pushing Mimi up against the wall and kissing her Virgin lips. Saintly. The two of them laughed and shrieked, their voices echoing in the stairwell.

"Ahhhh" Tom said, " you are the treasures of *my* church".

Harry smiled and turned back to his painting. Is blackness absence or presence? Does it draw one in or leave one out? One light. That's all anyone needed. A pinhole, a crack, that lets everything flow in. The boat on the black water seemed to move about on the black canvas, changing course. He blinked several times.

More crashing and stumbling followed by laughter on the stairs.

"For God's sake," Harry called "get up here, all of you, and fix some breakfast. Or at least open another bottle of wine."

Clarice walked into his studio. Her costume was altered. Yesterday morning when they had headed out to celebrate, she had a shoulder harness cleverly rigged with birds on wires. They'd fluttered around her head in a beneficent manner. Now she looked like something out of an Alfred Hitchcock movie. Birds at odd angles, all askew. One caught in her hair. Her sandaled feet caked with dirt.

"One of your birds has built a nest," he said, plucking it out of her wild mass of dark blonde curls. The morning light made her appear to be fuzzy, an ochre color that only Italian air could provide.

He grabbed her thick rope belt and pulled her towards him. She felt very real and solid. He kissed her, dipped his fingers in blue paint and smudged it on her cheeks. When she stepped back, momentarily startled, the paint throbbed. He saw it more clearly than he could see her cheek.

"You've been up all night painting!" She said

"And you've been up all night carousing" he replied. "After breakfast we'll call up the God of Sleep and see what he brings. Food before sleep for now."

" What do you mean, see what HE brings? The Goddess of Sleep is a woman. Man has to wait on her whims, to be let in, to be drawn in, enfolded by her dark wings."

He held her tight by the rope, wound it around his wrist and kissed her deeply. She tasted like marzipan and wine. She tasted like the color yellow.

Mimi interrupted them, banging on a pot. "Buon giorno, buon giorno. Pasticceria. Cafe latte. Served on the balcony!"

They sat down and watched from the balcony as the rising sun poured pink and yellow into the sky and Monday changed to Shrove Tuesday. Many of revelers were still out in the street below. Harry tried not to think about the black painting and the little cork boat bobbing on the surface of the paint.

Instead he thought about the review in "Art News" of his latest show at the Steadman Gallery. They had commented on his changed palette, the heavy usage of dark colors. He found it amusing that the critics noticed via his paintings what his friends and family turned a blind eye to – his dimming sight. The visual image of the retina appeared constantly in his mind: the delicate innermost layers of tissue lining the eye, layers of light receiving cells. Layers. They peeled off like old paint. A poorly primed canvas, perhaps. Some days he watched from the corner of his eye as another layer separated and drifted off, floating beyond the frame.

Clarice took his hand and led him to the bedroom. She removed her costume and collapsed on the bed. Before Harry could remove his clothing and join her, she was asleep. His fingers traced the familiar lines of her body. With his eyes shut he could still see her. With one stroke he saw her arm, another stroke added the softness of her smooth thigh, another her slender throat. He outlined the angular features of her face and then added color as if color had a life of its own. He added layer after layer, starting with the blues and moving to pink working in color as a function of memory. When he touched Clarice he felt color. He slid an arm up her back and twined a hand in her hair, the color of burnt caramel. Then he placed himself in the crook of her arm and slept until late afternoon.

The increased noise in the streets below woke him. He kissed Clarice but she barely moved, swatting at the air as he slipped out of bed and put on his St. Jude robe. He tugged at the brown scratchy cloth, pulled it over his chest and fastened it with a rope before walking into the kitchen.

Tom and Mimi had already returned to the street. The kitchen table held a platter of cheese and a half bottle of red wine. He broke off a piece of cheese and washed it down with the remnants of a glass of wine someone had abandoned on the table. He had no idea whether day was beginning or ending. Time felt as smudged as the edges of the world he viewed with his damaged eyes. He picked up his thick wooden cudgel and headed out. The cudgel with its knobby top made a fine walking stick.

The day had turned again to dusk. Masqueraders gathered in gondolas on the Grand Canal. It was a maze of bobbing lights, refracting rainbows into both the water and the sky. Crowds of costumed revelers coursed along the cobbled streets. A huge butterfly wobbling on giant stiletto heeled shoes spread her iridescent wings as she passed him in the street. Her wings opened then closed, folding over her naked breasts.

Harry followed the flow of the crowd over the bridge to the next island.

A juggler perched on the rail of a footbridge tossing tiny balls in a blurry circle. A fire swallower's face glowed from the flames that shot out from his mouth. Harry kept moving. He crossed one bridge after another, jostled by kings, queens, Casanovas and beggars.

"Bless me, father" a man said, grabbing the hem of his robe. Harry kissed his fingers and applied them to the petitioner's forehead. He kept moving. He was looking for something specific.

A little girl in red Elizabethan dress slipped her hand into his, "Come with me, father" she said and curtsied. She tipped her head from side to side, bobbing her blonde ringlets. He opened his mouth to speak but nothing came out. He eyed her curiously. She seemed very familiar and must be someone he knew. Her eyes were two ebony stones and her lips a shiny red. She gestured for him to come along. As if hypnotized, he followed her through a series of vaulted archways. She skipped a few steps ahead and then turned to make sure he was following. They entered a brick courtyard where a stage had been erected.

"Carry me on your shoulders" she commanded.

He hoisted her. She barely weighed anything. He held onto her lightly by one ankle, which a short white sock covered. Her feet were encased in black ballet slippers. She directed him towards the stage. It was heavily draped in red velvet and lit by torchieres. Off to one side a piccolo player dressed like a wolf in a clown suit played, accompanied by a drummer in a royal page outfit. Their music mixed with the noise of the gathered crowd.

In the center of the stage stood an abnormally tall figure in an alchemist's hat and a robe that glowed in the dark. He had a long grey beard in which twinkling red lights were embedded. Flames burst from his fingers as he flashed his hands in front of the audience. He spun in circles. Flowers appeared as he closed then opened his hands, and tossed the flowers to the audience. He closed his hands one more time, then released several lizards that scattered through the crowd running up the vine-covered walls on the three sides of the courtyard. Pinwheels of color shot from fountains on stage then hovered over it, forming a dragon in the sky. Harry stared at the dragon. He could see the lines of its body, clearly defined. It had no fuzzy edges.

The magician pointed into the crowd – he pointed at Harry. His eyes met Harry's. eyes. His face melted and Clarice's appeared in its place. The magician/Clarice gestured again and the crowd fell back a step. The magician balled up his hand and threw something invisible towards Harry. The knobby top of Harry's cudgel burst into flame. Harry felt electricity travel down the staff but held onto it and raised it into the air. He'd forgotten the little girl on his shoulders so mesmerizing was the orange/blue color of the flame. He let go of her ankle and, as he did, she evaporated and the sky above the courtyard filled with white doves. Dozens of them. They rose against the darkened sky and vanished leaving behind puffs of white smoke. The fire from the cudgel stopped as quickly as it had ignited, leaving only a black smudge on its tip.

The crowd roared its approval and the magician, his gray face restored, bowed and disappeared through a trap door on the stage. Harry stood still as the crowd dispersed, as they vanished around him.

A dwarf dressed in the brown sackcloth tunic and cowl of a Benedictine monk hobbled up to him. "*Nota benem*" the dwarf repeated over and over and gestured that Harry should follow him. The spell of the night was still cast so he complied.

They staggered along the cobblestones on a twisting path around and between buildings and along the canals. Everything acquired sharply delineated edges as they traveled a labyrinthine route. Harry could see more clearly than he had in a year. They boarded a number 82 vaporetto, water taxi, at San Zaccana. The night contained a thousand different shades of black and gray as the vaporetto cut across the water. He was enthralled watching them swirl into focus, each shade delineated.

The dwarf monk stood guard next to Harry, not speaking as the noise of the crowds carried across the water. Its pandemonium sounded like no language Harry had ever heard before. The sound became a fabric – a scroll unfurling, the sound issuing from the throat of a mythical beast. He felt it and saw it. Clearly. They exited the vaporetto on the island of San Giorgio at the first stop across the canal. The glowing face of the San Giorgio Maggiore church stared at them as the dwarf monk led Harry out of the light, around to the church's backside.

They arrived at a low door, which the dwarf monk unlocked with a key from a huge rusty ring. The stooped gray weathered wood door was the right height for the monk. It contrasted with the gleaming white facade on the front of the church that reflected lights from the lagoon and had a doorway that reached to heaven. The monk shoved the door and it swung open.

We're entering through a courtesans' door, Harry thought as he ducked low to enter the church. Something he'd read about in books. A secret entrance for intrigue.

The monk scurried through the corridors with Harry following close behind him in the dark. When they entered the basilica, it was illuminated only by candlelight. The monk carried a wood chair over to one corner and motioned for Harry to sit in it. It faced the wall on which a painting of the Last Supper was hung. He recognized it as a Tintoretto. The enormous picture was dark but filled with flashes of color. Harry could see it clearly. Two light sources emanated from the painting. It was the earthly light source, an oil lamp, which produced angels from out of the flames and the smoke. The supernatural light that flowed from Jesus was being passed like bread and wine to his earthly disciples.

Harry felt both lights exit from the painting and penetrate his field of vision. He was pinned to the chair as if he were a part of the painting. He felt paint applied to his body. Each color producing a different sensation and the light grew in intensity.

He sat still until a hand touched his shoulder. "Mi scusi, signore" a properly dressed gentleman spoke.

Harry was confused. He looked around for his escort, but the dwarf monk was no where to be seen.

The gentleman switched to English. "What are you doing here?"

Light was entering through the glass windows as Ash Wednesday dawned. It flooded onto the floor in rainbow colors. Blood red bleeding into greens and blues. The air glowed yellow. Harry had no idea how long he had been sitting there. A monk had brought him here to see the painting, he explained to the gentleman who seemed to be some authority.

"Ah no, signore, that is not possible. This monastery was last opened in 1806. Napoleon destroyed it. It's now the Cini Foundation. We maintain it as a museum." Angelus bells rang from multiple directions. Harry thought of Clarice back in bed and of the light emanating from her body as he exited the church alone. He felt the colors illuminate around him as he walked towards the vaporetto docked by the canal. They were unlike any color he had ever seen. He stopped at the water's edge, marveling at the layers of orange and purple lapping against the sea wall, certain that they weren't there before. As he boarded the vaporetto he felt the paint brushes in his hands and saw Clarice leaning over the balcony, her hair a cascade of roses, waiting for him to come home.

Martini's Bar and Grill

Ralph moved with her across the dance floor. She picked up his rhythm. A sort of slow samba. She responded to him in a way that made the drinkers scattered around the lounge think that they had been dancing together for a long while.

He placed his hand on the small of her back. Small was not the right word. She was a plump woman. Not fat. Just evenly plump. Her arms were smooth and her body was squeezed into a backless black cocktail dress. Mother-of-pearl earrings dangled from her fleshy lobes. Her back was different from the backs of other women he had known. Her flesh met in a crease, a line between her shoulder blades as if marking where wings had been surgically removed. He guided her with his hand, purposefully placing it on the crevice as a signal to follow him. In spite of the spiky high heels on her feet she appeared to float along, turning this way and that – matching his every move.

The band played classics. That was their name, "The Classics" - just in case it wasn't obvious from the tunes. The bandleader had a pompadour and wore a red suede jacket with a polka dot tie and a black shirt. His cell phone kept ringing. He let the pretty young girls at the closest table answer it. "Say whatever you like," he told them. "Take a message. Tell them you're my mother. Speak Italian. Whatever."

At each pause in the music Ralph escorted the young woman to the nearby tables and introduced her. "This is Vicki, my sweet wife. It's our second anniversary tonight." Vicki smiled and studied the pattern of the wood on the dance floor, averting her eyes.

Ralph Samuelsson was an elderly gentleman. His thick white hair sleeked back from his forehead, and his pale skin made him look almost like an albino. He was quite tall and moved with the grace of a much younger man.

When the band struck up "Theme from a Summer Place" he drew Vicki close to him. As they danced he slid her away, pulled her to him again and with a dip their legs entwined. He held her close a moment in his arms and sniffed the top of her head inhaling her scent as if she were a newborn or a flower. Only two other couples were out on the dance floor and they struggled with the beat.

It was snowing outside. A football game without sound played on two screens over the bar. The regulars sat there, watching the game, punctuating the music periodically with a whoop or a howl or a moan. The yellow light of the Super 8 Motel sign shown through the window. The freeway noise, muffled by the winter weather, mixed with the music. Diesel and doo-wop. Ralph kept his hand on Vicki's back as he led her to their table. He could feel a vibration deep inside the indentation, something like a low hum. His home in Florida felt far away.

Florida turned some retirees the color of old shoe leather but Ralph had just become paler, as if bleached like driftwood by the sun. Even his thick eyebrows and lashes looked like snow.

Ralph cupped his hands around the drink in front of him. The cool glass made the room stop spinning. This evening was not what he had planned for their anniversary when he'd realized that he would be in Detroit. He'd imagined Top of the Pontch. A river view. Lights gleaming across in Canada. White tablecloth. Romantic lighting. Fine wine. It was as if he led two lives – one envisioned and the other in real time. Dancing with Vicki helped him glide effortlessly between the two worlds.

He pictured her back home on San Marcos Key, helping seniors create jewelry out of seashells at the Center. Her smooth hands gently guiding the gnarled fingers of her elderly students. For a moment everything turned black and out of focus and then he saw her, and only her, suspended against the bluest sky.

Often he flew into Detroit, back home, at the request of his daughter. Demanding Debbie he secretly called her. "Please, Papa" she'd begged. "I need you to be here." Ralph couldn't remember if she had been like this before his first wife and Debbie's mother, Mildred, had died. Debbie would cross her brows and stare at him as if trying to see inside his head with x-ray vision.

Twice a year, as a routine, he returned to Detroit to tend Mildred's roses. They had been called Mildred's before she died and Debbie had him transplant the bushes to the front of her bungalow when he moved to Florida. A deep coral 'Brigadoon'. An apricot 'Yankee Doodle'. And the dark red 'American

Beauty'. The roses kept him tethered. Debbie could not remember from one year to the next the proper way to tend them, she said. How to wake them up in the spring by pruning them when the forsythia bloomed and how to bed them in the fall. "One more year, Papa, I need you to care for them. One more year." And he returned faithfully.

He had bedded the roses three months earlier in October, removing their dead leaves to avoid fungus, watering heavily, protecting the stems with dried oak leaves. And then Debbie called again. Worried about him and needing his presence. He'd returned again to give her some peace.

Vicki took Ralph's hand. Her plump hand felt warm. "You're daydreaming," she said, looking into his milky blue eyes translucent like a celluloid piece of the sky or the inside of a shell.

"I'm sorry," he answered, refocusing on her moon face. "I was thinking of the roses. How much I miss them this time of year. When the roses are blooming Debbie seems so much stronger – less needy." He shook his head and stared into the drink before him. "In the winter everything up here looks like an old black and white movie." This trip, in fact, even Debbie looked like a piece of an ivory chess set to Ralph. Everything was turning alabaster.

The bandleader returned to the stage after his short break and spoke into the microphone. "We've been told an Alberta Clipper is blasting through here tonight folks, dropping temperatures to the coldest of the year. The band would like to see you all out on the dance floor making the heat rise. We're playing some mighty hot tunes this set so... Let Me See You Shake Your Tailfeather." The bandleader struck up the tune and the synthesizer followed.

The rhythm guitarist put down his guitar and grabbed one of the pretty young girls seated at the table nearby. She giggled and blushed as they grinded around the floor, hips pulsating. A half dozen other couples joined them on the floor. Ralph stood up and was about to dance when loud voices in the entryway caught his attention. A man stood in the doorway, a familiar hunched over shape. He wore a long tattered coat and a hat with one earflap. A rag around his head covered his other ear. On his hands were pink acrylic mittens and a dirty green and black plaid scarf was wrapped several times around his neck.

"You know you can't come in here" the waitress with a blond bouffant scolded him. "We've told you that time and time again. No beggars. No vendors, either." The bartender inched his way over to the door, placing himself nearby in case his help was required.

"Just this once. Just tonight. It's so cold," the man pleaded. He carried a white bucket. Ralph remembered where he'd seen the man. Each day, at the morning and evening rush hour, the man would stand at the entrance ramp to the Jeffries Freeway down the street, peddling roses. Deep red ones, American Beauties. The kind Ralph liked best. He'd never seen anyone purchase one though.

"No. Next thing you know, you'll be wanting to sleep out back. You gotta go right now," the waitress said.

"Just a minute," Ralph said, moving between the waitress and the homeless man. "How much for the roses?"

"Five bucks," the man lowered his eyes to the floor.

"No, no. I mean for your whole bucket."

The waitress stared at Ralph. Her name was Marge. It said so in scrawling script across a badge shaped like a martini glass pinned to her uniform. She placed a hand on her hip and rolled her eyes. "OK, you guys. Take care of business but then he's gotta to leave."

The man smiled a toothless lopsided grin. "How 'bout twenty-five bucks. But I keep the bucket."

Ralph paid him and rescued the frozen roses. Their color was only slightly damaged along the edges, like a black petticoat showing under a red dress. He plucked off the bits of ice that clung to the stems and handed a rose to Marge as he turned toward the tables.

The bartender leaned over the counter. "You know he'll just spend it on rot-gut or a dime bag." Ralph nodded politely and weaved his way toward the back of the room. He handed a rose to each of the pretty young girls. They blew him a kiss. When he reached his table an empty glass sat there. Only an empty glass. He looked around, confused, and then placed the roses into the empty glass.

"What is it, honey?" Marge asked him, noticing his expression.

"The woman who was here, where is she?"

"You mean that young one you were dancing with earlier, Samantha, the dame in the tight black dress?" she asked. "Why she left ages ago! Would you like another drink?"

White light blurred his black field of vision. He couldn't focus his eyes for a moment. "No, no thank you. I'd better be getting home." He walked to the coat rack and stood in front of it. None of the coats looked familiar. He waited. Finally, he spotted one that looked like something he might wear. He slipped it on and it fit. As he started toward the exit he reached into the pockets. His hands came out empty. No gloves. The wind and the snow hit him in the face as he forced the heavy door open. His hands were numb and cold. He scrunched his chin down into the collar of the coat. The Arctic air was pouring across the border from Canada propelling the snow sideways. It beat against him as he walked and made a sound, a hum, like the noise of wings flapping as if some creature was rising up into the night sky.

Ten Mile Road

I'm starting to think in rhyme. My friends just roll their eyes and shake their heads. Sometimes they laugh. Mostly they're puzzled by this middle-aged, slightly plump (well-endowed, I like to think), white lady who lives just north of Ten Mile, bakes cookies for her grandkids and volunteers twice a week at the old folks home and is really a super-star in disguise. Or at least a potential super-star trying to bust her way up to the big time. I've got my believers too. "You can make it, Shirley," they tell me. "Get down, girl," they holler as I climb onto the stage for open mic night. *Ain't got but one dream. It's mighty fine. Ain't got but one trip and it's mine, all mine.*

It started one day when I was doing the dishes. An ordinary day in an ordinary suburb. I had finished drinking the second pot of morning coffee. I couldn't stand still, twitching away. The words just started to tumble and flow. They summed up my existence. *It's a bitch that Tuesday looks just like Monday and Thursday and Friday don't even rhyme. Up in the morning. It's such a bore. Do the dishes and sweep the floor. I take out the trash, cook more hash. Talk some trash. I'm talking trash. Kiss my trash. I'll kick your trash. Big, fat trash. Shake it now. Shake it fast. That big, fat trash. Shake that ass. Shake it now.*

That's just the opener for my act. I've got the shake-it costume too. A silver-sequined tube top. Lets my cleavage show. Lets everything else show too. It's good for shaking it and I've got lots of "it" to shake. Since I've started to perform I've cut and dyed my hair a spiky blue. During the week, when I'm disguised as a suburban grandmother, I wear a wig. If anyone notices that it's fake, they assume that I'm a cancer survivor.

I never wear the wig when Richard stops over. Richard is my ex-husband. I love to rub his nose in it. He has peanuts for testicles. And no rhythm. I should never have married a guy who couldn't dance. Unfortunately, it appears that both my grown children have inherited his two left feet. They can at least clap their hands in time to the beat once I get it going, but they have to work at it. Richard is one of those guys with a briefcase and a pocket protector who wipes the phone with a hanky before using it and probably wouldn't ever sit on a public toilet seat. How he got that twenty-something-year-old bimbo to move in with him, I'll never know. Lorraine. What a name. What a shame. *Bimboland is mighty cool. It's a real fine place for ex-husbands, ex-boyfriends and fools. You gag 'em, and you choke 'em and hang 'em on the wall. Let them out for supper and a tumble and a paw.* The bimbo makes him constantly late with his checks so lots of things are broken around my house.

Often I have trouble with my wheels. Wheels are a big deal in this town. American wheels. Japanese ones could get you stoned, or worse. You dream about wheels until you're sixteen, then spend a lot of time and money getting hold of the right looking machine. It's part of the mating dance like peacocks spreading their tails. Cruising the streets looking bad. That's how I met Richard. Richard drove a Mustang years ago and I was a Mustang style lady. Now I drive a Ford Escort. I've named her Jane, as in Plain. Trouble is that some days she runs and others she won't. I take her to the mechanic and she works just fine. Mike, my mechanic, looks at me blankly when I come in one more time with a loud noise that disappears as soon as I pull into his driveway. "Sounds great, Shirley. No problem with that engine." I think that means it's all in my head. *Rev' your wheels, open your door. I'll do it in the backseat. I'll do it on the floor. If your chrome don't shine, we are through. So baby, oh baby let me double hemi you.*

Today, Jane refuses to start and I have to take the bus. And I mean The Bus, as in The One and Only. If you miss it, kiss it good-bye. I've seen movies where you stand on the corner and, whoosh, bus after bus will sweep by and pick you up. No way. Not today or any day in this town. The wind is trying to shift to the north and I'm dancing from foot to foot to stay warm. I have my costume bag with me. The "City Times" wants to do a shoot and I have to be at their office by 1 o'clock. A centerfold piece, they told me: "MC Mama mixes it up in the Motor City".

I see and smell the bus approach. It has an ancient advertisement for "The Lion King" on its side. And a public service message about the vices of smoking. It makes me want to light up right then and there. I board, and insert a dollar into the receptacle. The driver barely glances at me. I feel like one of those science kits for the barely Visible Woman. A transparent body that the light shines through. The driver sees a slightly stale middle aged woman on her way to nowhere. If he only knew!

It's the middle of the morning and the bus is mostly empty. I sit in the middle. I prefer the middle – the middle of anything. So I can really mix it up. Leave open all my options. It's like that child's rhyme about the crazy Duke of York. *When you're up, you're up and when you're down, you're down but when you're only half way up you are neither up nor down.*

A young man sits in the back. He's wearing a satin jacket and a baseball cap pulled on over a headrag. He's wired to music. I can tell because of the beat. *Boom-da-da-boom-da-da boom* can be heard in spite of his earphones. He taps with his fingers on the metal bar of the seat in front of him. *Boom-da-da-boom* but he stops and looks me up and down a couple of times before rising from his seat.

"Hey!" he calls. "You that crazy white old lady rapper? I know you! You bitchin'. You one bad mother. Wanna hear some fine beats?" He offers me his headphones. It's XLDaddy2Cool. My palms start to sweat. Daddy2Cool *is* too cool. Thinks he's so ghetto that no one can touch him. Certainly not some menopausal wrinkly suburban white lady. I'm in training though. I'm almost ready. I offer the young man some oatmeal raisin cookies from my bag and give him a flyer for my Saturday show at the Juke Hall. It's billed as the Biggest, the Best and the Baddest get down in Motown. I'm not sure which I am, but I want to be all three. Get down in Motown is my fast track out of here. Rumors are that a Japanese promoter will be there.

Daddy2Cool left a message for me on my answering machine. " Yo, mama! Yo ass is so big – it ain't something that Japanese dig. You white rice, you stinky fish. I gonna make you sushi on a dish."

The bus lurches its way into the City. Old newspapers and plastic grocery bags blowing everywhere – in all the weedy fields and abandoned buildings. We pass one strip with viable stores. An auto repair shop, a wig store, a nail salon, a drugstore, and a bar-be-que joint that looks tempting. Just thinking about a slab of short ribs makes me start to drool. The branch library stands off to a side with boards over its windows. The trees have lost most of their leaves and they point at me with their bony fingers. *Stay in your place, Ms. Wrinkly-Face, it ain't a question about race. It's who wants a gramma who shakes her bootie and can jam' wit ya. Like the brother down the road drivin' a Lincoln or a Ford, or a Caddy or a Hummer, or a dope 440 Porsche. Rev it up! Burn some rubber! You might not get it. You a sucker.* It sounds like a whammy Daddy2Cool might try on me. He's like those trees pointing with their fingers. He's got nothing on me, I tell myself. And this weekend I'll get to prove that – showdown at Juke Hall. A duel with Daddy2Cool. One that will let me take off on a 747. I sure hope that they like cookies in Japan.

The bus lets me off a few blocks from the City Times office. I try to hurry and when I arrive Marcia (pronounced Mar-see-a), my DJ, is pacing the hallway. She's young and oh so trendy.

"God, Shirley. What took you so long!" she says.

"It's the awful buses." I take my coat off and throw it on a chair. "Can't wait for my first real contract. Then I get my Mustang and look out – its ride, Sally, ride. Cruising Belle Isle on a Friday Night. Taking off to Chi Town for the weekend. And I get to tell Richard to shove his pitiful allowance up his ass. How's my hair look?" I have on shiny blue press-on nails to match the color. I run my hands through my hair to make it stand up and look electrifying.

"Hair's great. Come on," Marcia says. "I'll help you with your clothes and make-up." We've got the routine down to fifteen minutes. Like Clark Kent in a phone booth, I become MC Mama. Good thing the steam heat is on high in this old building. Goosebumps wouldn't photo well, I think.

I walk into the room, which is set with bright lights for the shoot. Marcia is telling me something about Saturday. I catch just a part of it. "Shirley, Bernie said that those Japanese promoters are in town. Saturday's for real money. It's the Big Time – our break! Wham. Bam. And we are out of here."

"Shirley, baby, good to see ya." George, the city editor, comes over and stands on his tiptoes to kiss my cheek. I am a big woman, like I said. Both wide and high and, with my spiky heels on, I'm a virtual tower of power. George is a small, affectionate guy. I give him a big squeeze. The click of the cameras tells me they are shooting this too. A pseudo stage covered with Christmas lights is set up in one corner with a mic.

"We want this to look like the Juke Hall. We'll be out on Saturday too for extra shots of the crowd, and of Daddy2Cool. We asked him to come down today and do a photo op with you. He 'don't do that,' he said. 'See my agent.' So, honey, you are it. You're the centerfold. The City Times playmate of the month. One color shot and the rest black and white." George looked out the window. "That about sums up this town too. One color shot and then black and white." He shook his head and left the room as the photographer went to work. He took a lot of shots from below. I'll probably end up looking like Paul Bunyan or his sidekick, Babe the Blue Ox.

Marcia takes charge of the beats and scratches while I rap a bit to loosen up. I get nervous in front of a crowd. Nervous pumps me up. Gets me going at 99 miles an hour. Makes my brain shimmy and slam. It feels odd to be rapping in a room with only a photographer and a light man. I think about Daddy2Cool. Whooping and hollering and grabbing his crotch. That gets me nervous enough to start jammin'. Saturday's show is not a head-to-head open mic showdown but a three act, coin-toss order of performance. Me, Daddy2Cool and this kid, SlamJamJoey. The kid is ok. Uses some pretty worn retreads and isn't a showman. Daddy is my competition.

"One more shot, please," the photographer begs. "Just lean over. That's right. Thanks baby." I squeeze my arms against my chest. They press my big bosom further towards his cyclops camera. I lick then purse my big red lips. Shut my eyes. Blue glitter falls out of my hair, cascading towards my cleavage. Marcia is good at these touches. The blue glitter. I find it everywhere for days after the shows.

"Come on," Marcia says after the photographer has finished. "I'll give you a lift home. I don't have to be at work for a couple of hours." Marcia waits on tables at the Great Lakes Bar and Brewhouse when she isn't working shows for me. It doesn't seem like much of a life but she's young. A friend of my daughter's introduced us and we've been a team for the last couple of years. MC Mama and DJFineBody (her stage name).

We head north up Woodward, across 8 Mile Road and into the burbs. She whips her car into my drive and screeches to a halt. We sit for a moment and stare at the porch. Someone's been there. White chalk is rubbed everywhere and something that looks an awful lot like blood is smeared on the stairs. I unfold my big self and jump out of her car, slamming the door.

"Goddamn it Marcia! Look at this." A dead chicken with its neck twisted has been deposited right at my front door. "He wants me to be afraid. Daddy2Cool. I'll fix him. Send all these bad vibes right back at him. He shouldn't mess with me." The beats were pounding away again. *Snakeskin. Frog legs. Eyes of newt. Chicken leg gonna tear your suit. Wave your hand, grab your balls. Your face will crack and your voice will fall. Voodoo gonna get you. Gonna get you soon. Voodoo gonna get you. Make your life a cartoon. So grab your crotch, what's in it's mighty small. Wave your hands, but I'm the one that's tall. 6 plus 7 gonna make you fall. Nothin' save you - You warty juju man. Nothin' gonna save you - not even yo' mama can.*

I go inside as Marcia drives off, leaving the mess for later. My answer machine is flashing red. I push the button. "You have two messages" the voice drones.

They're both from men. One is from Richard and it's some mumbled explanation about why his monthly check will be late. Bimbo probably needed new breast implants. The second one is an insane cackle. "Yo, yo, you 'hoe. Don't bother showin' up Sattaday. I'm the man. I am the baddest and the best. I've got words to make lips burn and pussies howl. I gonna beat you with the hippest bop. No way you gonna make me stop. I'll throw you to the floor, 'til you holler 'no more'. No dried up old lady gonna shove me out the door. Hey babe – you there? You hear me? Just forget it. Forget I said. Go back to bed. You 'most dead." More cackling. Sounds to me like I've got him worried. Otherwise, he'd be ignoring me instead of going to all this trouble. I feel so satisfied that its time to bake some cookies. Double Chocolate Chip Chunks, my favorite kind.

That night I dream I'm taller than the Colossus of Rhodes. I'm standing straddling several islands – one foot on the north, the other on the south. My electrified blue hair lights up the night sky. Below me people are scurrying to and fro talking excited in a language I don't understand. They point at me and blow kisses, then bow. I wake up shouting " Konnichi wa!"

Saturday arrives before I have much time to think about it. The Juke Hall is just east of Downtown. It's a neighborhood bar during the week with some of the finest entertainment around on weekends. Only special shows, like tonight, have any cover charge so it's real popular with the young crowd. The Hall's hard to spot as you drive down the street. It's on a block that leads to the river. All the buildings are a dilapidated gray. Most are abandoned but somehow the Juke Hall survived. You have to know it's there. They don't advertise but you don't need to in this town. If the music is good, word of mouth carries it around. Plain Jane decides to run so I've got wheels to get me there.

'Hey there Mama!" Joe, the bouncer greets me at the door. With a deadpan face he asks me for my ID. "Gotta keep things legal here." he says, pretending to scrutinize it. "Go on upstairs. Marcia's been here and set up. She's up there worrying if you'd make it on time."

I climb the rickety stairs to what passes for dressing rooms, costume bag slung over my shoulder. I have to duck at the top of the stairs so as not to bang my head. Someone said the Juke Hall used to be a stagecoach stop on the Chicago-Detroit line but it looks more like an old whorehouse with a sink and a toilet in each of the upstairs rooms. Layers of yellowed mismatched wallpaper are peeling off of the walls. I could write my name in the grime on the windows. I throw my bag onto a satin couch in the room Marcia has claimed for us. There's a thermos of dark roast coffee waiting and

I start to slug it down. The twitching in my head begins. I pace around the room throwing off my clothes. In my head I picture a scene from the movie "Rocky". Come out punching, I remind myself. Swing hard. Hitting below the belt is legal.

Marcia DJFineBody walks into the room. She's dressed all in black, slinky black leather. Her entire body is Ninja wrapped. Only her eyes show, thick with black mascara. "Clothes, Shirley" she reminds me that I am naked. Her voice sounds muffled beneath her headgear.

"Grab a shoehorn and shove me in," I say and we run the fifteen-minute transformation drill. Glitter covers the floor everywhere as Marcia tosses it in my hair. I hear SlamJamJoey kickin' downstairs. The beats come right up through the floor. He must have drawn number three, the opener. It's a warm up with the crowd still arriving.

"I got your prop," Marcia whispers. "Brandon kind of 'borrowed' it from work. It's got to be back, in one piece, on Monday." She motions over to one corner of the room. A huge old jackhammer is leaning against the wall. "It's your lucky night, big lady. We drew number one. You get to close." She dusts my chest with a last dash of blue glitter that clings to the adhesive she rubbed on my large expanse of exposed skin. The excess sinks between my breasts. *I've waited so long to bust out, bust outta this house, bust outta that door. I been blind, been deaf, but I'm ready to roar.*

"Let's go listen to Daddy2Cool. I'm ready," I say and we go down the stairs, through the bar and into the dancehall. We stand way in the back behind the soundman, Bobby. He smiles and winks at us. "Go get him Shirley," he says.

Daddy is up on stage, arms waving, foam flying from his lips. Heavy gold chains swinging around his neck. The front of the audience is his fly girls. Scantily clad and moaning with pleasure, they writhe to the music. "Do me, Daddy!" they cry. Daddy is real rubbery, like a snake. He slides around the stage, hissing and crotch grabbing. I see him scan the audience. A mistake. He's looking for me, I can tell. I stand tall, blue hair glowing above the crowd packed sweaty shoulder to shoulder. Smoke is pouring from his smoke machines on stage. Fingers of white smoke wriggle through the audience –Daddy struts this way and that, then points at me and starts bobbing. *You blue bitch you give 'em blue balls. I gonna laugh when you fall. I gonna Huh-huh-huh and nasty nasty. Whip it in your face. Watching you bleed raw. You ain't nothing but one big tittie. All shriveled up and no no pretty. Watch me whip it. That's it baby, whip it. Watch me now, Oh baby. Feel it.* He's crotch grabbing like wild now and the fly girls are screaming. One climbs on the stage and they dry hump. The smoke gets thick as he wails and carries on.

Suddenly three canisters onstage explode, shooting whipped cream into the air. Lights crash and Daddy is gone. Really gone. So gone, he doesn't even know it yet. The crowd whoops and hollers. But I am ready. Daddy2Cool won't even know what hit him. Marcia slips away to open in her Ninja disguise. My words are sharp as Ninja fighting stars. Damn the torpedoes. I'm a mountain of a woman coming at ya. Ready, aim, fire.

Marcia opens with the beats. We buy them from some high school computer music geeks. They are special. Anyone can move to them. She is scratching and spinning and playing while I shimmy through the audience to the stage. Buckets of blue glitter confetti have been rigged over the audience. Marcia pulls a cord. It tumbles over the crowd and they scream and go wild. I'm shaking my bootie moving towards the stage, wailing and howling into the microphone I'm carrying. *Oh yes baby, I'm ready to fight. Get down tonight. This here is Motown. Listen to my lowdown. This here is Motown, where the weak are eaten alive. I'm one bad Mama coming at ya. Get down tonight. Get down. I'm coming at ya.* Finally I reach the stage and six young men in the audience give me a one-two-three boost up. I'm wearing 6-inch neon blue platform shoes. I look way larger than life like a statute or a visitor from another planet. Someone's fantasy of the Great Mother. I grab the jackhammer. That's when the trouble begins.

I mount it and when I reach the line *I like 'em big and strong. Full of action. You gotta a little weenie that you've been packin'* all hell breaks loose. Out of the corner of my eye I catch a black and gold flash, realizing too late that it's Daddy2Cool looking like Ferdinand the Bull.

"That's it Mama. I won't take no more insults from some old white lady. You too big for your britches. I'm cutting you down." He gets off one good swing that catches me in the eye. He tackles me and we topple to the ground, rolling around the stage. I may be old but I'm big and strong and he is blubbery. When I punch him in the gut it feels like a giant marshmallow. I manage to incapacitate him with a knee to the groin by the time Joe the Bouncer and some other beefy guy make it up onto the stage. The crowd seems to think its just part of the show. They haul Daddy2Cool away. My head is a whir and the beats are a blur.

I holler to Marcia "Skip to the finale" while I pant and try to catch my breath.

She's rigged a swing that drops from the rafters. I jump onto it and rap while swinging over the heads of the audience handing out chocolate cookies baked by yours truly. I don't spot anyone who looks remotely like a promoter, especially one from Asia. Maybe that's for the best, considering the night's events. When we hit the last note the entire dancehall is rocking. We exit the stage, leaving on a loop of repeating music playing for the crowd to dance to. I feel my eye swelling up. If it turns blue I guess it will match my costume.

Upstairs, I change my clothes then sit back and let Marcia remove my make-up and tend my eye. She has removed her Ninja suit and put on some old sweats. Phil Jacobs, the club owner comes in with a concerned look. I'll bet he's thinking lawsuit. Worrying about it. Not my style.

"Look, Phil. Daddy2Cool's a baby. He isn't worth the time of day. I don't want to spend one more minute thinking about him. Let's just not put him on any bill with me ever ever again. And I mean that. Never ever again. He's no artist – just some thug." I don't have to convince Phil. He's with me on this one.

I take my cut of the door. After I pay Marcia it's enough to get me through the week even if Richard stiffs me on my allowance check again. I feel like I'm stuck in one of those repeating music loops myself, waiting for another chance to break out.

"You want a ride home, honey?" Marcia asks, looking at the puffiness shutting my right eye.

"Naw. As long as Jane starts I can make it north of Ten Mile in no time. I might try slapping a steak on this eye. I've always wondered if that really works. Although slapping it on the grill sounds better to me right now." I realize that I'm hungry and thirsty and deflating quickly. Time to hit the road home.

The twenty-minute drive north goes quickly. I've barely walked in my door and thrown my bag on the floor when the phone rings. It's Marcia.

"What's up now?' I ask. "You just can't stay away from me, is that it? Or do you want to come over and have steak dinner with me at 3 in the morning?" There's noise in the background. Obviously she hasn't gone home.

"Shirley, he was there! The promoter was at the show. He wants you. He wants you to tour Japan." She stops speaking for a moment. I can't believe it. My lucky night. This is great. It's like a crack opening and I can bust in, I just know it. Finally.

"There's a catch though." and she pauses again, waiting for me to ask.

"Money?" I ask.

"Nope. There's plenty of that. You'll never guess. Sit down." She waits a proper length of time.

"Ok – ok. I'm sitting. What is it?"

"Shirley, he wants you BUT..... he wants you with Daddy2Cool. The whole show. Choreographed, like tonight." I can't speak. "Shirley, you there? Goddamn it, say something. You ok? This is for the big bucks, honey."

"Wait a minute, give me time to think." I sit there and imagine wussy Richard standing in the doorway, writing me another check and whining all the while. "Bimbo needs new clothes. Bimbo needs a trip to Vegas." I imagine letting him write the check. I stare at him with my icy blue eyes and draw myself up tall, inches above Richard. I take the check and let him watch as I shove it in my mouth and eat it, chewing ever so slowly, never once losing eye contact. I can't resist this picture.

"It's OK, Marcia. It'll be OK. Let's do it." Bring it all on. I am the Biggest, the Best and the Baddest ready to roar out of Motown. Look out, Japan.

The Manual

I married Stuart because of the pearls. The strand he gave me in a black velvet case looked identical to the pearls that Jackie Kennedy wears. Jackie is the perfect lady. She lives a magical life, illustrated in all the glossy magazines, smiling alongside her handsome husband Jack. In the only photo I have of my father, he looks like President Kennedy. The one thing in focus in the blurry picture is my dad's straight white teeth, reflecting the flash of the camera. I want to think that he looks like Kennedy even though I never met my father or Mr. Kennedy. I foolishly thought the pearls meant Stuart understood something about my soul.

I worked at Babes Bar & Grill, as its one and only singing waitress, when I met him. I've been told I sing like an angel, like a bird, like a diva. It's what I do best. The waitress uniform at Babes was a starchy high-buttoned pink cotton one piece with my name, *MaryBeth*, stitched across the top, right at the full swell of my ample breast.

I've always been able to find restaurant work. Any diner will hire someone built like me. I have my mother to thank for that. It's my inheritance, my endowment. It's the only kind of trust fund a kid like me has. The trust fund caught Stuart's eye. He came in one night, nattily dressed. His trousers pressed with creases, shiny leather shoes, a jacket without a tie, his shirt unbuttoned enough to show off the little hollow in his throat. His slender frame, long sideburns and blue-blue eyes like Elvis gave him that sort of larger-than-life look.

He sat at the bar smoking a cigarette in a holder, and became a repeat offender, appearing every night at the same time, sitting in the same seat. His blue eyes fixed on my every move.

I'd spent six months working at Babes, saving up for my escape. Previously, when I left home in central Indiana, I imagined I would go to

Memphis to start a new life. I pictured myself singing in one of those famous singing diners and being discovered. *The Mah-velous Miss Mary Beth* in lights on a marquee of a big time club.

Only it wasn't in Memphis, Tennessee I ended up. Like an idiot I found myself in southern Indiana, not far from the Ohio River in Memphis, Indiana, home of Babe's Bar & Grill. I hadn't been specific asking for my bus ticket. My obsession with manuals hadn't expanded to include atlases. I still have dreams of Memphis, Tennessee even though my marriage to Stuart only got me as far as Louisville. Memphis isn't that far away. I know because I bought a pocket atlas after that mistake. I could raft downriver from Louisville and get there in no time.

I hadn't known Stuart but a couple of weeks when he got down on his knees in the diner, with the pearls, right in the middle of my shift. The pearls shone in their case, plump and full, each milky white pearl pressed against the cheek of next one on the necklace - and he had a bouquet of red roses in his other hand. He was so convincing, so lovey-dovey and he showed me a picture of his house, a magnolia tree blooming in the front yard that I said yes and quit the job on the spot. It all whispered magic to me.

We crossed the state line into Kentucky and were married, in less than four hours. I hummed "Going to the Chapel of Love" all the way there.

Afterwards, we parked Stuart's turquoise Thunderbird alongside the curb in front of Mama Sadie's crumbling gingerbread Victorian house. He opened the car door for me like a gentleman and we walked up the path. I suspected nothing. The house listed slightly to the right, as if leaning towards the sun. The opposite side stood in the shadows of an old oak tree. In spite of it being mid-summer, some of its branches were bare.

Stuart knocked at his mother's door with his arm around me, waiting until she opened it a crack leaving the chain fastened – checking for burglars or rapists, I imagined. She stared. I held out my hand with the gold band on it and her eyes lit up. She chortled, opened the door and gave me one of her smudgy red lipstick kisses that leave traces for days, kisses that no cold cream removes. I peeked in past the vestibule and saw a dark staircase and a chandelier with mismatched bulbs and missing crystals. The yellow air in the house behind her swirled with dust motes.

"Welcome to The Family, girl," she said without asking my name or what have you. The ring was enough. She didn't invite us in. Not then, not ever. Stuart says she hasn't had any company over since his Daddy passed on years ago. She walks into *my* house though, without an invite, without even knocking.

It's fall housecleaning. *Good Housekeeping* tells me this is crucial work to be done every fall and spring. When we were newlyweds, cleaning was not what was on our minds. Now I have plenty of time.

When I poke my broom into the back of the linen closet I find a small notebook hidden behind a mound of hand towels and scads of dust bunnies. I sit on the varnished wood floor, lean against the wall, staring at the satin, glittery cover. I rub my hands across its ribbony sheen and try not to open it, knowing that it isn't any of my business. Yet I sense that the book is intended for me.

User's Manual –it says in a curvy feminine script, inked on the front. *Gina Akins Von Stern* (his last name, now mine). Gina, the first wife. The lovely Gina with her long legs and tiny breasts (his words).

Honey, the opening page addresses me, *if you are reading this it means that I am long gone. The back of this closet is a place Stuart never touches. This journal is safe, unlike me. I have no hiding place.*

And you need my help. If you knew what was good for you, you'd skedaddle without reading another word. Pack up your bags and hightail it back to wherever you came from. I'm sure you aren't local. Locals here got his number. But this boy has charm charm charm and I'm betting you are hooked. So here it goes. I recommend you take this one page at a time. Don't worry about what follows since page one is plenty for you to contend with, for starters.

I hear the door open downstairs and shove the book into my apron pocket. Someone clears their throat then hollers. "Yoo-hoo, Mary Beth, girl! You up there?" The voice rises and falls, yoo-hooing like someone calling a pig. It disintegrates into a coughing fit. Mama Sadie. At least that's what she's had me call her since the day Stuart and I eloped.

I'm relieved that the yoo-hooer isn't Stuart home early from A & G Tool and Die. He would not approve of my find, I'm sure. And it will not be reported in the "How was your day, honey?" dinner table conversation if he makes it home in time for the meal. Many nights he does not.

Sometimes I think he's more married to that job than he is to me. He's explained a thousand times what he does. Molds and casts. Forms. Metals. Instrumentation. Demand. Supply. He pours it into my head and it pours out the other side. He's assured me he's important. A big man. Invaluable. Almost an owner of the shop. I don't ask him too many questions. *Only ask questions for which you want answers - whether they are good, bad or awful,* the Pocket Book of Manners counsels me.

"I'm coming, Mama Sadie," I singsong back to her, standing up and smoothing my apron. I look like the perfect little wifey, I tell myself, tucking a stray lock of my wispy blonde hair behind my ear and moistening my lips. I work hard at looks. I know they can be deceiving. A little bit of deception can be stimulating, I read in the *Happy Husband / Happy Wife Handbook*. Let Mama Sadie think I am the pretty air-brained pre-packaged wife.

I don't want her to come up here, snooping around, as if my affairs were her business. When I reach the bottom of the stairs I find her thumbing through our mail, having scooped it up from the floor below the mail slot. I try not to be suspicious, wondering if she's stuffed anything into her pocket, especially anything that looked to her like a personal letter. I am sure she'd love to intercept my mail if she could.

My sister writes me letters from Arkansas. It's the only connection I have to my own family. I can't picture exactly what she looks like any more. Margo raised me after Mom died when I was fourteen. She stuck it out for two or three years. I didn't make it easy for her either and she left town married, pregnant and relieved to be free of me. I remember her scent, a heady floral perfume. And the black lacquer of her dyed hair piled high on her head, reflecting light, looking like a mirrored helmet. I assume Margo and I share the same deadbeat, name-never-to-be-mentioned, Dad. No one ever hinted otherwise.

I was in the middle of a blizzard of hormones when Mom died. I didn't care about anything, only boys. Even my mother's death barely punctured my heart. This sounds callous but it's the raw truth. I could lie to myself but I'm not so good at that. A fact is a fact. I told my sister I could take care of myself. And these years later prove that I have.

I don't understand families. Either they are suffocating like Mama Sadie or ephemeral like this distanced one that ties me to my sister. Margo writes me letters. They are usually a litany of the wrongs done to her by her children, by her husband number two or three or four, by her boss, her neighbor, the dog or the cat. And recipes: *The Best of the West, Tuna Pot Pie a l'orange, Road kill Redoux,* or *Chocolate Orgasmic Surprise.* The last recipe was one she suggested I try on Stuart for Valentine's Day or our anniversary or anytime I think he might have a case of the wandering eye. It would fix him good, she reassured me. And not to worry. She's an expert. If they stray, they come back with their tail tucked between their legs begging for it after one taste of *Orgasmic Surprise*. I wonder if she tried it on any of the first three husbands.

I don't want Mama Sadie reading such sage advice. I don't want her poking into my tenuous family relations. It's none of her business, although she thinks anything I do is automatically her business and subject to her approval whether it's my clothing, my housekeeping, even our life under the bed sheets.

"Looking for them grandkiddies," she says repetitively, nudging me and squeezing my arm. "Y'all got them hiding somewhere? Get on with it, gal." Stuart may be forty but I am only twenty-three and in no hurry. I am not a biological time bomb about to explode. The last six years, on my own, have blurred the past and the future. I'm in the here and now living in my beautiful house with my successful husband in a lovely genteel town. I am modern though. Modern enough to understand the value of those new little pills, dispensed monthly in a round plastic container. Yellow and white. One a day. And the value of keeping them a secret.

Mama Sadie slaps the mail down onto the hallway table when she sees me walk down the stairs. She wipes her hands as if they were in contact with something diseased and sniffs the air.

"Where's Stuart?" she asks, as if she doesn't know.

"Took off on a river boat," I reply, letting her eyes bulge a little bit before correcting myself. "I'm teasing, Mama Sadie. The man works too much to have time for that sort of thing. So far as I know. Would you like some tea?"

"Only if you got a little extra to put in it. Something good." She knows I keep a bottle of Jack Daniels tucked away for her visits.

Three hours later she has inspected the bathroom, the kitchen, the dust on the windowsill. I expect to get a report card with grades. I remembered to crook my pinkie while we drank the tea, like they tell you to do in all the books. I've taught myself manners from manuals. I do believe you can learn most anything from a manual, including how to cook, or how to garden, or compose a proper letter, or fix a leaky toilet. *The Ten Thousand Positions of Love* is one of my favorite manuals. I love the names of the positions: *The Laughing Chihuahua. The Swinging Pretzel. Venus Descending.* Stuart has no idea what can be learned from a book. He thinks it's all from my experience. I finger the manual in my apron pocket wishing it was Braille and I could read it with my hands.

Mama Sadie finally leaves after ordering me to sing her a song. "My little canary," she calls me. Probably she's forgotten my name. I warble a little bit of *Amazing Grace* to satisfy her. I don't think she wanted Elvis or Buddy Holly or any "tight underwear music" which is how she refers to music she doesn't like. I lean on the door when it closes, watch her teeter down the walk on her skinny bowed legs, heading home, and I squeeze my eyes shut for a minute before going upstairs. Etta James is rumbling in my head. "*Something's got a hold on me, OOOHHH it must be love.*"

I change my clothes quickly before Stuart comes home, squeezing into stretch pants and a red flouncey top. Stuart has commented on the few extra pounds that make my pants snug. He doesn't complain about what the extra pounds do to my breasts though. I reapply my make-up. This is another tip from one of my happy homemakers' manuals. *Make yourself fresh before your husband returns from work. He will feel refreshed too. No man wants to come home to a scullery maid.*

Before I hang up my apron, I feel the satin notebook in its pocket. Something tells me that this will have to be kept a bigger secret than *The Ten Thousand Positions of Love.* Once I had a diary that I didn't keep hidden, a diary of my fantasy life. My mother found it and went through the roof when she read the entries. The entries were a bunch of adolescent lies, sort of. Let's say they were embellishments. Big ones. However, she thought the lie was me saying the diary was only lies. She kept a belt on a hook by the door and walloped me. She locked me in the house at 6 p.m. every day. I guess she figured that since she wasn't about to send me to a convent and she couldn't guard me every minute either, maybe the belt would knock some sense into me. She stopped when she forgot why she was beating me. One day it was like she woke up. She wiped her hands after whacking me a dozen times and declared that she hoped now she'd cured me of my sinful ways.

The only sense that it knocked into me was that I figured if I'd already been punished for the events in the diary, I'd darned better start experiencing them. First came the punishment then the crimes. Petty theft, blowjobs, hooky from school. It felt good to be bad. I learned to be stealthier and more secretive.

The only truthful entry in the whole damn book had been my fantasies after watching Elvis' gyrations on the Milton Berle show. When I watched him swivel those sexy hips in his tight black pants and sing *Blue Suede Shoes*, it changed my life forever. I'd lower my voice and sing, "One for the money, two for the show, three to get ready now go-cats-go.... you can do anything but stay off-a my blue suede shoes." I wanted to get to Memphis anyway I could, and sing duets with him. When the FBI and the pope couldn't stop his wiggling, Uncle Sam drafted him. That nearly broke my heart. That and his marriage to Priscilla.

I plop onto my bed, sinking into a feather comforter. The canopy overhead makes it feel like a nest. I open the *User's Manual* to the first page. "Gina, Gina, Gina," I sing to myself. "Getting to know you, getting to know all about you." I sing as I read. Singing calms me.

The first sentence hits me: *Have you ever seen this A & G Tool and Die Shop, where he supposedly toils for such long hours? Have you??? I haven't, either. At first he'd change the topic whenever I asked to take a ride to see it. Finally, one day he grabbed my arm and dug his fingers deep into my flesh. It left marks for days. He made his eyes into little slits as he glared at me. Look Missy, he said. I pay the bills. The shop is protected. Against industrial spies, and wives.*

A door slams downstairs. I go to my dresser and shove the diary inside a box of Sanitary Napkins. That's the last place a man would look. Feminine privacy, supreme. I stash my sister's letters there also. My youth has served me well. I keep my string of pearls in the drawer too, in a silk pouch alongside my little pillbox hat just like the one that Jackie wears. I get prickles thinking about her, she is so beautiful. Jack and Jackie. I picture her waving a white-gloved hand to the adoring crowd. She is more than a queen.

"Coming, dear," I singsong to him as I gaily traipse down the steps, a welcoming smile pasted on my lips. Stuart is bending his lanky body to peer into the hallway mirror. He's licking his finger and slicking down his eyebrows. I know for a fact that he uses shoe polish to hide the gray hairs sprouting on them. He turns his head this way and that, oblivious to me.

The next day I wait until I'm sure Stuart is gone. He comes back five minutes after he has left and hollers upstairs, "Forgot my hat!" The door slams again and I open the *User's Manual.* Gina's handwriting is beautiful. Loopy and sinewy. She is elegant, a real lady, I'm sure. I can tell from the script.

Chapter two has a title: **Spy vs. spy vs. spy**. *Do you feel like you are a character in Mad Magazine? One of those spies spying on other spies? That's because it's time to put on your trench coat and investigate.* She's written each word, perfectly formed, in a straight line. Her capital D is intricate, like Old English. *Are you being watched? Are you checked up on? By him, or by his wretched mother? And do you have a clue why? I bet you haven't been having an affair or even thinking about escape, until now. Every year it's gotten worse. Quiet accusations became loud ones. And then he tried restraints. You must turn the tables. Don't wait. I'm sorry I didn't try sooner. I didn't know how.* Poor Gina. Here she wrote a manual but it sounds like she had never read one. They are so empowering. I fiddle with my wedding ring. It's grown tight but I can still twist the band on my finger.

Stuart does reappear often for items he's missing: an umbrella, globes, keys. It happens almost every time he leaves for work. He looks around and stalls before leaving again. Perhaps he thinks I have a man hiding in a closet. Or several of them. I've found his jealousy flattering. I figured that he'd get over it one day, develop a little confidence in our lovey-dovey relationship. Maybe next year, I remember thinking each time as he returned home, opened doors, and peered in closets. A year hasn't even passed and Miss Gina makes it sound like it will only get worse.

If I had time, I could tell you more, offer you a real solution or maybe even prevent you from having to read this. I fear that I haven't long to write. I can hardly breathe. The world is closing in on me. I wake at night in a cold sweat and don't know why. I have no family to turn to and Stuart has forbade doctors. He insists that they are quacks and that my illness is hysterical. Tonic will cure me, he says.

Let me tell you about hysterical. My last trip away from this prison, my one and only attempt to figure out what is what, I followed Mama Sadie back to her house. Secretly. She deserved it for all her snooping and prying. I am sure you know what I mean. I went around to the back of her house where the overgrown pricker bushes are so thick that they block the light from penetrating the windows. It was the dining room that I found myself looking into. I ignored the scratches from the branches, and the mosquitoes gnawing on my legs. I watched Mama Sadie set the table. She moved in slow motion, blowing on each utensil and polishing it before setting it down. I watched her take a white napkin and shake it in the air. Once, twice. She folded it into a triangle and tied it around the neck of someone in a chair. She kissed the top of his head and stroked his shoulders pressing her flat chest against his back. She rolled her head backward and moaned as she rubbed on him. Then she fed him his soup a spoonful at a time. When Stuart turned his head, I left in disgust and went home to write this. I don't imagine there will be more to say. The fevers are getting worse. I'll take a double dose of that nasty tasting tonic tonight. I want you to know, you are not alone ever. I am with you in word and deed. Do what you need to do and do it for me.

Gina's manual feels heavy in my hands. My life is like a *What's Wrong With This Picture* and I have just spotted it. Stuart. I have to steady myself even though I am sitting down. The notebook doesn't tell me how to do anything, yet it explicitly says "manual" on its cover. I feel as if I just had a tooth extracted. There's a humming in my ears. I have to be sure that this isn't a fantasy of a sick woman. I think of my mother's belt on the hook by the door and my resolve hardens. I was never one to freeze and hide and be sorry later, wishing I'd had the foresight to know what was going to happen. Hindsight is a waste of time. It only shows you the pimples on your butt. I close the *User's Manual.* It tingles in my hands. Poor Gina, no foresight. Get up and go investigate, the book whispers to me.

The clock next to the bed ticks louder than usual. It sounds like a metal shovel clinking on stone. I wait an extra hour, to be sure that Stuart won't return, before I scoop up spare change for the bus. I pull a knit cap over my hair and put on sunglasses as a disguise. Subtle, I think. Theme music from *The Pink Panther* pulses inside my head. If I owned a trench coat I would wear it with the collar turned up. I pause a moment and try to decide. I take Gina's manual with me buried in my purse.

I have the Metro bus brochure, a manual for riders with maps and easy directions to follow, clutched in my hand. I've heard Stuart refer to the street intersection by his shop a million times. 75th Street and Columbus Drive is a dot on the far edge of the bus riders' map. I walk a half-mile to the bus stop and wait on a wooden bench carved with initials and names. Gordon and Jill. Bobby and CeeCee. Bill and Theresa. Bill and Patty. Bill and Cindy. W.T & L.M. Everyone loves somebody or everybody or anybody. The bus pulls up and the doors whoosh open. The driver is chewing gum, looking bored, his Louisville Transit cap pushed back on his baldhead. I board and ask politely to be let off at 75th and Columbus. He raises an eyebrow and shrugs.

75th Street and Columbus Drive, the pinpointed location of A & G Tools, isn't in the better part of town. Stuart speaks of the area in ominous tones. He's told me that drug deals go down on the streets around his shop and that prostitutes linger on the corners. Gunfire sounds daily. The tool and die shop has a mechanized gate protecting their yard, large illuminating floodlights and a 24-hour security patrol, he says. A pack of Dobies on guard. They have filed teeth to go with their pointy ears. I have a visual of the place in my mind, industry and commerce reigning over an encroaching slum. A moat protecting a castle. Dark and light.

I get off the bus near the end of the line. The driver nods and points to the corner as I hesitate on the stairs. "Dat's it, Miss. 75th and Columbus. Ain't no other one."

I step down as the bus door exhales behind me, and the bus pulls away from the curb. I turn in circles. Mostly there are empty lots filled with blowing newspapers and garbage. A pile of abandoned tires. Rusted out appliances. Other than a stray mangy-looking brown cur nosing through the garbage there isn't another soul around. The dog looks up for one moment. He has one lop-sided ear raised. He sniffs the air and goes back to scavenging, dismissing me.

I don't see any prostitutes. There's a liquor store on the corner. Adjacent to it is a brick apartment building that has seen better days. It sits on top of a shoe repair shop that has dusty windows and a gated door. The sun is directly overhead. The November noonday sun is still bright enough to bleach everything white.

A sign almost fills the shoe repair store window. It's handwritten in crooked black ink:

I WILL HEEL YOU

I CAN REPAIR YOUR SOLE

I WILL EVEN DYE FOR YOU

Another window is covered with a sheet.

I don't see any tool and die shop in any direction, or any sort of industrial warehouse. I pick the shoe store over the liquor store and cross the street. I try to peer through the grime of the shoe repair window but see only a blurred image of myself, finger rubbing the glass, touching my own finger. Even though it looks like it's dark inside, I ring the bell. If anybody is around I can ask about A & G Tools. I have to proceed with this mission.

Two stumpy fingers part the crooked yellowed blinds on the door, a pair of eyes peer out and I hear the sound of several locks turning. The static of a radio crackles in the background. I hear a muffled voice holler, "It's a white lady."

The door opens only a crack. A voice says "Lady, don't you know he's been shot? They done killed the President. Lest that's what people's saying. Praying otherwise, but he been shot down in Dallas 'cording to the news. We closed. Everybody closed. Might be the end of the world. You suppose to go lay low. Wait 'til they sez what's what. Who done it."

For a moment I lose my sense of up and down, sky and ground. I must be hearing the man wrong. Who is "they" and what president? I feel the hush and a buzz in the air. I stagger and catch myself on the doorjamb. "What president?" I ask like a fool.

The door opens wider. "You real pale, m'am. Maybe you best come inside and have a glass a water and a sit down. You ain't been listening to no radio, for sure."

I enter the shop feeling lightheaded. It smells of leather and dust. The shelves along the walls are lined with old shoes and boots. I can't tell if they are decorative or in for repair. There's a glass case counter filled with cleaning supplies. An adding machine sits on top. And a receipt pad. I steady myself against the cool glass and leave a smudged handprint on it.

The man who let me inside waits while I catch my breath. He's very dark-skinned and has a large head of glowing snow-white hair. When he smiles at me, I see a gold tooth in the front. In the dim light of the dusty shop the tooth looks like the star of Bethlehem.

"It's O.K. honey, we as shocked as you. This here's America. Nobody supposed to shoot the President like they do in them backward countries. Somethin' ain't right. I tells you, it's the end of the world and we best pray hard for salvation. "

There's a striped curtain hanging across the doorway to a back room where a radio is playing loud. I can't make out all the words. Urgent. Bad. Shock. Chaos. More shock. Voices on top of voices. An overhead fan turns slowly making the curtain wave.

"Georgie," a woman calls from behind it. "You bring that young lady in here and I'll fix her some lemonade. Perk her right up. Lemonade gonna make her feel better than your praying will."

I step through the curtain into another world. Twinkling Christmas lights hang along the walls infusing the room with blue, red, and green light. A deep red velvet sofa sits against one wall. A coffee table covered with lace. A picture of Jesus, exposing his bleeding heart, hangs on one wall. A collection of crosses, large and small, hangs on another wall. Their metals reflect the lights, which bounce off the bodies of Christ. An ancient Victrola sits atop a radio cabinet from which the news emanates. "Shot three times," it says over and over. "No official word on condition. Reporting live." My head reels.

The tiniest lady in the world is at a fridge, holding the door open. She's dressed in black and is almost invisible. "Sit yourself down," she says. "Over there, on the sofa, and I'll git you a glass of homemade. It's the real stuff. It cures whatever ails you. It's got the sweet and the sour. Marry them together, that's what's lemonade. That's me and Georgie too," she chuckles. "Him's the sour, me's the sweet."

"Get out, old lady," he says. "You the sour. I give you sugar." He gives her a peck on the cheek, takes the glass from her hand, and brings it to me. "You feelin' better, young lady? Mebbe you want to pray with us for Mr. Kennedy."

A familiar voice on the radio comes through the crackling noise. "This is Walter Cronkite. No official word yet but we've been advised by KLRD in Dallas minutes ago that the President is dead, shot by an assassin. This was reported to the station by a doctor in tears. The last sacraments were administered by a priest." He pauses, a catch in his voice. "There's no official word yet. However, our correspondent in Dallas, Dan Rather, has confirmed this report." The air is exiting the room. More radio static and then his voice again. "Flash just in, from Dallas, Texas, the official report. At 1 p.m. central time. 38 minutes ago, the President, John Fitzgerald Kennedy, died."

The sweet and sour slips down my throat, momentarily clears the cottony pressure around my head but not the aching feeling in my chest that the whole world has changed in one moment. Something's lost forever. I feel old, that's what it is. Older than I've ever felt before. Older than when my mother died and the rest of the world went on as normal. It's as if this death has stopped the world, stopped time. Chills run up and over my shoulders. Georgie and his wife drop down onto the sofa next to me. Their eyes well with tears and they clutch hands.

"God rest his soul," Georgie murmurs.

My mind's eye sees that horrendous moment the President was shot. The radio described Jackie as crawling out onto the trunk of the limo. I see the Texas sunlight bouncing off her pearls. I don't think she knew where she was going, except away from the scene. I don't know if I am outside of history or inside it.

I taste the lemonade on my lips. I hug the wizened lady as my tears start to flow. She turns to me. I don't even know her name but she's no longer a stranger. "There, there," she pats my back. "There, there, honey. We all lambs in Jesus' flock. He loves us. Don't go forgetting that." She strokes my hair. Her bony chest is comforting.

When I sit up she hands me a hankie that smells of lavender. I wipe my eyes. The gratitude I feel is overwhelming. I'm so glad that I'm not alone. Or at home with Stuart who always has something smart-alecky to say about the President. I roll my eyes when Stuart starts in on politics. At least Stuart likes good music. That was important to me when we met.

I stand up and dab at my eyes again. I wonder if all these tears are going to flood the Ohio River. I'm sure that the entire population is crying at the same time, regardless of politics.

"Thank you for your hospitality. God bless you both, too. And keep you safe. I'd best head home. It was silly of me to have come here. I should have known. I thought there was an A & G Tool and Die shop nearby. Or something like that. It was something my husband said." I don't need to ask.

I know.

They look at each other. The little old lady smacks her lips and makes a tsk-tsk sound. "You tell her, Georgie," she says.

"Honey, you ain't the first to come looking for that place and you ain't gonna be the last. It weren't ever here. Sometimes we get mail, letters and whatnot, addressed to whatever they is. This gentleman comes, collects 'em. Don't peek, he says. We don't. He pay real well for that. Harmless enuf. His business, we figure."

Nothing surprises me. I don't even blink. Georgie walks me back through the shop. Shelf after shelf loaded with shoes. Shiny leather, canvas, suede. I stop at the door and ask him, "Do you have any blue suede shoes?"

He laughs and shakes his head. "That white boy sure can sing. Gotta special order blue suede. Shoes, vest, any of it. Blue don't grow on any critter round here 'cept mebbe once in a blue moon." He opens the door. "Honey child, you take care. God bless you."

There are clouds overhead. I see all kinds of creatures in them. Even one that might be the soul of the President. I imagine JFK trying out his new wings. The blood drying. The wounds closed. Sorrow for what's left behind, what's left undone. Sorrow for those of us earthbound, stuck with loss. Every loss leaves a hole. At least it does in real human beings. I know this because I have plenty of holes. I hear the wind blow through them. The songs come to me through the tiniest of the holes in my heart. I'd rather think about the songs than the holes. The songs ease the aches.

I'm in luck that the buses are still running, that the world hasn't really ground to a halt. I run and catch one going uptown. There's only one other rider, an old man talking to himself, spittle flinging from his mouth. Out of breath, I flop onto a seat way in the back where I can be alone on the return trip to my false life. I fish Gina's diary from the bottom of my purse and cling to it for a moment. I kneel on the cracked leather seat of the bus and press the two metal clips together on the window so I can raise it a crack. Cool air floods in as I shove the manual out. I watch it tumble into a weedy ditch at the side of the road as the bus moves forward.

I force myself to watch street signs so I won't miss my stop. I don't need a manual to tell me what to do next.

When I enter the house I'm relieved that there's no sign of Stuart. No hat hanging on the front hallway rack. No umbrella upright in the stand. Apparently "the factory" hasn't dismissed its workers due to the national tragedy. I'm certain that would be his story. He'd stare at me with those blue eyes opened wide, cracking his knuckles all the while as if to challenge my skepticism, daring me to doubt him. Hurry, a voice inside me urges. I push the image of him out of my mind. He is not a good man, and certainly the wrong man in my life. I don't want to know where his money comes from. There's a word for it that I want to avoid at all costs – accessory, and it doesn't refer to handbags or jewelry.

Mistakes are wrong only if you don't correct them. I am starting to sound like a manual myself.

"It's now or never…tomorrow will be too late," I sing it in the lowest register I can muster. I imagine Elvis' sonorous voice urging me on. I hear Gina over my shoulder say - *Do what you need to do.* I throw only what I need into a suitcase. No manuals. I leave behind the pillbox hat, my white gloves, all of my accessories. I lay my pink MaryBeth waitress uniform out on the bed in the shape of a body, along with a frilly apron and a box of Kleenex. I fluff the pillow for him to cry on. Memphis, I think, I'll keep going until I really reach Memphis.

Spikes O'Death

George Haas was busy eradicating grubs from the Major's front lawn. Attached to the bottoms of his shoes were *Spikes O'Death* - a metal platform with spikes that penetrated the ground as he walked. He tottered up and down the sloping yard. Straight rows of little puncture marks appeared in the grass behind him. The spikes dug into the earth, aerating it and, he imagined, skewering the blind white grubs as they munched on the tender roots just below the surface. The intrusion of the grubs infuriated George – as if they were a personal insult, as if they were an infestation of his own body. He clenched his teeth, growled to himself, and tried to focus instead on the red, white and blue annuals that he'd planted to frame the Major's circular driveway.

The humidity, with its threat of imminent thunderstorms, distracted him. It was almost tornado weather, when the air is sucked out and a sickly yellow-green hovers on the horizon. George's greying hair trailed down his back and matted along his forehead. He felt the pressure drop behind his eyes.

George stopped working and looked up at the brownstone directly across the street just as the woman tenant left her house. She locked her door and slipped the key into her jeans pocket. She flipped her black hair behind her ears, sweat stains already forming on her blue cotton blouse. George watched carefully as she disappeared around the corner.

He gave her a few minutes, just to be sure, then walked across the street moving stiffly on the spikes o' death. He liked the robotic sound they made as they struck the pavement. When he entered the woman's backyard, he scowled at the overgrown bushes, untrimmed junipers and sparse hemlocks scattered throughout the yard. A scraggly dogwood, inappropriate for the climate, stood in one corner of the yard with its arms spread in miserable supplication. He forced himself to focus on the task at hand. Low rumbles of distant thunder approached as George overturned a metal trashcan beneath a window. The overgrown yard protected him from prying eyes.

This was not his first time. His youth had been spent honing just these skills – the quick entry, the vanished objects. These search and destroy missions had sent him from foster care to an assortment of reform schools and finally, to avoid prison, the army. He hoped that this job would be the one to provide for his escape from ten years of tending the Major's garden while sleeping on a cot in the carriage house and cooking on a hot plate. Ten years of Mr. Major bailing him out of trouble because George was a meticulous gardener and difficult to replace. Every time that happened, George's debt to Mr. Major grew. Last year Mr. Major had seen to his release again. George fancied that Mr. Major was rather gleeful, chortling as he paid bail and worked his behind-the-scenes connections to have the charges dropped. George owed him and he did not like owing anyone for anything. Maybe, this time, he'd find the means to flee and leave everything behind him.

The window opened easily, as he knew it would. The spikes o' death on his feet dug into the sill as he hoisted himself inside. The interior of the house was chaotic. The woman appeared to be a painter. Unfinished canvases leaned on every wall. They were all paintings of a woman, maybe the same woman, he couldn't tell. Each painting showed only a part of her body. One depicted the right side. Another, the left. Another, one eye, one ear and a huge gaping hole for a mouth. He lost his balance and tottered on the spikes o death, barely staying upright. The eyes in the paintings seemed to watch him.

The sound of rain already falling on the trashcan reminded him to move on. Reminded him what he had come for. The bedroom door stood open. He moved quickly through the drawers, cursing her for her disorder. Her valuables were not apparent, except for a ring on a vanity top, which he slipped into his pocket. Another sound caught his ear – the front door opening. He hadn't predicted this either. Adrenaline boosted his pulse. The front door closed. Footsteps approached the bedroom. A woman's arm appeared in the doorway.

He grabbed her.

"Don't move," he shouted way too loud. "Don't move or you'll get hurt." His knuckles were white and tense on her brown arm. He felt her muscles tighten but she made no other response.

"Quiet or I'll kill you!" He dug his fingers into her flesh.

Although she seemed surprised, he couldn't smell or feel anything except that an odd vibration filled the air.

"Wait," she said calmly. "Wait, one minute."

He felt dizzy as the vibration increased. He looked into her dark eyes and let go. She stepped back, one step only, and fixed him with her black eyes. Pinned him like a specimen on a collecting board. Slowly she began to unbutton her blouse, one slow button at a time – never lowering her eyes. She dropped the blouse to the floor. She reached behind her back and undid her bra and let it fall – it fell in slow motion over and over and over again. He stared at her chest. Her chest was a delta, a map, a bunch of lines and cords; some still red and welted where her breasts ought to have been.

He blinked:

He is walking through water over the knees of his uniform. Damn, he thinks. He feels a leech attach where his pant leg has come out of his boot. His body is a maze of welts, some infected, some not - from assorted bites. He constantly removes ticks from the warm crevices, especially from the soft spot where his balls press on his thigh. The chemical smell of burning rice paddies fills his nostrils. The copters whir overhead. The constant rain. And he trips. He stumbles over something and catches himself in a panic. Here, in Da Nang, one can't be sure of the ground or the sky or the air you breathe. The landscape doesn't translate. Something bumps his leg again. It's a young woman. It had once been a young woman. A very young woman. Her translucent skin detaches where her naked body bumps his and he sees her breast. Her one breast. The other breast, a wound, an empty space over her heart. Pieces of her skin float on the water like pages of a book, messages without a bottle. She stares at him and he can't turn away.

George backed slowly away from the woman. She kept her eyes on him. Not moving. Maybe, not even breathing. Her chest didn't seem to rise and fall. He backed out of the room. The spikes o' death made no noise now. He backed out of the hall over to the window. He climbed out backwards, never taking his eyes off of the woman in the doorway. At the last moment, half way out the window, he wanted something, anything. He stretched his arm into the room and grabbed a small canvas. He stumbled into the backyard and ran, turning the corner without looking back.

The rain had slowed to a drizzle, the pressure had stabilized as the front passed through. Many blocks later George walked into a pawnshop, one he knew well. A buzzer rang as he pushed open the door. He wiped wet hair from his eyes with the back of his hand. The spikes o' death scratched the floor as he approached the bulletproof glass. He pushed the ring with its blood red stone through the opening. The pawnbroker held it up to the light and rubbed it with his thick meaty fingers before pushing a handful of bills under the glass.

George clung to the painting of the woman as he shuffled out the door. The painting depicted one side of a face, one eye, a long slender neck, and a sloping shoulder. It was the hand that mesmerized him. A delicate hand, palm opened.

Outside the pawnshop he removed the gardening device still strapped to his feet. He flung it into the alley as he walked towards the bus station with the picture tucked under his arm. "Boston", he said, talking to himself, shuffling as he walked. "Maybe Boston's the place." He boarded a bus, East Coast bound, still clutching the picture of the fractured woman and sank down into the faded vinyl seat. The air smelled like sweat and antiseptic. From some dead sleeping place deep inside his chest he felt for the first time in decades, desire.

Fish Hunting in Vermont

Dave ran his hand along the shiny red flank of his Chevy pickup as he tossed his fish hunting gear into its bed. The fenders arched high over the extra large all-terrain tires. He could almost start the car with the energy he felt flowing from the metal to his palms. Almost. He hopped into the cab, and turned the key. The truck responded immediately. He backed out of the drive, headed down the gravel road, leaving a shower of pebbles in his wake.

LuAnne, the secretary at St. George Elementary School, had laughed when he called in sick. She'd already phoned for a sub. Hunters are creatures of habit, you know, she told him. After eight years at St. George, she had him covered for the opening day of fish hunting season. She only wished that she could read his mind the multitude of other times when he called in on a whim.

Dave had been to every March opening day since he was nine years old, old enough to go with Grandpop out to his special fish hunting tree. They shinnied out onto the branches with their rifles, waited patiently until the fish swam close, and brought home supper. Dave kept up the ritual. Every year, though, he missed Grandpop more than the year before.

The snow at lower elevations had melted. The trees stood bare, leaving the view exposed up and down Lake Champlain and across the water to New York State. Higher up, the mountains stood snow covered, a reminder that winter lingered above the valley, not yet ready to release its grip. The fine line between seasons made Dave feel as if he harbored two different people inside himself. One burrowed deep, curled up, hoarding provisions. The other busting out, ready to walk trails or grow wings and fly. He didn't know which one he inhabited at any given time. It changed from moment to moment, like most of his thoughts on the nature of the world.

As daylight inched towards the valley, Dave descended towards town. His truck fishtailed rounding the curves, vibrating to the beat of his subwoofer. "*It kills and thrills like the horns of my Silverado grill. And the girls all sing, save a horse, ride a cowboy,*" pounding over the airwaves of WOKO. Dave patted the dashboard as the truck clung to the road. Reliable. There weren't many things in Dave's life he labeled that way except for Grandma Nona and his Chevy Silverado. Not reliable, was repeated over and over to him, relationship after relationship, as the women in his life moved on. It didn't matter to them that he had a reliable truck. They wanted more. *Not reliable* stamped on him, USDA inspected and graded.

He reached Highway 7 where motorists were heading both north and south to work. Their headlights poked holes through the morning fog like portholes to another world. He turned north up the lake and pulled into the parking lot of *Mabel's Diner*, a glorified doughnut shop. The neon window sign blinked, Open 24/7, in blue and red lights. His Grandma Nona, who raised him, referred to it as the 24/7 Shop.

She'd worked the early shift as far back as Dave could recall. Since she was always up before dawn each day she might as well be doing something useful, she said. Grandpop's disability from his bum knee had covered the rent but it didn't cover the extras like bingo or ladies night at the Indian casino. After Grandpop died five years ago she kept working, mostly out of habit.

Dave entered the shop. A couple of truckers and the regular early morning geezers sat on stools at the formica and chrome counter drinking mugs of coffee. The regulars turned towards Dave, their heads nodding in unison like plastic bobble-headed dolls. "Morning Roy, Jim," Dave bobbed his head in reply.

Everything in the shop was blurry and steamy, except for the florescent light illuminating rows of metal trays filled with doughnuts. A fingerprint smudged glass case on the countertop held three pieces of soggy apple pie, probably the same three pieces as every other time he'd been in the shop. Ordering pie in a doughnut shop seemed like ordering a hot dog in a pizza parlour.

Dave's Grandma Nona looked up from the coffee she was pouring as he walked in. "Dave, honey! Gimme a peck." She leaned across the counter so he could kiss her powdery cheek. Her white hat was embroidered *Mabel* across the crown. No one remembered who Mabel was, whether it was a former owner, a former owner's girlfriend or a dairy cow like the ones dotting the Vermont landscape.

She reached under the counter and extracted a white bag. "Got your provisions. Put in a couple of them old fashioneds that you like best. Don't go feeding any of the good ones to the fish. You got some stale ones in there for that. I put in one of Grandpop's favorites too. A lemon one. Be sure he gets it." She looked towards the front window that reflected back the interior of the shop and shook her head. "I miss that man. You tell him that too, if you see him. Cranky bum-legged old grump. I miss him a-lookin out for the both of us." She tried to straighten her permanently wrinkled uniform and managed to smooth the apron down a bit. "Go on now, Dave. I hear them fish calling your name."

Dave left the diner and walked across the lot, kicking at the gravel with his steel-toed boots. Although Grandpop had been gone over five years now, Dave felt him hover above their fishing tree every year on opening day. Sometimes he thought he actually saw him. Sometimes he heard him dispensing advice. "Shoot carefully in front of the fish's nose so the explosion shatters its air bladder. Carefully now, don't want that bullet hitting the fish. Get it all tore up. No good for eating that way."

Dave decided against peeling out of Mabel's parking lot. He waited to put the pedal to the metal until he'd downshifted around the first curve heading towards the marshy shores that lay beyond Burlington. He loved the way his truck grabbed the road as if its tires were studded with claws. When he revved the engine, it emitted a low throaty growl that felt like it came from the back of his own throat. The road followed the lake. Dave traveled with it, leaning into every curve, moving in and out of the low-lying fog until he reached Burlington. He tapped time to the music on the steering wheel as he drove.

Burlington was barely waking up as he slid through town towards Main Street. Stately old homes, mostly used as fraternity houses, lined Willard Street. When he approached the intersection with Main Street, sirens started and stopped and started again, in short bursts. The reddish blonde hairs on the back of his neck prickled at the thought of another traffic ticket. Next time, the judge had told him, he'd suspend Dave's license. He leaned over and turned the music down low.

He started to turn right onto Main Street and glimpsed a police car with a hairy knock-kneed monster running in front of it just below the intersection. The beast towered over the parked cars. It ran uphill like it was driven by a diesel engine. For a moment he saw the red and blue lights spin. In his side mirror he recognized the shaggy creature by its shoulder hump and huge rack, shaped like the spreaded palm of a hand with short pointy fingers. The moose paused, raised its nose and flared gigantic nostrils; the officer turned on his sirens again. As if offended, the moose swung its head from side to side, then lowered it and ran towards Dave's car. Its hoofs clomping on the asphalt sounded like a cavalry charge.

Dave felt an uneasy calm as he jerked the wheel farther to the right. In his entire life, roaming over the Vermont countryside, he'd only once seen a moose and then not up close. Grandpop had cautioned him that he wouldn't want to, either. "All them dozens of yellow signs on the highways – *Moose Crossing*. They put those up like magic charms to keep away what moose's left in Vermont. It works purty well, see – you ain't never seen one! You hit one of them with your car, and mebbe the moose'll survive but you sure as hell won't. Them critters got long legs. They come right on in through the windshield, and you got a half-ton critter sitting in your lap."

The smell reached him first through his open truck window. An odor like an old rug a wet dog had been sleeping on. Mildew and compost. Dave stomped on the accelerator trying to avoid contact. The moment stretched out as the truck moved in slow motion. Dave noticed the beast's brown coat – mottled in spots, a few ribs sticking out, and a trickle of drool trailing from the corner of its big flabby lips onto its beard. The animal closed in, with the police sirens wailing behind.

Instead of accelerating to safety the Chevy hit the moose or the moose hit it. It was impossible to tell. Dave felt the crunch of the door panel as the moose fell against the side door of the truck. He heard a crack and the hiss of air escaping from his left side. The moose slid across the hood of the truck. A hoof struck the windshield. A tire exploded as the truck bounced off the curb. A crackling fanned out over the window, running at him as if he were stranded on the lake with the ice breaking up. The webbing spread and then paused for a moment before the entire window gave way, collapsing into piles of crystals covering the dash and tinkling onto the floor. The truck listed to right and bent forward on flattened tires.

Dave wanted to move. It was entirely thought and no action. He wanted to breathe. Air transformed to fire. A knife turned in his side. The last thing he heard was the buzz and static of the police radio. "Code 1050. Code 1050. Main and Willard." He leaned back on the twisted seat.

A translucent extra eyelid clouded his sight. Green northern lights shimmered. They stretched out across the lake below him, brighter with each painful breath. Grandpop crawled across the top of the cab. "Davey boy.

Don't let your prey escape. Them shot up fish floating ashore gives fishhunting a bad name. Especially with all those crunchy granola town folks. Best to be good with your net, hit or miss." He extended his arm. It grew longer and longer and he reached in through the missing windshield for the bag of doughnuts that still sat on the seat. "Hope you saved the lemon one for me, sonny." He grinned, a gold canine tooth glowing bigger and brighter until Dave had to close his eyes.

The next week he spent swimming underwater, surfacing at times then retreating, until breathing came more easily. Faces floated across his field of vision. Their lips moved and he saw bubbles escape from their mouths. The burble and sucking noise of the machine hooked to his chest sounded like words. "Hoooome, gotcha gotcha gotcha, hooooome."

Nurses and doctors dressed in white, poked, turned and prodded him. Relax and sleep, they said as they injected medication into his IV. He felt his left side where the machine drew air from the space around his flattened lung, making room for the beating of his heart, making room for the rise and fall of his chest. He understood the reason people spoke of heartache.

He thought that it must be Christmas one evening when his mother Wendy appeared in his hospital room. He'd always lived with Grandpop and Grandma. His mother was a bodybuilder who lived to travel and compete. She sent him ribbons and trophies as proof of her accomplishments, appearing when Dave was little once a year at Christmas time with an armload of presents. Whenever he'd asked his Grandma who his father was, her reply was that "only the Lord knows, and he's not telling."

Now Wendy paced nervously around his hospital room, crisscrossing the white and tan linoleum squares. He watched her taut body stride as her tawny hair swayed from side to side with each shake of her head like a catamount about to bounce. "Just don't get trapped," she warned him, her eyes circling, on alert. "There's quicksand, everywhere, sucking at your feet. You can't stand still." She told him she was moving again, to St. Bliss. Somewhere in the Caribbean. One of these days she'd settle down. Soon. Someday. She'd call him. Dave had heard it all before and nodded. His mother crouched low to the ground, sprang straight up, over the bed and out the window. Dave woke covered in sweat.

He remembered his mother's last visit, many years back. When it ended and Wendy moved on to wherever, his grandparents sat for hours on the rusty porch glider, their gray heads touching, wrapped in an old quilt. In the fading light that bounced off the mountains in yellow streaks and dribbled down into the lake, they rocked and sighed. Their 'tsk-tsk-tsk' sounded to Dave like it came from their bones.

The night after the doctors removed his chest tube, Grandpop appeared in the glow of the dim light above his bed. Grandpop stood at the foot of the bed dressed in overalls and rubber waders. He shook the hospital bed. Dave closed and opened his eyes. Then tried to close them again. Grandpop rattled the bed.

"Fishing time, Davey boy, rise and shine. Day's a-wasting. Up and at-em. We'll head out before the sun rises. I'm a gonna need a boost to get up that old tree. Big strong lad like you to give me a hand. If you stay in here, the fish will never come."

Dave sat up. His breath caught and Grandpop swelled up until he appeared to fill the room. When he exhaled Grandpop shrunk to the size of a tiny gnome. "Come on boy, your legs is working fine. With your keen eyes and my varmint gun we're ready. Let's go." Grandpop returned to normal size. He gimped over to the door, peeked both ways and motioned to Dave. "Coast's clear. Hurry it up."

Dave slid his legs over the side of the bed and sat a moment on the edge. The quiet of the late night hospital felt thick in his ears. He looked around the room. Everything whirled, got thinner and taller and toppled to the left then the right as he struggled to hold up his head. After things stopped swaying, Dave spotted a small metal locker on the opposite wall. He teetered toward it, the linoleum floor spongy under his feet. Ever so slowly, without making a sound, he pulled open the metal latch on the locker. Inside he found new camouflage gear – a set of pants and jacket hanging neatly on a hook. He slipped them on, felt around the bottom of the locker but didn't find any boots or shoes. So he retrieved the blue hospital slippers and put them on.

The camouflage clothing made him feel invisible. They hung loosely on his bones as if the clothes were a too big bunch of skin. No one can see me, he thought, I can barely see me. At the last moment, he remembered something from a movie and arranged the bedding to appear as if someone was asleep in the bed. The visible made invisible and the invisible made as if it could be seen. He held up his hand and thought that he could see right through it.

The hallway was illuminated at night like a deep-sea aquarium, a watery glow bouncing off pale walls. Years of tracking in the forest had taught Dave how walk soundlessly, how to place his feet softly on the earth. He pulled up the collar on the camouflage jacket and scrunched down as he approached the nurses' station. "Invisible," he reminded himself. "Leave no tracks."

A middle-aged nurse sat sideways with her profile facing him, reading glasses perched half way down her nose, thumbing through a stack of charts on the desk before her. She muttered to herself as Dave drifted passed. "Breezy. A bit too breezy tonight. North wind bringing back snow. MaryAnne!" she called to someone out of sight. "Better check to see if there's a window opened on the floor. Cold spell's coming, I'm feeling a draft."

Dave glided down the corridor, holding onto the metal railing along the wall for balance, and pressed the automatic door opener at the entrance to the unit. For a moment he paused, panicked. "What am I doing here?" he thought. "Wounded and adrift." There wasn't anyone to ask. Grandpop was nowhere in sight. He straightened up and walked through the door.

The lobby was almost deserted. A digital clock over the door read 3:15 am. A woman sat at the information desk in front of a Rolodex, a white haired woman in a striped apron with a starched white cap on her head. She smiled at Dave as if he reminded her of someone. A son or a grandson perhaps. "Button up that jacket young man. It's nippy out there."

"Yes, ma'am." He fumbled with the buttons. For a moment, in the distorted half-light, he thought she was Grandma Nona. He shook off the image and veered out through the revolving doors. He felt fluid oozing out his side. With his left arm crooked tight against his chest, he waved to the woman with his right. When he exited the revolving door and looked back, no one was there. Only a deserted lobby pulsating in dim light.

There was an odd sensation of being carried, swept along in a current headed towards open water, which felt better than walking. He leaned towards his wounded side, protecting it and went with the flow. One foot in front of the other, he drifted into the parking lot where a smattering of cars were parked.

The night air was clear and brittle. A full moon illuminated the lot and the purple mountains off in the distance. Light spilled out of the sky. Its icy blue color burned and pressed on the wall of his lung. Viscous warm liquid seeped from the side of his jacket. He squeezed his arm tighter to his chest as a breeze gathered around his bare ankles.

Dave looked down and saw Grandpop, tiny as a chipmunk, scurrying around his hospital issued felt slippers. Grandpop stopped running and stood up on his hind legs, squinting at Dave. Then Grandpop ran faster and faster in circles and, poof, became smoke. The smoke rose until he couldn't see it any more and it blended into the Milky Way. It became a smudge that looked as if someone had smeared a gigantic finger across the sky.

Dave sat down on a curb. His side ached and his fingers were wet where they pressed on his chest. He felt himself rise, floating. One eye on the sky, the other on the water below. His body felt porous and free. Above him, he spotted the three bright stars in Orion the Hunter's belt. There was Orion, chasing a dream with his club raised, ready to strike his prey. Dave's breath rattled. The picture changed and he was seated back on the cold concrete. Orion retreated.

He lifted up his head and spotted what he needed. An old beat-up dusty black Ford station wagon. It was covered with stickers. *Greenpeace. Save the Whales. Free Huey, Duey and Louie.* A car as unlike his Chevy Silverado as possible.

With his good arm he forced himself up and shuffled across the asphalt. When he reached the car, he rubbed condensation off the station wagon's dirty window and peered inside. A set of keys sat on the seat, rural Vermont style. Opening the door, he slid in and fumbled with them until he found the right key with a Ford logo. He turned it in the ignition. The engine coughed and complained, died once, then started up on the second try.

In the darkness Dave drove slowly, relieved that the car was an automatic and easy to drive one-handed. He turned the car towards the lake. The stars were fading and clouds covered Orion. Light snow began to fall. He drove to the far side of town and headed out Swanton Creek Road. The overpass above the interstate was lined with orange barrels topped with blinking warning lights, waiting for the morning construction crew. He bumped along the rough road, knocking down one of the barrels.

At the trailhead he parked the car, got out and tossed the keys onto the seat. False dawn was breaking, giving everything a glow. Dave felt as if he were inside a snow globe. He tilted his head back and opened his mouth, tasting the snowflakes. For a moment he stood like that, with his eyes closed, savoring the cool drops. Then he waved his good arm and brushed the snow from his face as he entered the woods following the trail.

Pine needles, decomposed leaves and patches of snow matted the ground. The hospital slippers afforded little traction. He dug his feet into the ground, making toeholds to avoid falling. His footprints would be easy for any tracker to follow. He moved slowly and breathed with difficulty. Daylight was melting the snow and rivulets began to flow by him, forming little streams that headed towards the lake.

He reached a clearing and stepped out from the shadowy path onto the shoreline. The blue sky reflected and multiplied the sunlight. Echoes reverberated across the valley. He heard the whine of a truck engine carrying a heavy load to the work site back down the road. The crystal clear morning air tugged and pulled at his chest.

Along the shore stood a thick old tree with low branches leaning far out over the water. Dave hobbled over to it and put his arms around the trunk. For a moment he stood there, leaning against the bark of the tree listening to it breathe. It made his breath come more easily. He had never missed a fish hunting season and here he was. He was reliable, dependable. He'd proved it. "I'm here, Pop, coming up to see you," he said lifting his head.

He felt with his toes for a hold and boosted himself up, like he used to boost Grandpop when he'd gotten too old to shinny up by himself. Dave crawled up the tree and out over the water on a sturdy limb inching along on his belly. Underneath the branch, brown water lapped and rolled towards the bank. Circles formed on the surface as a fish crested, snatched an early morning skimmer off the top of the water and sank back under the waves.

There's a moment when the hunter and hunted inhabit the same skin, when they breathe each other's breath and see through the others eyes. There's a moment, one thin silvery moment, when that transmigration happens.

Time froze. Nothing hurt Dave anymore. His breath came easily. He stood up tall and stretched open both his arms, balancing on the limb. Off to one side he heard a loud percussive noise, an explosion, and he leapt out into the blue.

What You Don't Know

Hero lies at my feet while I shred papers, everything at your hospital from important documents to the daily prayer bulletin. He barely looks around until someone enters my kingdom. Then, in a manner unlike most seeing-eye dogs, he greets them ecstatically like an overgrown puppy dog. He slobbers and drools and is occasionally obedient. We first became partners five years ago. He's my third guide dog and we're a great team.

You think I can't read what you hand me to shred. That's why you decided this was the ideal position for me. I spent eighteen years in the radiology darkroom developing film, bringing pictures to light. Now you hand me things to destroy. Papers from your desk and files, things marked confidential in electric pink envelopes, emails both official and personal. I've shredded numerous soiled copies of the Sports Illustrated swimsuit issue. Pregnancy tests. HIV screens. Health department citations. Motel receipts under aliases. Fluttery little slips labeled While You Were Out, so-and-so called. You don't know it but my fingers decipher them all.

When you enter the room I can tell by the vibrations of your feet if you are carrying papers of interest. I smell the perspiration in your palms. Your breath has this certain corrupted odor. Something like cabbage or brussel sprouts.

"Hey, Charlie, how's it going?" you greet me. Hero doesn't rise to welcome you, another tip-off. You leave the documents in a big bin for me to feed to the grinder, a metal beast with a taste for paper. From those five words you speak, I know a lot. Whether you've had a rough night fighting with your wife, or the other lady - the ever so young one you think no one knows about. Or if you had another bad meal from another Chinese carryout. Or if you lost money over the weekend playing slots. Or if you are preparing a round of layoffs.

Ordinary sighted people are often kind but ignorant. They think I am disconnected, cut off from the events swirling in the air around me. They don't know that Hero is a special dog. When he curls up on the floor his eyes close, but mine open. I become powerful. I hold the papers in my hands but fleetingly. That's all the time I need to absorb their content. Each color has a specific feel. Sometimes a paper is so hot it leaves blisters on my skin.

I sort quickly. Into the machine goes everything mundane. Even the swimsuit issues, although for a small moment I can't resist running my fingers over the partly naked bodies of the models. It's a small thrill.

The rest of the papers I salvage. I'm saving them in a 3-hole binder, neatly punched, ready to present to you. When I walk into your office, my demands won't be negotiable. You will meet them all.

Weather

When Davis walked into the *Stormy Stormy Night* I was seated at the bar chatting up Nate, the regular night-shift bartender. I'd offered Nate a joke again, in exchange for a drink. Punch lines are my problem. Most often I forget them and end up paying for my own drink. This one was a complicated joke about one of the seven dwarfs, Dopey, and the Pope and black nuns in Alaska. Nate leaned on the polished wood counter, waiting for the kicker. As I tried to recall it I bit my coral red lip and tasted fruit punch from my lip-gloss. My eyes traced the pattern of Ursa Major in the twinkling lights shaped like constellations that decorated the ceiling. I shrugged.

That's when Davis strolled over and sat on the stool next to me. He looked as if he'd been awake all night though it was early evening. His hair stuck out every which way and his geeky black glasses perched on his rather large nose, a cool, hipster nerd style like a Ghostbuster or a batty professor.

"Buy you a drink?" he asked. Straightforward, no come on line. I liked that.

I ordered a *Gale Warning*. Davis cocked his head, thought a moment. His eyes were a beautiful shade of stratus cloud grey. "OK, I'll have a *Wind Shear*," he said. That stopped me. He hadn't bothered to glance at the menu.

"Nate," I said, "give me a *Ridge* on the side.

"Make mine a *Trough*," Davis replied. "Opposites attract." Either this guy was really smart, or he was one of us, a First-Degree Weather Freak. It didn't matter. I was hooked.

He tossed a navy blue jacket onto the back of a chair, sidled up to me and ran a hand through his hair in a vain attempt to make it behave. I wanted to reach out and stroke it but restrained myself. Every once in a while I hold myself back. Restraint can be a good trait in small doses. Sometimes you just have to let go. Otherwise it means that you miss the train, miss the boat, miss the plane, the whistle blows, the man leaves, you don't answer the phone, or return the call and that can weigh heavy on your heart.

Nate placed two drinks in front of us. The frosted glass of my *Gale Warning* sweated onto the paper coaster, a puddle forming over the Newcastle Ale logo. Nate arched his eyebrows. One corner of his mouth smiled, or smirked. Davis extended a hand and introduced himself.

"Davis Raymond. It's reversible. Everyone gets it backwards. I migrated down from Marquette a month ago. Transferred, promoted I suppose. I work for NOAA out at White Lake." He retrieved his jacket, turned it over and showed me its logo, a circle with a white ghost bird, flying between the dark blue of the sky and the ocean blue of the water. He was a real meteorologist, not an amateur weather freak like me but an authority, an expert, a professional.

"Janina Borofsky, not reversible," I said, shaking his hand. "I work at St. Agnes Hospital as an ER clerk." I paused a moment, unsure how much to say.

Nate chimed in. "She sings. Lead singer for The Cut-Ups. She's good. I'm one of her groupies. Friday nights they play at the Pig Pen."

"It's a only a part-time gig. Maybe one day we'll break out, or maybe not. I'm a weather spotter too."

"I guess I spotted a spotter." Davis laughed and stretched his long legs out in front of him, ankles exposed below his khakis. Seven and half feet tall, I imagined. My mind elongating his lanky body.

"How did you become a spotter?" he asked. "I got into weather from Boy Scouts. I still have my meteorology badge, a yellow bolt of lightning on a field of green. Some people start because of movies, like *Twister* or *Wizard of Oz*."

I loved the *Wizard of Oz* and told him I dreamt of being be sucked up in a flying house and deposited in the Emerald City to sing and dance with the Munchkins in Lollipop Land. And how I grew up on the Texas coast where everyone follows the weather with maps and radios, tracking hurricanes every season as if weather was a member of the family. I'd moved north and weather obsession stuck even though my Texas accent didn't.

The *Ridge* on the side kept me talking. I told Davis that my mom had brought me to Michigan when fleeing a bad marriage, her third attempt at matrimony, and returned to her childhood home. She taught me to speak like a Yankee. Said she didn't want me to sound like my dad, Texan number two.

I'd taken a weekend course here in order to follow storms and discovered that weather addiction was more permanent than a tattoo or a tooth extraction.

Davis was a good listener. Our hands brushed and I let mine linger, relishing the electric current I felt.

We set ourselves up in a second floor apartment, above a novelty shop and a pizza store. The flat tarpaper rooftop housed our private weather station. Davis retrieved discarded instruments from White Lake. It was the last station in the country to update from radar to GPS readings. We reaped the benefit. Old instruments, still functional.

We also installed antique weather apparatus from flea markets where we browsed, sometimes traveling hours from Metro Detroit to the far reaches of the state or south to Indiana and Ohio. Brass weather vanes shaped like a half dozen creatures, a menagerie of roosters, dragons, goats, and winged horses were posted along the low wall of the roof. Blue liquid barometric pressure gauges hung beneath a small lean-to alongside Banjo barometers, with varying lengths of necks. When they were in synch all the elements of the universe harmonized. I felt their rise and fall in my bones and behind my eyeballs. I heard tunes, *Foggy Mountain Breakdown, Shady Grove, Keep on the Sunny Side*. The music was subtle and Davis unaware of it.

Davis used the instruments to determine the likelihood of storms by plugging in temperature, dew point and pressure to a K-Index. I adjusted our lives in response, serving vegetables and fruit when the pressure raised, red meat when it dropped. I hunkered down in advance of storms, excited to ride them out. We drank champagne at the stability point, toasting our relationship.

Charts covered our bedroom walls with their wavy lines, contours and measurements. Isobars, temperatures, dates. I coded our sex life alongside them, a curious graph whose pattern followed the weather's rise and fall.

The moon can change anything. I know that from my work at the hospital where every full moon more babies are born and the ER fills with lunatics. Luna, lunatics, loony, words that roll around on the tongue. We feel the impact once a month inside our plastic bubble of a hospital building.

I feel the moon's tug and pull when I stand bareheaded soaking in its fluorescent light. I feel the ebb and flow of the tide. At these moments I become a different person. Anything can happen.

My band, The Cut-ups, tries to schedule gigs accordingly. We're hot when the full moon arrives. My voice is not my own. It picks up another octave. Wailing and moaning. The crowd goes berserk. It gives me shivers to think about it.

Davis has never heard me sing except in the shower. The gigs over the last six months have occurred on nights when he's had to work. Too busy, he says, training three interns. He's promised to switch shifts with one of the other meteorologists next time we play The band insists that he's a phantom, some sort of peculiar weather phenomena. They know my inclinations.

Even my mother doubts that Davis is real. She's way too busy to come by and check him out, steering her own impending shipwreck of a relationship off the ends of the earth once again. I've met him, C. J., and I'd be willing to bet he has a wife and ten kids hidden away somewhere. Even his name sounds phony. Only initials. She is so damn repetitive and predictable. I fear that my genes are cursed. I rarely return her calls.

I've created imaginary lovers in the past, which is why everyone finds Davis' existence suspect. There was Tyrone, an agent from Columbia Records who was going to bust us all out of here. And then Daniel, a soap opera star, a super hunk. Davis is staying below everyone's radar. He's so real that it's unreal. So solid that I begin to chip away at him. Subtly, I think. I wash his white underwear with my flaming red sweatshirt. He doesn't flinch at his pink socks. I exchange the salt with the pepper in the shakers and wait for a reaction that doesn't come. Not even a blink of the eye when I sprinkle the bed with sand from the beach. An invisible force propels me to press for any sort of reaction.

At breakfast, I surreptitiously watch Davis as he opens the newspaper where I've cut out every third article. I pretend to cook at the stove, waving the spatula and sprinkling spices into the eggs, talking all the while to the frying pan, fiddling with the knobs on the stove. I notice his jaw clench. I see it. A tendon in his neck pulses a few times and then the tension passes like a rampant cloud heading over to the other side of the world.

"Mice," he says. "I think we have mice nibbling in this house. Better set traps." He folds his napkin and smoothes the creases before getting up from the table.

I think of Davis' name. He is reversible in ways that I am not. He's so calm that if you threw a stone into his water, there wouldn't even be a ripple. I'm not like that, especially at this time of the year, my moods swing high and low. Once the pressure falls, a storm moves in. I look forward to it obliterating the boredom of continuously calm weather and high-pressure blue skies. I want roil and change. Davis is not like this. Perhaps there's some place we can meet in the middle like two intersecting lines.

I refuse to have sex with Davis. The charts aren't right. It's not the first time.

"Don't do this," he begs. "Come on, Janina darling. I need you, baby." All the standard dull lines he's tried before. He can't argue with the charts he has created, no matter how hard he tries. He cracks his knuckles and I sense something like anger. I'm starting to doubt his dedication to the weather, or to me.

I stay in bed late and count the tree cricket's chirps. Dolbear's Law lets me calculate the temperature. I count for 15 seconds, add 40 and I know that it's 72 degrees outside. I don't need a thermometer to tell me the heat is rising in here.

On Sunday I walk across the Ambassador Bridge, heading south to Canada. The border sits in the middle of the bridge. It's a white stripe painted on the walkway where both flags fly, a no man's land. I step onto the stripe, putting one foot in front of the other and turn sideways. I am either in both countries at once or nowhere at all. I have to pick which way to go.

I stand with my arms spread and look at the strait that separates the countries, watching sailboats below wave like white hankies bobbing on the water. Stratocumulus clouds flow overhead. In winter chunks of blue ice break away, heaving up from the frozen river and float towards Lake Erie, beyond Lake Ontario, into the St. Lawrence and out to sea. The air today is thin on the hump of the bridge as if it were a mountaintop where I am suspended between two countries and between sky and water and the cars whizzing by ignore me.

Davis sends me roses but they are the wrong color. White roses. Roses without blood, drained of everything. Ghost flowers. I send him a box of candy with the little brown wrappers emptied of chocolate and filled with whipped cream.

He doesn't show up at our gig, after promising me. Even my mother has come to a show, for Christ's sake. I don't get it. This one's at the largest venue we've ever played, in an old river district warehouse. A text message arrives just before we open, he has car trouble. Dead battery. Waiting for a jump. I am so mad at his no-show that at the end of our set I kick in Josh's bass drum and knock over his high hat and snare. I tear off my clothes, toss them to the crowd, and storm off stage in my underwear and leather boots. The audience thinks its part of the act and goes wild. It's nearly a full moon, which I'm dreading because it's a blue moon, an extra full moon. An unlucky moon. Josh will never speak to me again. I am sure this is all Davis' fault.

When I walk into the apartment, ready to do battle, ready to demand an emotional showdown, there's a note on the fridge. "Gone back to Kansas. Good luck, Dorothy." I can't decide if this is a coward's ending or simply a change of seasons. His side of the closet is empty. I'm not sure what I feel. It isn't loss but the arrival of the inevitable. Weather is like that.

* * *

I wake confused. It's a "dark and stormy night" like a page torn out of a cheap novel, near the end of tornado season. The full moon has come and gone and wreaked its havoc. A green-black sky sucks out the air on the other side of my window. Sounds, like a freight train, roar overhead. Sirens activate but my weather spotter's radio has not. I sit on the side of the bed and fumble for a flashlight. It's dim beam illuminates the steps as I hurry barefooted to the top of the stairway. I pause and shake the flashlight, hoping for a flare up of light. I whack it on the palm of my hand. It dies for a moment then returns, faintly. I force myself down the stairs towards the basement, with its spiders and cobwebs, to take cover. My ears ache as I feel the pressure drop. Outside trees fall, branches bouncing off something metallic. Glass shatters. Electricity crackles and vanishes. One by one the lights go out. An empty trashcan tumbles down the street. On the last step I slip and fall. Something is on the stairs and that's the last thing I remember as I land flat on my back and my head strikes against the riser. A red and yellow pain. I wonder where everyone else has gone. Am I alone on a crashing planet?

Dawn seeps under the front door, filtering in, a mist, a gas, an eddy of ground fog. The pale light throbs behind my barely opened eyes. I am lying at the bottom of the rickety steps. I move each limb to see if anything is broken. Nothing noticeable, except for a knot on the back of my head. No blood. The dim beam of the flashlight still shines in the corner of the doorway, illuminating a discarded gum wrapper and a crumpled advertising circular. I leave the flashlight lying there to fade out and die, like a morning star.

I drag myself upstairs to the apartment. Its bare walls astound me. Then I remember that Davis is gone, swept away by a rogue wave. A typhoon with my name. There's a calendar on one wall. *The Forces and Faces of Weather.* This month's picture shows a cactus in the snow with flowers blooming on its sagging limbs. Today is circled as another workday. The circles and the Xs over each day help me pace my life.

I throw on a pair of jeans and grab my shirt, which is embroidered with the hospital logo of a heart wrapped in bandages. I take my keys from the hook next to the door and lock the apartment. There's nothing sitting on the stairs this morning. Outside, no evidence of a storm. Everything stands placidly in place, trashcans lined up against the side brick wall, newspapers on the door stoop. My tongue feels thick. I grab a paper and open it. Stare at the forecast. Partly sunny or partly cloudy. Take your pick.

I drive away, even though I am hours early for work. From Woodward Avenue I notice the water tank that stands high above the Detroit Zoo. It's been painted with a parade of animals. A jolly circular parade, like the peaceable kingdom on display. I make an illegal left turn into the parking lot. The zoo has just opened. A few women push kids in strollers, heading for the gated entryway. An elderly woman with tightly wound gray curls, carrying a knitting bag, waits in the line to enter in front of me.

I hand the cashier a wadded ten-dollar bill, fished out my jeans pocket. Her hair is pink, a snake tattoo peeks above the collar of her shirt. She barely looks at me, already bored with her job although the day is just beginning. "Have a nice day," she drones without making eye contact, pushing two singles back through a small opening. She's my age and could be someone from the audience of any one of our shows.

I head towards the Arctic Ring of Life at the far end of the zoo. In the pool next to the artificial tundra there are two polar bears standing in water up to their necks chomping watermelon rinds. A coconut bobs nearby. One of the bears dips under the water, swims over and retrieves it. He paddles with giant white paws.

A red-jacketed docent walks towards me, eager to speak to a visitor. She greets me and launches into her speech without even a good morning how-do-you-do.

"Polar bear hair has no color," she says and pauses for effect, hoping to note my surprise but doesn't see any. "Their hair merely reflects light. Look at this closely and you'll see - their hairs are actually translucent." She pulls a piece of fur from her pocket and holds it out towards me. I stroke the thick clump of hair. Each individual hair is like a hollow crystal reed.

"If you see some yellow or green, it's due to algae. Otherwise, what you see is a white bear that's actually colorless. You can see the absence of color. Or the presence of sunlight. It's a cloak of invisibility. The bears appear to vanish against the ice. When they hunt they cover their black noses so that light simply bounces off of their fur. Then they're invisible to seals until after their prey surfaces. The bear's mouth and tongue are black. By then it's too late for the seals to notice."

The bear with the captured coconut is swimming with it held between his black gums, unsure what to do. He swims in confused little circles, away from the other bear, hoarding his coconut.

I doubt that these watermelon-eating bears would know how to behave in the wild, in a storm. I lean on the railing and watch. The wide nostrils of their black noses flare as they sniff the air. Black tongues loll out of their mouths as they swing enormous heads from side to side as if trying to pick up sonar messages. One bear turns and stares at me, his ears flick. I know what to do.

I walk away carefully covering my nose with my paw. Invisible. Safe. Alone. I look up at the sky and I see clouds. Only clouds, white puffs without scientific names. Some are shaped like polar bears turning somersaults underwater. Others float in wisps across the sky, changing on the run. The wind picks up and blows sideways as I leave the artificial Arctic Circle and cut across the zoo to the exit. My pace quickens. I'm floating. As I near the exit I recall the punch line to the seven dwarfs joke: "Dopey fucked a penguin." I laugh so hard I have to stop and sit on a bench to catch my breath.

After work I'll go home and paint the ceiling of my bedroom bright blue, bluer than the eyes of God. Maybe I'll enroll in a Yoga class or an Italian class. Maybe the Cut-ups can be pasted back together. I'll write some new songs. Maybe I'll call my mother and invite her to dinner.

Feline Domesticus

FlatFoot Floogie is a big alley cat. So big that, in my old neighborhood, people who spotted him called the police thinking he'd escaped from the zoo.

"Ach," the desk sergeant said, after receiving several calls. "That must be Roseanne Costello's cat from over on Valencia. It won't harm you none." Many of my neighbors had my phone number memorized. And they didn't call to join the Floogie Fan Club.

The phone would ring. Hysterical Mrs. Buckley would scream into my ear "Roseanne, come and get your damn cat. He's killing chipmunks all over the block. It's a bloody mess."

Or Mrs. Turnock would call. "Tommy got a real fright yesterday. Came around the corner and there was your cat. Big as a mountain lion, that thing is. That beast ought not to be prowling the streets! "

Moving was the best thing for Floogie and me. No one in the Avenues knows my phone number. I'm keeping it unlisted.

Floogie was just a kitten and I wasn't more than ten years old when we got him. My great-uncle Joe, a merchant marine, gave him to me one Christmas morning. "Might grow a bit," he cautioned, handing me a yowling fur ball. "His mother was the Queen of Siam." Floogie looked like any other grey alley cat, for a while. Then he grew as if he were in a 1950s horror movie. His weight reached forty pounds.

Even the vet didn't know what to make of him. "Maybe his hormones have gone wild," he said. "I wouldn't count on this kitty living a long life."

We gave him a dog bed in the kitchen. When I left home at eighteen my parents referred to him as my cat so off he went with me. They were relieved to have the curse of the neighborhood removed to a distant part of town by their eldest daughter.

That was more than twenty years ago. So much for modern veterinary theory. Floogie has shown no signs of aging, although I have. A few wrinkles around my eyes, nails that grow like claws - yellow and curled at the tips, dark hair streaked gray at the temples shedding everywhere.

I stare into the mirror. The sweat on my brow is intensely bright. Little droplets of jewels that hurt my eyes. I can't see my mother's face, even though everyone says you're supposed to as you age. My face is more feline. My parents seemed old from the beginning. They grew alike in voice, manner, and appearance as they aged. They lost their boundaries and dissolved. Melded into a single being. Floogie and I might be like that, I think as I force myself to turn away from the mirror. After all, I am otherwise alone.

Throughout the years boyfriends have come and gone. Even the ones that liked cats didn't seem fond of Floogie.

My last boyfriend, Mark, was a gem. A true gentleman. Too bad he didn't survive the cat test. We couldn't even make love in the missionary position. Just as he would reach orgasm, Floogie would pounce on him and sink his claws deep into Mark's buttock. Needless to say, this sort of cat behavior has cramped my love life. I don't know what became of Mark. He seems to have left town. Flown the coop like one of those pigeons Floogie is fond of snatching out of mid-air. Mark didn't leave so much as a feather behind as evidence.

Floogie doesn't care that Mark's vanished. "Good riddance to that dirty dog," he said. "I didn't like him panting and drooling around here, anyway."

Currently we live our lives, Floogie and me, in a sunny flat out in the Avenues not far from Golden Gate Park moving quietly through the days and weeks. It's a better neighborhood and we're able to keep a low profile. I support us with occasional temp work to pay the bills.

Today is Friday, which means it's time for our special liver dinner. The rest of the week it's either chicken or fish. I reach into the china cabinet, forcing open the warped doors, and extract Floogie's special china liver dish. The red china dish has a picture on it of a calico cat wearing a pink ribbon. She looks right out of the dish with big sexy eyes. We've named her Betsy and she's Floogie's hot Friday Night Date. I cut the cooked liver into tiny cubes and arrange them in a semi-circle on the plate. Floogie arches his back and rubs against my leg.

"OOOH Betsy" he croons impatiently as he circles around me. "Betsy!" he moans. I place the plate on the ground and he crouches low to eat. When the liver is gone, he cleans Betsy and her plate, scraping his tongue over her beautiful face. Then he wipes himself with his paw, tips his head and thanks me.

The neighborhood has been buzzing recently with talk of a burglar. They refer to him, or her, as a cat burglar. Mostly small items are found missing, jewelry, silverware and such. This worries me. I think they look at me funny now when I leave my flat and walk down the stairs and out into the street. And it's the *way* they look at me - out of the corners of their eyes. Shifty-like. As if they know something and want to speak to me about it, but they don't. I go about my business and keep my eyes focused straight ahead, looking away at the thin line of the horizon. I plant my feet firmly one in front of the other, counting as I walk. One potato, two potato, three potato, four. I have a worry spot on the back of my hand that I've rubbed raw.

The worst of it is that Floogie stays out later and later each night. I don't really know where he goes. He seems tired when he squeezes back inside the apartment through the opened kitchen window, collapsing onto his bed. He refuses to discuss any of this with me. "Mind your own business, Missy," he says to me. "A cat has to do what he has to do."

As if that were not enough, within weeks of the cat burglaries, the kidnappings started. Well, baby snatchings might be more accurate. Flyers have appeared throughout the neighborhood, particularly around the park, warning mothers to keep a close eye on their babies. Babies are being lifted from strollers, cribs, sandboxes, playpens. Different locations each time. The babies are in good health when recovered. Usually a passerby hears them crying in the bushes. One was found in the park under a six-foot tall rhododendron bush. Another mewing pitifully in a grove of eucalyptus. Another under someone's front porch steps. Very clean, healthy. Except for some scratches. And teeth marks on the backs of their necks. I like the smell of babies. I use baby talc around the litter box and in the bathroom as a deodorizer. It's the tops of the babies' heads that gives off that odor, along with the scent of apples and rain. When I see a baby I think of the world as being very small, something I can hold in the palm of my hand or carry in my mouth ever so carefully. Some people like the smell of bread baking. They say that it makes a person blissful and content. But I would rather have *eau de bebe* sprayed everywhere instead.

Mark did not like the baby talc smell. It riled him instead of calming him. He brought me flowers to cover it up. Roses of the most fragrant varieties.

Beautiful, but thorny things. I set them in vases around the house. The next day, as soon as I'd leave to work or to shop, Floogie would go on a rampage. He'd pull the roses from their vases, tear off their petals and scatter them all over the house. When I returned, I'd scoop up handfuls and toss them into the bath water where I'd lie in the tub for hours by candlelight, smoking a cigarillo, studying the cracks in the ceiling. I knew that the cracks in the bathroom ceiling contained secret messages. Floogie perched on the edge of the tub, twitching his tail, helping me decode them. He nudged me with his leathery nose to keep me focused and awake. Maybe, one day, I'll find a message about Mark sent from the missing person's bureau between one of the cracks.

After our liver dinner, I recline in the tub even though there are no roses. I've sprinkled the water with Eurasian mint instead. The smoke from my cherry-flavored cigarillo drifts up towards the ceiling. I stare at it and the distortions take shape. The squiggly lines become ghost writing, visible only by the candlelight. The light flickers across the ceiling and I read: *Sell the jewelry.* Another wispy line takes shape and reads *NOW!* I sit up in the tub, my heart pumping away like a tattoo needle.

Floogie paces in the doorway. The candle casts his shadow larger than any mountain lion. Just last week a lioness in the Oakland Hills pounced on a female jogger. The jogger, a petite young woman, crouched low to the ground. A mistake. She turned her back. Another mistake. I do not make mistakes. I fix my eyes on Floogie as I get out of the tub and stand up tall as I rub my body dry with a fluffy white towel watching Floogie slither back and forth across the doorway flicking his tail. He seems agitated.

I paw around in my closet until I extract a red dress with a wide flounced skirt and a scoop neck bodice. I tuck my sallow thinning hair under an Orphan Annie wig and throw a black cape with a hood over it all, to blend invisibly with the night. However, I need to locate the jewelry. I dump out the drawers of my dresser trying to remember where I've put it. As I'm crawling around on my hands and knees, tossing clothes everywhere, I remember that the dresser was last year's hiding place. The sweater boxes under the bed are empty too. I empty out the kitchen cupboards and finally locate the stash in the pantry behind a dozen cans of Campbell's Tomato Soup. I stuff fistfuls into a plastic shopping bag.

It's almost 2 a.m. and I'm not sure whether I can find an open pawnshop. Floogie has already vacated the premises as I slip out into the darkness to catch a streetcar downtown. While the car rattles and shakes its way along the track, I decide that South of Market is my best bet. I exit quietly out the back door of the streetcar at the first stop past Van Ness and turn to my right. It's a little bit like Atlantis at night. Alive with an underwater other-worldliness. The streetlights give off a gaslight glow, a foggy yellow light. No one pays any attention to the pat-pat-pat of my soft shoes as I wander up and down streets, past warehouses and after hours clubs, looking for the pawnshops. I stop occasionally to sniff the air. Fish and salt. Roasting coffee. Urine. Human sweat.

I spot the exactly right shop. I know it's right because it has a neon sign that once said *Pawnshop* but the fourth letter is burned out and reads *Paw shop*. There are no lights on inside. The metal shutters are rolled down to the ground and locked. I know they're locked because I shake them and knock to see if anyone will answer my call.

A light comes on in the apartment over the shop and a head appears in a window. "God damn it! Shut up! No one's there until morning, you goddamn drunks and crack whores! Can it, will ya? I gotta get some sleep." He slams the window and vanishes.

I walk around the block, watching. Two times around to the right. Then three times around to the left. The air is hollow and quiet. Only the hiss of electricity as it moves along the power lines. The fog is pouring out of the ocean and layering the streets like cream swirling in a dish. Little fingers of it stalk the street. I stand in front of the pawnshop, and then position myself in a corner of the doorway curled up to wait until morning.

I'm awakened by a brown leather shoe poking at me. I look up and see a one-eyed man. He's cocking his bald head to the right and peering down at me to get a good look with his one functional eye. The morning sun has burned off the fog and a faint baking smell has replaced the evening's odors.

"What'd ya want, girlie?" The man asks grimacing as he turns and struggles to raise the metal shutters. "Up kinda earlier, ain't ya? Too much party last night, I'm betting." He waits a bit and moves close to me. He lowers his head close to mine. "Cain't ya speak or the cat got your tongue?"

I stand up, straighten my dress, adjust the wig on my head and stare him right in his eye. I fish the shopping bag out from under my cape. His expression changes.

"Oh, it's business, is it little lady? Wait a moment 'til I'm opened up right and proper here." He fusses a bit more with the shutters and lifts up the bundle of newspapers that was heaved into the doorway some time during the night, carrying it inside.

We transact our business and I'm soon on the streetcar lurching my way back out to the Avenues, a tidy sum in my pocket. I get off the car several blocks from my apartment. It's still early in the morning and the world has barely begun to stretch. A few people are out walking dogs. A couple of women in business suits with sneakers on stride toward the bus stop. I can hear into the houses as mothers wake children for school. The air smells good, a new day, a rebirth smell. Then it reaches my nostrils. The irresistible *eau de bebe*. A jackhammer feeling creeps up from my toes to the tips of my ears. They swivel this way and then that, listening. The mewing reaches my ears before I spot the pram. Just sitting there. I cannot help myself. I reach into the pram barely rustling the covers.

Somehow I'm able to climb my steps and open my door with my arms full. It doesn't seem like my home though. It's deserted. And chaotic. Several plants are dumped over. Dirt kicked around. Food is strewn about the kitchen. Floogie is not here. I look around, all over, even on the ceiling for a message. Finally, I spot something attached to one of the houseplants. He's left a note. In his clipped but careful handwriting I read that he has run away. He's gone feral and joined a gang in the park. He hopes that I will be able to find some other company for Friday night liver dinners. I'm not shocked that he's gone – I'm too feline for that - but I am shocked that he would go feral. That appalls me.

I squeeze the bundle in my arms to my chest. It whimpers a bit. I drop onto a chair and slide the shoulder of my red dress down, exposing my breast. I make purring noises as I put the baby to my breast and encourage it to suckle.

I Slept with Monica Lewinsky

ꕥ

I consider myself lucky to be writing my story in this fleabag pink stucco motel, the *Good Night Inn* on Woodward Avenue, the main drag in Detroit. Detroit's the birthplace of the auto or the tar pit of the industry, depending on your point of view. And my point of view changes daily.

Room 215 at the *Good Night* is small and comforting in spite of being dilapidated. It's a weekly lease with a tiny hot plate kitchenette. Everything in it is a variation on brown or tan – the walls, the chairs, the rug, the ceiling - except for the lime green 1950s corduroy bedspread. There's a small TV with basic cable so I can watch football. The season is starting, although I don't think I'll become a Lion's fan. They've had too many years of being losers. I'm looking to root for a winner. And it's not only the Lions. The entire city of Detroit is more down on its luck than I am. Decades of neglect litter miles of the main streets. Broken buildings, weed filled lots. Not even the Feds want anything to do with it. It's an edge on the map that's sliding towards oblivion.

Six weeks ago I walked into *Tweaky's Bar*, my usual Saturday night pit stop at home in South Fremont, New Jersey. The lighting was dim. Smoky with a yellowish gin glow. I paused to let my eyes adjust to the light. At the bar was this Marilyn Monroe look-alike, alone, sitting on a stool. I've always had this thing for Marilyn. Norma Jean Baker, Queen of the Castroville Artichoke Festival who transformed to Marilyn Monroe, Queen of the Silver Screen.

When I was a kid my dad had pinups of her all over our garage. Wrenches, welders, drivers, and a whole assortment of Snap-On tools laid out on the workbench underneath that famous photo where her skirt billows up around her waist. I can still see her white silky underpants. I can even feel them. She was my first paper whore back when I was thirteen in my own private Hollywood Heaven – a garage in South Jersey. Now a bleached blonde with red lipstick, cleavage and a pout can wiggle her little finger at me and I drool.

Marilyn was sitting off to one side of the bar stirring a Mai Tai with one of those paper girl-drink umbrellas in it. I sidled up to her and tried to control my breathing. The perspiration along my hairline blended with the gel and I hoped it made me look slick.

"Has anyone ever told you that you look like Marilyn Monroe?" I sat myself on a barstool alongside her and placed the heel of my boot on the rung of her stool, posing western style. The bar had a black light over it that made my white T-shirt glow and my pecs look tight and toned. Just like James Dean, I thought.

"You can buy me a drink if you like, it's my birthday. And go ahead, call me Marilyn," she said. She bit her red painted nails and twiddled strands of her platinum hair. There was something familiar about her but I paid no attention since I had already mentally transformed her.

It was a hot evening in July and getting hotter by the moment. All that anyone in this part of Jersey thinks of on a day like that is how soon can they get to the shore. I felt the surf pounding. Marilyn wound a strand of that very blonde hair around one of her luscious plump fingers and puckered her big red lips. Oh Baby, I thought, Papa wants you!

I tried to look at her face when I talked instead of at her barely covered voluptuous chest. I had read an interview with Marilyn in which she complained that men always talked to her breasts instead of to her face.

I introduced myself as Jack. That's my real name even though I'm no Kennedy. Jack Albert Orlovsky, III. Born and raised in South Jersey, a true local guy. I've even got the bowling jacket with my name stitched on it to prove it. The back has a flaming wheel with our league sponsor's name, *Gerry's Monster Wheels, Inc.*

New Jersey is the Garden State but not the Garden of Eden, or even the Hanging Garden of Babylon, although that's much closer. The Garden State is the place where you reap what you sow. In the movies those reapers often are gangsters but I've never met any of them off the screen.

"I work at *Fanucci's Ford* as a Warranty Manager," I explained to Marilyn, "trying to keep everyone happy. A regular five-day a week gig except I go in some Saturdays to work on my own car. She a beauty - a classic 1974 Ford LTD with a two-tone paint job, one of the finest machines in town. Gave her a lube job this afternoon."

Marilyn crossed and uncrossed her legs. She shifted her weight from side to side on the stool. She was a real looker, maybe twenty-five or six. Slow down, I told myself. Small talk is like small change. It grows until it is money in the bank. The longer you wait, the more you collect. I can be a sincere sensitive guy if I work at it and take my time. I let a woman know that I'm ready to look deep into her soul, to see beyond the tempting outline of her oh-so-fine body. It's all in the eyes. That's the message I tried to deliver to Marilyn by baring my soul.

Marilyn returned my intent look. "Sounds like you have a real thing for cars." She stroked the glass and ran a finger around its rim.

"Really," I said, "what I always wanted was to be a mechanic. Tinker with engines all day long. After my dad died, my mom made me go to Millville Community College to get ahead in life – you know how that is. I'm just a blue-collar guy in a white collar disguise."

Marilyn nodded and stirred her drink. "You bet I know. I wanted to be a simple housewife but my life got mixed up. Something awful. I'm here looking for a way out, hiding out, in fact." She winked at me. "I've got a little summer sublet in town."

She took a pen out from a glitzy black evening bag and wrote a phone number in pink ink on a cocktail napkin. Folded it in half and handed it to me.

"You're so sweet. Call me and we can get together soon. Maybe real soon?"

I left the bar that night, taking it slow and being cool. I liked the idea of a summer romance, no strings attached. It sounded almost perfect. I should have been suspicious of anything that looked perfect. Perfection is an idea that some dude on top of a pyramid invented to frustrate the rest of us in our daily lives. At that time I forgot that. A perfect-looking dame leaves me running like a horse with blinders on. This Marilyn-like creature seemed so familiar and so familiarly enticing.

I walked to my apartment, one room with a kitchenette off Main Street, past small framed houses painted ridiculous colors like pink and green. The three block walk felt as if it took hours. I was lost in my erotic fantasy of her milky body in my hands.

South Fremont, New Jersey is a small town with only one main street but it has a half dozen bars. When you turn twenty-one you sign on at one as a regular, like picking a college I suppose. *Tweaky's* was my place. It was small, personal and I liked their jukebox best. Oldies. Slow dance tunes.

I phoned Marilyn a couple of times that week. One odd thing was that when she answered the phone she wouldn't speak. I'd hear her breathing on the other end but no voice until I'd ask, "Marilyn, baby, are you home?" Then she laughed. If I'd been a detective like Philip Marlowe that would have been a clue. Marlowe had a real way with dames, which I liked. But I was still James Dean stumbling towards ruin and destruction.

We talked for hours. None of her stories made sense. One day she was a farm girl from Wisconsin, a runaway. The next day she was an heiress from New York City hiding out from the paparazzi. I didn't care. I tried to be casual even while I imagined her in a strapless summer dress with the wind blowing up around her thighs. I could see her grabbing at the flimsy material and squealing. A faux wholesome babe, winking at me.

Other women have caused me regrets. Talkers. Weepers. Clingers. Ones with angry spouses, boyfriends. Occasionally a disease, but nothing fatal. I acted out the script and moved on to the next role. I did not suspect that this would be different. Marilyn should have been tattooed, branded with a hazardous warning sign.

We arranged to meet again at *Tweaky's* the following Friday.

I arrived first and ordered champagne, Marilyn's favorite drink. I took the chilled bottle and a couple of glasses over to a booth. Black plastic, circa 1950s. In fact, the booth probably was from the 50s. The torn spots were covered with duct tape on the worn vinyl cushioned seats. It was as intimate as you can get at *Tweaky's.*

"Angel Baby" was playing on the jukebox as I waited. I sang along in falsetto "Uhoo, I love you, Uhoo I do-o-o. Angel Baby, my angel baaaaby." I imagined my hand slipping down Marilyn's backside, fondling her ass. Big and full. I almost lost it right there, alone in the booth with two champagne glasses sweating on the table.

An hour passed. I didn't mind the wait. Marilyn always kept people waiting – photographers, reporters, film crews. Probably even Jack and Bobby. Some women you can forgive anything. Even suicide. Marilyn stopped the hands of the clock.

Then she appeared wearing sunglasses, a red scarf tied around her bouffant hairdo and a white dress which made her painted lips even more appealing. She untied the scarf and tossed it onto the seat in the booth.

"Jack," she said "the aliens have escaped from Roswell and are trailing me." She glanced towards the front door as she sat down.

"Don't worry, hon, I'll protect you." I said as I twisted around to look at the door. A man in a black suit leaned against the jamb, trying to blend into the dark wood walls. He had a newspaper rolled under his arm. For swatting flies, I supposed. He didn't fit into this picture. I knew he was watching us because he didn't once look our way. Probably he thought that was subtle. I've seen enough movies to know that undercover guys can behave dumb as dirt. Black suit and shiny shoes didn't fit in a small South Jersey town either.

She sat with her back to him. I figured out that this was so he couldn't read her lips. She downed a glass of champagne as if it was a chaser.

"You really don't know who I am?" she asked.

"Sure," I said. "The girl of my dreams. Fantasy stuff. Marilyn. Cinderella. Venus. Beauty, but then I hope you don't think I'm the Beast." Somewhere in the deep recesses of my mind, her face was familiar.

She leaned toward me and her perfume erased any connections I might have made. "How about coming over to my place?" she asked.

The layout was perfect for our escape. Just past the restrooms, an exit door opened into the narrow back alley. "Ladies, first" I said, gesturing with my eyes towards the rear of the bar. She exited leaving her red scarf draped on the seat of the booth. I waited a few minutes. The man at the door glanced at his watch, leaned back and appeared to be whistling. I headed towards the restrooms, then veered out the back door.

She was waiting for me in the alley. Standing on one foot, leaning against a brick wall, head tilted to the side, blond hair cascading over an eye. Our lips met as I took her in my arms and pressed my body against hers. She dug her fingers into my slick black hair and wrapped one leg around me. This was a scene from a movie and I knew the part well. The throb and hum were loud by then. I disconnected all brain controls.

We stumbled along Fourth Street, our bodies bumping as we walked. Her apartment was up some rickety backstairs over *Fifi's Pet Grooming Salon*. We took off our clothes without speaking a single word until she stripped to her panties, which were white with *Sunday* embroidered on them, across one of the hips.

"I know it's not Sunday," Marilyn said. "But any day can be Sunday now, according to my underwear. I lost my "Friday" panties. Some dumb-ass detective took them as evidence." She looked at me, waiting. I still didn't get the exact nature of the challenge in her eyes.

Women make me behave poorly. The problem isn't my brain; it's my prick that's dumb. It gets me into a lot of trouble as it leads me down that proverbial path of sin. I could hear dogs barking faintly below us. Poodles, I imagined.

I couldn't wait any longer. I took her there and then on the kitchen floor with its black and white squares of tile. Her red lipstick, platinum hair and white-pink body squirmed under me. That moment of thrill shot me back to adolescence. I saw Marilyn step off the wall of my dad's garage and give herself to me. My whole body spasmed. Marilyn, the queen of my dreams, in my arms!"

When I came to my senses she was wrapped in a white terrycloth bathrobe, lighting a cigarette, seated at the Formica kitchen table. She blew out a puff of smoke and it hung in the air like the backdrop for a black and white noir movie. Particles of dust and light blurred my vision and suddenly it came to me. Monica Lewinsky was grinning at me through the haze. Monica, but as a dyed blonde. This was not the Technicolor romantic Marilyn scene I 'd been imagining. After the scandal with Bill, five years ago, Halloween partygoers wore blue dresses with stains and dark-haired Monica wigs. Trick or treat took on a whole new meaning. "Monica," I said out loud. "Why didn't you tell me?"

She launched into a Monica explanation. About all the men who'd taken off once they'd realized that she was the President's other woman – *That Woman.* How they practically ran out the door as if she were diseased. About the rest of the men who wanted to sleep with her only because the President had. About the secret agents following her all the time, opening her mail, harassing her friends and family. It made for a rotten sex life, she claimed. She was working on tears at this point. I can't stand to see a woman cry. My mom cried for a full year after my dad died, so now I do anything she asks to keep the tears away. I looked at Monica and tried to appear sympathetic.

She said she'd liked it that I thought of her as Marilyn. "We could have a great future," she said. "Lots of fun. True romance. We'll have to be very careful." Her voice dropped to a husky whisper. "Bill told me lots. The truth about Roswell and the alien landing. About the mafia controlling congress. About money changing hands, assassinations. Just like Jack and Marilyn. There are agents out there suspecting this. Don't talk to them, no matter what."

She opened a big red and white plaid scrapbook that had been stacked between *The Joy of Cooking* and *Asian Meals Made Simple.* There was a picture of Monica wearing Chelsea's beret on the front cover. She had titled it in black magic marker with large loopy cursive letters *The Book of Me.* Inside were newspaper clippings, bunches of photos, old White House IDs. There were even blurry photos that the paparazzi had shot through the window of her bathroom of her sitting on the can. Not very classy. Some of her baby pictures were in it too. Kind of like a before-and-after collection.

"Bill liked those, the baby ones," she said. "And so did Hilary." Then she covered her mouth with her hand and her eyes got bigger. "Forget I said that, please," she asked. "I don't know why I'm telling you all this."

I spent that night with her even though the fantasy bubble had burst. Her dark roots were showing through her platinum dye job. If I had been able to spend a night with the real Marilyn Monroe I would never have woken up with regrets. I would have died a happy satisfied man. Regret is too kind of a word for this affair. With Monica I was trapped. I wanted to return to my snug small apartment where I felt sane and safe.

I watched her that night, half-sleeping. Several times she tiptoed to the window and peeked out between the slats of the plastic blinds. I watched at one point while she rifled through my pockets, examined my wallet, and even checked the soles of my shoes. I couldn't wake and I couldn't sleep. I dreamed of aliens landing, green and slimy with big bug eyes. I envisioned men in black suits, armed and dangerous, loitering under yellow street lamps, waiting for me.

And the reality that followed wasn't all that different. Monica brewed me a cup of weak as piss Maxwell House coffee in an old percolator on the stove before I headed out to my place. There was still some fog in the early morning air that hadn't burned off as I walked the half-mile or so to my apartment. The fog made a greenish glow like a backdrop for a sci-fi thriller but I didn't meet up with aliens. Only a couple of shopkeepers opening their stores, a newspaper deliveryman zooming by in an old Buick station wagon, and some homeless guy in torn Bermuda shorts and a New Jersey Nets T-shirt digging through garbage bins. I walked quickly.

When I unlocked my door and entered my apartment I stepped into my new and altered life. Everything was a mess. A total trashing had taken place overnight. The apartment was engulfed with clothing, papers, food, pots and pans – everything I owned strewn on the old wooden floors. I couldn't even tell if anything had been taken.

I walked towards the phone, which was next to the bed, stepping over my scattered belongings. Its red message light was flashing. Four calls, it said. I erased the first two, which were hang up calls. The third one was muffled as if someone had their hand over the speaker. I could make out some of the words. "Sorry. No longer able to ignore. The dame. Official notice. Don't call police. Twenty-four hours."

I saved it and moved on to the last call. I recognized a sobbing Monica. "Jack, my love, I am so-so sorry. You must forgive me but you're in honest, truly, cross my heart, real life danger. Get out of town quickly. They think that you know everything, that I babbled secrets and stuff you're not supposed to know. They followed you. You know, the guys in the black suits. I peeked out the window and saw them. They have ways of finding out everything so don't tell anyone where you are, no one, nobody not even your Mom. Go quickly. I'll meet you in Reno, October first. We can get married at *Tinney's Love Chapel.* It's a drive through, so it's perfect. Check in at the Best Western and there I'll be. I'll be yours, forever. Just go quickly, my love."

I sat on the floor in the middle of the mess. This sounded like a really bad movie script but it was too much to ignore. I needed a plan. A sort of stopgap one, so I could have time to think. I was used to my routines, my orderly life. Five days a week at *Fanucci's Ford.* Weekends on the prowl. Sunday brunch with my mother. The same little apartment for eight years. I like small spaces. Enclosures. When I was a kid I would take two chairs from the dining room, place them back to back and drape a sheet over them to make a tent. I'd take a pillow, a blanket, a pile of comic books, a flashlight and I'd hide. For days. This was not going to be that simple.

While I was sitting there, thinking, the front window shattered. A brick with a piece of paper rubber-banded around it landed on the floor. It sat in the midst of glass shards. I was relieved that it wasn't a bullet or hand grenade, although I picked it up as if it might explode. "Don't go to Reno, or else!" was printed in big letters on the crinkled paper. Nothing more.

All thoughts of passion and exotic nights with Monica/Marilyn vanished. I could see Monica now, naked, covered with thick black body hair, fangs, blood dripping from her ruby lips, reaching for me with her claws. A Creature from the Black Lagoon rising up. The airbrushed fantasy was gone. All her scars were visible, her flaws and flab and wrinkles. The dark roots beneath her oh-so blonde hair. It was the ultimate next morning, day after, rude awakening. This could make me impotent for the rest of my life. And the rest of my life could be very short, I thought. I wasn't even sure how to be careful.

I packed a duffel bag with my clothes and necessities, wrote out a check to the landlord for two months rent, and phoned work. I knew I would get a machine since it was the weekend. "Family emergency," I said. "Grandma is very ill. I need to go out west since no one else in the family can go. Save my job, if possible. I'll phone later." I knew this sounded pretty lame and if I got back alive I'd most likely end up unemployed.

I found out how serious this mess was when I phoned my mom at her place across town.

"Jackie! Sonny boy," she said. "Are you OK? Some men were here about an hour ago. Some guys with badges looking for you. What kind of trouble are you in? They wanted to come inside and ask questions, but I told them no. National security, they said. Not very well mannered men, either. Lady, they said, we aren't here to play games. They said they were going to get warrants. What did you do?"

I wanted to tell her, "Ma, all I did was sleep with Monica Lewinsky" but I doubted she'd believe that. She'd think that it was another one of my movie fantasies. The truth hardly mattered. The government agents could make me into any kind of criminal that they chose. I'd never considered that this could happen to an ordinary guy from South Jersey who voted Republican and minded his own business. I always figured that the guys you read about in the paper being harassed by the government had to be criminals in some way, that they'd done something wrong and deserved to be punished or exposed. And here I was – public enemy number 7,529. I could see my picture going up in the Post Office and in all the grocery stores. My poor mother!

"Ma, it's a mistake. A big one. A case of mistaken identity like you wouldn't believe." This was damn close to the truth. "Just tell them you don't know anything and don't let them in. I need to leave town for a while until they figure it out. You know, drop out of sight like in the movies. You might not hear from me for a little bit but I'll be fine, Scout's honor." I was relieved that she didn't cry. She'd always wanted to act in a movie and probably saw this as her big chance.

Six weeks ago I drove towards Detroit, checking at each rest area to make sure I wasn't followed. I didn't know anyone in the Motor City so maybe it never occurred to them that I'd flee in this direction, to the Auto Mecca of the world.

As I traveled I thought about Marilyn Monroe. Once I was west of Cleveland, the flat stretch of highway left a lot of room for my mind to roam. I thought about Marilyn's transformation. How she rose furiously and became a household word. And about how that destroyed her, how she burned. Monica rose too. Yeah. Her name's become as common as Lysol or Kleenex. Except people around her got burned and she just floated away. Last week I read in *USA Today* that she'll be hosting her own talk show in LA. Seems that *she* doesn't need to hide. Guess she'll be taking a day off soon for the big trip to Reno where she can pace around the Best Western waiting for me to show up. I hope she's really pissed off left standing alone at the altar. Then she can host another show and call it "Who Wants to Marry A Floozy." I can't believe that I got the two women, Monica/Marilyn, mixed up. Like the difference between the words *starlet* and *scarlet*.

I'm keeping a low profile in Detroit. I've hired on with a landscaper, *Mike's Grow and Sow.* Landscape, rake or shovel. They pay me under the table. We work the north suburbs. Most of the crew is Mexican or from someplace south like that. Maybe Guatemala or El Salvador. I'm the crew leader because I speak English. I feel safe and out of reach of the authorities. I think that the edges of the country attract people like us. Marginal survivors, barely hanging onto the fringe of the world. Hunkered down for the duration, whatever that may be.

Sometimes I wonder when it will be safe enough for me to try to get another automobile related job. Probably I'm on some black list that's circulated through the industry. I picture my photo on a poster with a black X through it. "Do Not Hire This Guy. Call the FBI. Wanted for questioning on National Security matters." The picture would not look anything like me, of course.

I drive down the Southfield Freeway and look at the *Ford World Headquarters*. I pass the giant wheel that was used as a ferris wheel at the World's Fair. It sits alongside the Freeway near a billboard with a clicker that counts the number of cars as they roll off the assembly lines. Elsewhere in the city there's the world's largest stove and a giant Morton Salt Shaker. I found this out in a book of travel trivia I picked up to fight insomnia. Detroit superlatives. These giant things make me feel more invisible. Even so, driving by is as close to the auto industry as I've let myself get except for tinkering with the company pickup truck which, I'm embarrassed to say, is a Chevy.

On weekends I drive down I-75 to call my mom from a pay phone across the state line in Ohio. Somedays I think that I'll just keep on driving south to Miami or drive north to the very top of Michigan. The same road takes you to either place. Or maybe I'll escape to Canada like a draft dodger.

Then I realize that I've become used to my routine, simple as it is. I talk with my mom but never more than three minutes at a time. I once saw on a cop show that they couldn't trace a call like that. The agents are persistent, she says. She sees them outside her house, loitering, and sometimes in the grocery store or even at her hairdresser. They've talked to everyone in town who has ever known me, it seems. Of course no one has seen me. I can sense them fanning out. I sure wish I were as important as they think I am. Or that I knew whatever it is they think I know.

I'm Ken Jackson now (as close to Jack Kennedy as I could come). I've even cut my hair to resemble his. No more of the James Dean look. I've outlived him already. I drink with the guys after work or pick up second-hand paperback books to read by the yellow light from the chipped lamp next to my motel bed. I don't pick up women though. They are something I'm avoiding for the time being. Too much trouble.

I have no intention of going to Reno next month. Probably they think they'll catch me there. Like a dumb tomcat sniffing the air unable to resist a female in heat. But they don't know me. I have all the fantasies I need right here in my small motel room. A stack of magazines by my bed filled with trouble-free paper ladies of the night, in all sorts of suggestive poses. Some dressed as pirates, some in babydoll pajamas, all beautiful, silent and very safe.

The Emperor of New York City

∽

I ride the "A" train as it jerks back and forth like a cattle car, dispensing advice to my subjects, collecting up their troubles to take home.

"Don't worry, Missus Wilcox, Sammy ain't gone far. When he come back, you just pretend that you the one been gone. Off to the Bahamas on one of them cruises."

At the end of the day, I'm just as tired as if I was sweeping up an office. This job didn't really change my life. No Sir! Being emperor isn't all it's cranked up to be.

"Missy Jones, you just hustle yourself down to that there Fort Greene clinic. They gots a cure for that rash to be sure. And I take it up with Legba when I get home. Light him a candle and pour him something good to wet his whistle."

I exit at Utica Avenue. Music floats out of windows and storefronts, drifting down in the heat from apartments that hang out over the street. All of it, blending with the garbage cluttering the sidewalk. Reggae and rap colliding. Two worlds making one sound. That sound moves me along until I reach Prospect Street and turn in at my palace. I climb up three flights of dusty stairs, pausing on each landing to catch my breath and encourage myself to go on. These old bones don't move like they used to. I rattle and click and huff myself up the stairs.

Today when I open the door I smell Fu-Fu and collard greens cooking. I hang my braided jacket with its chest full of medals out on the fire escape to air. The feathered hat, my crowning glory, I place on top of the TV making it look a bit like a rooster.

Maggie stands in the kitchen. It's shaped like a crooked little box, the floor sloping away. One grime covered window sits high over the sink. Maggie puts her hand on her big old hip and waves a spatula at me. "George, why don't you get a real job and keep it? Like you used to do. I don't know 'bout this emperor business."

I pull my beautiful Maggie Mae, my lovely queen, Erzulie, into my arms, sneak one hand around back and grab her ass and squeeze. I feel the largeness of her flesh through the worn flowered pattern of her dress. I feel mangoes and melons and I am far far away from Brooklyn.

She rests her graying head on my shoulder and I murmur in her ear. "Maggie Mae, some day you will have diamonds and pearls. And a crown of jewels." I want to tell her that being emperor is something that I'm stuck with. It's not the sort of job you just quit. The exit door is that old wooden box, waiting at the end of the road. And me carried through the streets on the shoulders of a crowd of mourners. I am emperor for life, regardless. I stroke her hair, feel her relax and let go. Life is good.

"George, you old fool, here." She straightens up and hands me a wet frayed rag. "Go wipe off that table. Set places too, while you're at it." Just like that I am back smack dab in Brooklyn instead of wandering down Ste.Pierre Playa drinking coco juice. I shuffle into the living room where a card table sits. An oilcloth with pink and orange swirls covers it. Thumbtacks hold it on. I sit down on a folding chair and lift my feet, one at a time, so I can tug off my boots. Can't figure out if my feets are growing or my boots are shrinking. Each day it seems I have to tug twice as hard as the day before, but off they come.

On the wall opposite the table and next to the fire escape is a mantle that is not a mantle. It floats above a fireplace that doesn't exist. It's a jumble of colored glass bottles draped with beads. Crumpled dried marigolds are scattered on a lace doily. A dozen half -burned candles sit on various plates and cracked china saucers.

I hoist my old butt out of the chair and hobble over to the mantle in my socks. My stubby fingers dig around in the bottoms of my pockets for the crumpled scraps of papers with appeals from my subjects scribbled on them. Writings on all kinds of paper, newspaper and napkins. Sometimes even on a dollar bill or on some beautiful colored paper money from lands where it never snows, where no one ever grows old, where they just wake up one day and find out that they've melted. Their old friend, Mr. Sun, done turned them into butter and they wash away in the rivers and out to sea. That does not happen here in New York City, no sir. Not in Brooklyn either.

I fish around in the lint down in the corners of my pockets. These cracked stained fingers aren't good for much. Mostly they just dangle off my hands.

Don't behave like I want them to. I stuff all the papers I find into an empty gourd that sits on the far end of the mantle. Then I pull a tarnished flask out of my hip pocket and pour some dark rum, dark as my sweet Maggie's skin, onto a dish and light it. The flame tells me that Legba is near. I offer him a pinch of tobacco, sprinkling it into the fire. A gift. One that Legba likes.

Before the government recognized my kingdom and that I'm emperor, I worked the nightshift in the Philco Center for years and years. Watchman for Philco, fortuneteller and advisor for the cleaning crew. That's how I trained for this here job. Nowadays the government sends me a check to perform my duties. I ride the "A" train regular from 9-5 rounding up all the needs and sorrows of my subjects. I put them in the gourd for Legba to distribute to the proper Loa. I do it right, with respect. Their main transactions lean towards missing husbands or sons, broken sewing machines, lost keys, neighborhood quarrels, and lovers' spats. Most of the folks - some short time, some long time out of Mother Africa – can't pay me for my work but they do fill my stomach instead. I get my share of sweet potato pie; it's almost as sweet as rolling in my Maggie's arms.

I rock and pray, "Grande Ai-Zan, salue Legba. Now silver breaks rock. I'm asking how you are? Salue Legba, Ai-Zan vie, vie, vie Legba. Creoles, sounde Legba's mirror. Legba vie, vie. Creoles sounde miroi Ati Bon Creoles. Legba! Mirror! Salue Legba." The fire dies out and I know he heard me. I close my eyes and hum and rock. His power fills the air around me. I feel like the tobacco smoke rising. Light. Shedding my skin. Legba is here. Then something catches my eye. A face. Out on the fire escape. It's half-black and half-white with a big toothy grin. The Baron, I think. A big old snake squeezes at my chest. Damn! I'm losing my balance. The ground feels like mush.

Somehow I find myself sitting on the folding chair, hands crossed over my chest. Each short breath sounds like cellophane paper crumpling in my head. When I turn towards the fire escape, no one is there. No Baron Samedi. No trickster. It's not my time. My breath returns to its usual rattlely old ways, shaking and grinding, huffing and puffing out my sunken chest. With each breath though the air tastes sweet. I roll it around on my tongue as I exhale.

"George, you OK?" Maggie stands in the doorway looking in at me. Her body is tense and rigid. I see under her skin to her bones. They look like white powder. Maggie, so dark and beautiful, the love of my life. With her white hair and white bones. We washed up on the shores here, this mighty strange land. We found each other. Made us shelter and a home. Raised up two children. Only to have them wash away. I see the fear bubbling under her skin. Twitching, ready to spill out.

I pat my bony knee. "Come here, baby. Sit on papa's lap. Gimme sugar."

A smile fills her face. Crinkles around her eyes like birds' wings. I feel it in my chest. Maggie shakes her head. "First food, then dessert. You gotta eat to keep some meat on them old bones. You gonna blow away one day. Whoosh! Like an old newspaper down the street, end up in some weedy lot being used up by bums to start a fire."

She goes back into the kitchen and returns with a feast for a king. I don't tell her about the Baron on the fire escape. She barely tolerates having these Loas hanging out around the house. I've got to feed them and calm them down on bad days. And the Baron! She'd be real upset knowing I'd seen him. I spend the mealtime describing my day riding the train. The troubles I've been asked to change. Maggie is like the gourd. I put the troubles inside her and it lightens my load. This gal is pure sunshine, sure enough.

"Sister Margaret Armbruiser," I tell her this, making up a name. I've got to make up the names for the supplicants as I go. Sometimes I remember their real ones. Most times, not. "This here lady got arms like a prize fighter. No one messes with her, to be sure."

"Sister Margaret, she be in bad shape now. Last winter, that low down Jesse run off with the neighbor lady. Now her boy missing. Not a bad one. A good boy, she says. Maybe gone off to look for work in Deeeetroit. Got some family there. But nobody letting her know what's what. Most likely that boy don't want to be found. I tell her patience, wait your time, wait two months and Legba will bring a message." I shake my head and sigh.

Sometimes, it seems that I'm caught in one of those hamster cages running round and round. The scenery don't ever change. "And Lulu Morgan, she put in for her mother. She's down bad with the flu, don't look good for her, Lulu says. Too old and too tired. Ready for the trip. Lulu don't want her to go."

After dinner, after our talk, I go out onto the fire escape for a smoke. I extract some papers and a tin and roll a fat one. The haze from the smoke makes Brooklyn look mighty nice. A curtain that blocks out all the grime. I lean against the no color brick wall. Below me several cats are prowling in the dumpster in the alley. Lots of the hullabaloo from the street drifts up. "Get your nasty hands off me!" someone hollers. "Enrique, Enrique!" His mama calls. I hear the clatter of dishes from the other apartments. Dinners coming and going. I hear Maggie humming a tune in the other room. The tiny patch of sky straight up is turning pink. I feel all the people around me. This time of day, it's no burden at all. I love their everyday sounds. They might not even need an emperor if the sun never set.

It's setting quickly as I finish the long smoke and go back in.

That night in bed, I reach for Maggie. She turns towards me with the same motion that's stirred me up all these years. Sometimes we make love in our sleep and wake not knowing if it was real or a dream. This time I'm awake. Hard to sleep with a squeezing in your chest and a hissing in your ear. So I reach for her in that old, familiar way, pull her chocolate flesh towards me and enter her. Then I look up. In a corner of the room, there's that Baron Samedi, dressed all in black – top hat and cuttail coat. He's there all right, dancing a banda, the humpety humpety dance. He's a grinning and chortling at me. Thrusting and shaking his skinny hips. Enjoying every moment. I roll off Maggie, blink a couple times and he's gone. That's it for me. Can't go on pleasing my wife with him lurking everywhere. I open my eyes off and on, seems like all night long. Checking out where I'm at – this life or the next. Maggie, lying next to me, mutters and snores. I knows my own bed when I hear it. The familiar is like a sleeping drug. I drift off before the sun rises.

Morning comes. Early summer day with the heat already rising up to our apartment through the floor. The walls, with their crookedy plaster, sweat. The shine changes their colors. Looks like a dark green mossy jungle in the bedroom. It's hard to make myself get up and dress for the job. That old red jacket with gold braids on the shoulders is equipped with medals galore, but no air conditioning. Gotta be a real man to carry it around. It's the sign of my office. The only emperor in town. This'll be one good day for riding the trains and escaping the heat. Maybe even head all the way out to Coney Island by end of the day. Ride the Ferris wheel and eat ice cream. I haul my sorry ass out of bed. Maggie's long gone. Market day on Thursday. She'll pluck a chicken and we'll have a stew pot tonight. I'll walk in the door and see the chicken feet in the sink and then I know for certainty that life is good. It's this routine that let Maggie get on with things after our kids were gone. Stewpot Thursday. Saturday Prayer Vigil. And Sunday choir. Lord knows that lady sings like an angel.

I hustle outside, my pocket full of subway tokens. The feather on my hat swishing like a horse's tail shooing flies. Morning folks on the street all bows and pays me homage. I squeeze onto the crowded train before I can catch my breath. Don't know if I'm dizzy from that or the heat or the perfumey smells in the car. Deodorants, sweat, after-shave lotion, cologne, someone with garlic breath. That's when I sees him again. Reading the paper on a torn plastic seat. Just sitting there like nobody's business. I spit three times and cross myself. It doesn't work.

Nobody's paying him the least bit of attention. Like it's every day a barefoot man in a top hat and cut-away tux (pants too small, up above his ankles) with a half black, half white face sits on the train. He holds the newspaper in front of him with white-gloved hands. Gives it a shake every now and then. And winks at me. I stagger a bit as the train pulls into the next station. Then I make a sudden move and get off. Don't really know what possesses me.

I cross to the other side of the platform, lean against a pillar to wait for the next train going home. There he is with the paper tucked under his arm, standing on the opposite side of the platform. All the rattle and hiss now coming from the tracks as the train approaches. I board it - more empty outbound. He's on it, though. Sitting. Reading the paper and chuckling. I figure it best to ignore him and sit with my back towards him until the train returns to Utica Avenue and I exit. I shake my head and discuss what it means to myself. Seeing the Baron like this. He's come for me. But I'm not going with him, no sir. I say it out loud. "No sir, Mr. Baron. I ain't ready. My Maggie, she be needing me. This ain't my time. You be here by mistake, I do believe."

The train lurches into the station and I exit. When I reach street level, I look back. He's following at a safe distance. Sort of floating along behind me. I move across the street and turn off by P.S. 108. So does the Baron. He floats about a foot off the ground. He doesn't walk. He sambas along, wriggling his hips, dancing all the way. Papers and trash blows about, caught up in a little whirlwind of heat and dust. Some of it catches onto the school fence. Candy wrappers, old lottery tickets, torn newspapers. I try to walk faster. I want to get home, lay down, drink some nice cool water. There's a throbbing in my head. I can't see clearly. Dust making my vision blur. Just barely make out the Baron shadowing me along the street. Dancing his samba.

I turn the next corner. My home and palace – straight ahead. I climb up the stoop and wait a moment to let my breath catch up to me before going in the door. Don't see the Baron anywhere. Must of realized he had the wrong address in his pocket. Must of listened to what the emperor said: I am needed here and now. Most likely he was in my head. Lord knows there ain't room in that head for him anyhow. Too crowded in there!

The stairs growing longer again today. Each day it seems one or two more sneaks in. I have to stop and rest a couple extra times before reaching the third floor. Number 3C staring at me. I open it with my shaky shaky hands. Can't hold 'em steady.

He's already inside when I open the door. He greets me, bows, honoring me and my position. No dancing, no laughing. His hat is off. Held across his chest real respectful. I look toward the kitchen. The chicken feet already in the sink, but I don't feel so good. The air's filled with the sound of crows' wings flapping. Their cawing is something dreadful. The Baron is floating again. He lies back with pennies on his eyes. He crosses his arms over his chest, holding onto the black top hat. He floats like that right out the window not bothering to open it. And I see her then. On the floor, all crumpled up. Her white hair streaming behind her head turned to the ground eyes opened. She's holding Legba's gourd. Her knees tucked up around it. Almost like she's asleep. But not. A riptide tears at me. I surrender and back out the door on tiptoes. I close the door, close my eyes and feel my way down the stairs blind.

The sunlight outside hits me like acid thrown in my face. I sleepwalk, floating the opposite way of the "A" train. A young mother bends over a carriage with a squalling baby. A teenager swaggers past, his pants hanging almost to the crack in his butt. The riptide pulls me along. My breath is erratic. The red feathers on my hat, the sign of my office, stick up above the crowd. The hot breath of the wind makes them sway. A rooster crowing, a rooster wailing, a rooster mourning. Maggie Mae, so far we came.

I find myself outside the "B" Line. I climb down to the station and board the first train. To Stillwell Avenue – Coney Island. The last stop. The very edge. Coney Island is a place that's both coming and going at the same time. Abandoned rides sit next to brightly-lit ones.

The heat has brought half of Brooklyn to the water. It smells of sweat and suntan lotions. The smell of young smooth skin and lips that speak of promises. I see none of it as I stumble along to West 12th Street where Wonderwheel Park stands. Something in my chest moans and hisses "escape!" And I squeeze my eyes shut as tight as I can so I don't see that empty shell of my Maggie curled up on the floor.

I pay $2.50 and wait in line. The Wheel turns above my head. I hear it. Sixteen swinging cars and eight fixed ones. Lovers kissing. Dreamers dreaming. Some folks all sweaty-palmed gripping the safety bar. High above it all.

Over the sounds of voices, yelling in languages I can't understand, I hear the ocean. The waves breaking. Whole and shattered. When my turn comes

I sit down in a car and fill my chest with lots of air. A bar fastens across my lap. Slowly the car rises. It jerks as it stops to fill each one with passengers. Swinging back and forth. And then the motion begins. The car moves around and around, from the earth to the sky. I'm gaining speed. I see everything rise. My past and my present. Sunbathers, out on the beach down below, lay with sweat pouring into their heat-bothered eyes.

The spinning wheel stops with me at the top. I let out my breath and stand up. The sky and the puffy white clouds suck at me. I raise my skinny black arms over my head and look to the South. Somewhere, way off beyond the horizon, I see an island. I see the endless motion of palm trees and taste the air. Its juice runs down the side of my face and I step towards it. Far below me no one moves. When they do look up, they will see a big red bird flying out over the ocean, the crest on its head fluttering as it flies out over the water. I exhale again and hold my arms out wide.

Leisure World

I assumed the message was about the dead rabbits when I saw Leisure World's phone number on a pink *While You Were Out* slip propped up on my desk. Leisure World is infested with rabbits since they drained the nearby lagoon to get rid of the gators. Apparently the gators had kept the rabbit population under control. Now they've reproduced like …well, like rabbits. Hordes of them run all over the place, hopping across paths and roadways, burrowing into the shrubs. I tripped over one while visiting Grandpa at Leisure World last week. It looked up at me like I was a dumb bunny in *its* way.

Grandpa runs down the rabbits with golf carts. Intentionally. He cackles with pleasure as he plows into them, full throttle, smearing their guts on the sidewalk. Then he drives the cart back to Unit 221, his own little utopia, where he keeps a tally that must be three digits long by now. None of the groundskeepers are happy with him because of the bloody trail of terror he leaves behind. They tried, once, to suggest that he clean up after himself. "Cleaning is women's work," Gramps sneered. I imagine him arching his bushy white eyebrows and staring down his royal aquiline nose at the male groundskeepers.

With trepidation I dial the number I know by heart. I don't need the pink slip. A cheery voice answers: "This is Leisure World, a retirement community for older seniors. Barbara Winchell, at your service." She's my least favorite person of all the smiley-faced camp counselor types that run the establishment.

"Sue Anne Eckstein returning your call." I sit at my desk and fiddle with my computer, calling up my email before she responds.

"Sue Anne, dear," she begins in this high-pitched artificial voice, drawling out the three words as if they are toxic, one long syllable at a time. I hate it when people begin with words like dear or honey or sweetie or sugar pie. It means they are pouring syrup over something nasty that will follow. "It's your Grandfather…"

An inordinately long pause follows, most likely for dramatic effect. Maybe she wants me to think the worst. Probably. I'm not sure what the worst would be. Death is inevitable. Our family knows that. We've dwindled to three – Grandpa, me, and my brother Charlie (and his largish clan of bible thumping in-laws who pretend not to be related to me or to Grandpa).

I open an email and wait for her to go on. I oversee a foundation that administers art grants. Queries and sad stories roll across my desk daily. Also angry letters which usually follows rejections. I have to deal with them all. I am not paid to deal with Grandpa. However, Barbara and the rah-rah crew at Leisure World are paid plenty for their 'care'.

The email on my screen is from an artist who paints breasts, literally breasts, only breasts, all shapes and sizes, in lurid neon colors. He's attached some photos to convince me of his artistic merit or to excite me. I can't tell which. The breasts look like candy mountain blobs.

"It seems that your Grandfather has vanished," Barbara finally intones.

With one click I send the breast artist a form letter and my best discouraging vibes. He will apply in spite of this, I can tell. I recognize it. If I could make him vanish instead of Grandpa, I would. I sigh and Barbara hears me.

"Sue Anne, are you there?" Her voice crescendos and I have to respond.

"Hmm – vanished how? A puff of smoke? A puddle of water, melted, perhaps? Like in Wizard of Oz. Or has he eloped with Natalie? How does one vanish leisurely?" I know what it sounds like to her and I don't care. For Christ's sake, it's a gated community, safe. They say so in their brochure. Peace of mind. Security. Paid for supervision.

"Young lady," she says from the playbook entitled *Stern Authority Addressing a Child.* The ridiculousness of it strikes me since she's no older than me. She may not realize it because she has one of those Florida tans that destroys skin and has left her looking like a prune. I avoid the sun. Especially since I've been into tattoos. They need protection, particularly in their early stage.

"This is serious. He's taken a golf cart and left our campus. That's theft, you know. Grand larceny in Florida." Her voice is rising higher. It's punching little holes in the ceiling. I figure that's how the acoustic tiles get their holes – puncture marks, from shrill voices, from thousands of Barbaras and their ear-splitting high decibel pronouncements.

If they try to revoke his golf cart privileges, I don't know what I'll do. He wants to believe that he resides at a hoity-toity resort, living a life of leisure. That's the picture my brother and I have painted for him. It's the carts, available on demand, that allow him to fantasize about his life. Those golf carts and the women residents - his harem - and the ornate glass chandeliers in the dining room. Evidence that he's living the good life.

"Call the police. Surely it can't be hard to find an elderly gentlemen on a golf cart." I study the most recent tattoo on my arm. It's a year old now, a willow tree bending over graciously. It looks Japanese. Its branches hang almost to the invisible water that I see below it in my mind. I hear the willow leaves rustling. I clench my fist and the branches move. Sway. More like hair than leaf.

"You can't be serious, honey," she snaps at me. She's starting to sound rabid. "Florida is riddled with elderly gentlemen on golf carts. Take away their car keys and bingo! They get a golf cart. There's a drive-in movie theater in Orange Grove that is expressly for golf carts. Row after row of them line up with speakers hooked onto their armrests. Every night. And they are all, *all*, driven by elderly gentlemen." Her voice is crackling. "Asking the police to find an elderly man on a golf cart would take the entire force a week or a month or forever. You *must* know where he's gone." I imagine her tensed mouth foaming, red lipstick smudged outside of boundaries. "Didn't he say anything to you? I'll bet you have a clue."

She thinks I'm a fucking Nancy Drew. I make the willow tree pulse some more, squeezing and releasing my fist several times. The willow tree was added onto my arm last year, after Mom died. She ran a restaurant, Willow-a-Way Diner. Pie and coffee were her specialties. And soups. Homemade bread, baked to perfection. A picture of a willow tree like this one, hung above the front door. It was a late night place, a hangout for artists and musicians. I grew up waiting their tables. That's how I got my start in the art world.

"Sue Anne, are you listening to me?"

"Sorry, Barbara, I'm at work. Distractions abound." Actually, there are only three of us that ever work in this office. At the moment I'm here alone, but she needn't know that. "What do you want me to do?"

I hit the delete button and the third letter in a month from one Mr. A. L. Johnson, artist extraordinaire, vanishes.

I agree to appear at LW the next morning, hoping he'll return by then and knowing that he won't without some corralling. That old man has caused more trouble in my life than anyone of my bad boyfriends. Barbara goes on and on about needing this signature and that. Visits, she thinks, should be made to the morgue to view unidentified bodies. Penalties. Loss of privileges. But it's obvious that she expects me to hit the road and find him on my own. And bring back her precious golf cart.

Hopefully I'll be able to cajole them into making another exception for Grandpa. The Leisure World management cuts a lot of slack for male residents. Men are a rare commodity, a handful at best. The women flit about Grandpa, cooing like a flock of pigeons. He loves it. He puffs out his scrawny chest and shuffles partners daily.

"They love to dance with me," he says. "Natalie tells me that I dance salsa like a Cubano. She says only Cuban men move the way I move to music. I'm *especial.*" He says this last bit with a flourish, kissing two fingers and flinging them into the air.

Natalie could be the oldest woman in the assisted/independent living complex (a very complex complex). She must be two hundred years old or pushing it. I'm not sure how she dances with her walker. Maybe she locks walkers with her partner while shuffling along the converted dining room dance floor. Sort of like teenagers locking braces while kissing.

Since Grandpa moved into Leisure World he dresses as nattily as he appeared in our old family photos. He wears ironed shirts – from the cleaners in a box, no starch. Starch gives him a rash, he says. He douses himself with *Canoe*, his favorite god-awful cologne. Shines his shoes daily. On his head he sports a straw bowler to keep the sun off of his face. "I've got skin like a baby's butt," he says patting a pock marked cheek, oblivious to his face in the mirror. In the evenings he wears a jacket to dinner, with a silk handkerchief in the pocket, regardless of the sweltering weather. He varies the handkerchief colors to match his shirts.

When I join him for dinner on Friday nights, he introduces me as his girlfriend. Suzy-Q, he calls me. Some of the women titter. Others glare at me as if I am robbing the opposite of the cradle. I pat his arm and give him a peck on his cheek, holding my breath so I don't suffocate from his perfume. Whatever I do, I don't contradict him. My mother used to do that, before she died - when he was living with us. She was the only one I ever heard talk back to him, the only person he ever let speak to him that way. With his huge white mane of hair, thick white eyebrows over icy blue eyes, and a cane that's more like a cudgel, no one messes with him. He says whatever he damn well pleases and to hell with everyone else.

I phone Charlie, across the border in Georgia. He always makes a point about it being a border, what separates him from us. I imagine it on some days as a barbed wire fence. On other days I see it as a brick wall studded with broken glass to keep out intruders, aliens, outsiders. I look for it whenever I drive north but it's been cloaked and made invisible. Charlie and I know it is there and it keeps us from face-to-face confrontation.

"Gramps has gone AWOL," I inform him when I hear his voice. I love his voice, low and soothing. It must be what my father's voice sounded like. I remember it only faintly, at night telling me bedtime stories and patting my back as I drifted off to sleep. Charlie's voice makes me drowsy. My eyelids grow heavy. I lean back in my office chair and let my head fall to one side as I clutch the phone.

"Suzy, I can't help you with this one." He sounds pained. "Beavis and Butthead have soccer games tonight. Marjorie has the Women's Group meeting at Church. I can have her pray for his soul but otherwise you're on your own. I ran out of ideas long ago on how to cope with that ornery old man. He's a damn mule. Mom was a saint, taking care of him all those last years. Gramps puts up with you because you remind him of her. Some days I think he doesn't even know who I am. He thinks I'm Dad and wants to kill me - as if it was me that ran off and left Mom and he might do it too, if I don't watch my back." He pauses, waiting for my reply. It sounds like I'm on my own. The Lone Ranger rides again. Heigh ho! Hit the road.

"What are you going to do?" he asks.

I glance down at my ankle. A serpent in red and green twines around my lower leg. In the right kind of light, its scales flash gold. I touch it for a moment before I answer him. I am powerful. I feel it in my fingertips. Poor Charlie, he has Neuticles for balls – nonfunctional implants. "Don't worry, Charlie, I've got it under control. I'm a one woman posse."

I leave the office and hit the road. I drive slowly, in widening circles, looking for an abandoned golf cart, using Leisure World as ground zero. The summer light bleaches the palmettos a pale green. Their fronds shake like feathers in the hot breeze. Heat refracts off the pavement in prismatic waves. It's a fry-an-egg-on-the-sidewalk kind of day. I hope the old man is inside somewhere cool, sipping on a lemonade and regaling an audience with tales of his youth. He can remember exactly what he was doing on August 3, 1939 at 10:17 a.m. Probably tarpon fishing, hauling in a sixty pounder after a lengthy battle or so the story would go like he was Ernest Hemingway himself.

I clench my teeth in frustration as time passes. I need something for direction. As I circle the section of town called Alphabetville, because the streets have letters for names instead of numbers, I pause in front of the *Inkspot* tattoo parlor. They know me well.

There's a parking space right out front, as if it were waiting for me. I get out of the car and peer into the front widow. Rosie is inside. She's a wonderful artist. I helped her with a grant to mount a show at Southernmost featuring tattoo artists of America. The opening night was a live exhibit of fantastic human canvases striking poses. The rest were photos. Some were accompanied by flat screen videos of work in progress, others by traditional works of art. She hung a photo of my willow tree tattoo next to a painting attributed to the Japanese painter, Hokusai.

I open the glass door and a chime sounds as I step onto the floor mat. "I know what I want on my back now," I tell Rosie as I head into her workroom, thankful that it's empty of customers. "A compass rose like that one, over your desk, between my shoulder blades." The decision feels like a great relief.

Rosie snaps on her gloves and pulls up a mask. I lay flat on her worktable with my back bare, my small breasts pressed against the white paper sheet. She traces the pattern between my shoulders. I leave my body as she works, pricking the skin quickly. I feel nothing. Three colors and the black outline. Blue and green for sea and sky and a red-petalled rose in the center. The black is crucial. It holds even if the colors fade over the decades. The shape and form will prevail.

Heat spreads across my back instead of pain or maybe the heat is the pain or the pain is the heat and that's part of my life in Florida. The two blur. Each prick appears behind my closed eyes as a neon green, a virtual Milky Way. I see Grandpa, his white hair glowing, driving his golf cart like a rocket ship through space. His hair grows longer and longer and flows behind him, the white mane of a comet burning, growing larger and brighter. Then he explodes.

When Rosie is done, she taps my shoulder, wakes me up, brings me back to the here and now and the mission at hand. I'll be O.K. With the new tattoo I'll be able to stay on track, locate Gramps and get back to my real/unreal life. I sway between the two, a woman in motion. *Poetry in motion* – the song that I used to think said *Oh, a tree in motion.* I imagined an oak tree doing the electric slide, a magnolia doing the bump and grind.

Hours earlier: The white-haired gentleman spots a billboard alongside Hwy. 51. It shows a woman in orange short shorts with a tight white t-shirt stretched across her ample bosom. One hand poised on her hip. Red painted pouting lips. *Hooters make you happy,* the advertisement suggests.

A mile later another board proclaims *Gentlemen, Truck-in here. Totally naked ladies. Stylish. The A-one All-Nite Truckers Club.* Gentlemen – the word captures his attention.

The white haired gentleman pulls up in front of the club in a golf cart. He parks it half on the grass, half on the broad expanse of the gravel lot then swings his legs sideways and looks around. It's 10 a.m. and there are only two other cars in its emptiness – a rusted out pickup truck and a 1970s vintage Cadillac.

He pauses a moment to catch his breath before dismounting from the cart. He totters towards the door assisted by a cane, the knob of which is a wild boar's head with its teeth bared. He rubs the tarnished metal with his fingers as he approaches the entryway, a screened door surrounded by red Christmas lights that burn all year.

It's a long walk and he's panting when he reaches it. His shirt is damp and wrinkled, much to his consternation. "What will the ladies think," he says out loud. "I'm a gentleman of leisure, a proper lady's man. A gentlemen's club. That's for me." He wishes he had brought along his bottle of *Canoe,* in order to mask the smell of sweat and mesmerize the ladies. He removes a pink silk handkerchief from the pocket of his shirt, dabs the perspiration from his brow. He stuffs it back into the pocket, his hands shaking all the while.

"C'mon on in, Pops," a burly man at the door holds it open for him. The man is enormous and the white haired gentleman can barely squeeze in past him. The place is dark and it takes a moment for his eyes to adjust to the dim light. There's a stage in the center of the room with several poles on it. Tables are set around its four sides, covered with extra long tablecloths. Colored lights swirl and a silver disco ball rotates over the stage. A tall lithe woman without any clothes on is winding her body around one of the poles. Her oiled flesh shines, light bouncing off of it. She throws back her head, her long hair touching her behind as she wiggles it seductively at two men who are seated at two separate tables. Her eyes are focused on something far away. She repeats her moves over and over, methodically. The men sit far apart from each other, one hand under the tablecloth, making barely audible grunting noises, eyes transfixed on the stage, a glass of beer warming in front of each of them.

A waitress sits slouched on a stool at the bar in a darkened corner. She has on only a g-string. Tasseled pasties hang from the nipples of her sagging breasts. Pointy high-heeled shoes pinch her feet. Her buttocks spread on the plastic of the padded barstool. There's a barely visible scar running across her abdomen buried along the top of her pubic hair. She's examining her fingernails, looking for chips in their neon pink paint. She nibbles the corner of one with her teeth. The day shift is the poorest of work. Few patrons and fewer tips. Salty dogs instead of sugar daddies. Two more months of this and she'll go crazy, she thinks.

The white-haired gentleman stops and looks around, confused. He's never been in such an establishment. But he was invited to enter so he must belong here. He expects there to be a folded card with his name on it sitting next to a rose in a vase on one of the tables. He can barely see anything. The silvery flashing lights look yellow and dim.

The bartender leans over the bar and flicks a damp towel at the waitress, catching her on her rump. "Go on, seat the gentleman, Margie." She scowls over her shoulder at him, sighs, and returns to examining her nails. He growls at her. "Go on, get your lazy ass moving. This could be your lucky day. He looks like a hot one."

She slides off the stool, stretches a bit and shakes her breasts. The tassels swing as she wobbles across the floor on her three-inch spikes.

"Good morning, Pops." She put an arm through his. "Let me find you a good seat. We got a couple left, I think." She leans against him and he can feel her flesh through the dampness of his shirt. A young woman's breast. Emotions he thought were gone surface. He wants to touch her. "Frances," he murmurs under his breath as she leads him to a table opposite where the other gentlemen are seated.

"Nope. I'm Margie. Thoroughly Modern Margie. My Daddy used to call me that. He don't call me much of anything now." She pouts her lips, pulls out a chair and helps him lower himself into it. "There you go, Pops. I'll bring you whatever you desire. We got some good specials." She hands him a printed sheet, steps back and swings the tassels fastened to her breasts for effect, smiling with what she hopes is a seductive smile.

"Honey, I can't see much in this light. Why don't you read them to me?"

She doesn't like to read the menu out loud, but some men require it. It stimulates them and they tip better, so she starts. "We got a Blow Job Gin Fizz, a 36-26-36 Tequila Temptation, a Black and Tan Two on One, a

Scotch Foreplay, a Tongue Job with a Tall Shot, a Lap Dance Daiquiri and a Whatever your Heart Desires."

Margie leans forward suggestively, squeezing her breasts together. They rise a little bit. She licks her lips, which are red and glossy. She smells musky and he wants her to stay just like that forever. That's what his heart desires. A suspended moment, time frozen. He recalls a younger self before his wife, Frances, died. She was so young when she was taken from him. She never had to grow old. Forever young, in his mind. He wonders what she'll think of him when they're reunited in heaven. Her being so young while he's become a cranky old man. Maybe she's even met someone else up there, a younger man, someone more suave, more debonair, more considerate. A deep breath slides out of his lips.

"That last one, the heart's desire, sounds right - whatever it is."

Two hours and several drinks later the lights swirl faster. Margie serves him again. She places another drink on the table and faces him, straddling his legs. He can barely breathe. She opens the top of her G-string and wants him to push the bills in there, against the damp curls of her dark brown pubic hair. His heart is thwacking against his ribs as he slips a $50 bill between the skimpy material and her skin. His fingers linger a moment. "Do you want more?" she asks.

He fumbles with his wallet and extracts another $50. "More?" she asks pressing down on his fingers, touching her breasts to the starch of his shirt and rubbing. This is better than she has done all week. She starts to feel giddy. She'll make her rent and then some today, she senses. This guy is primed.

I head out on the road again. The steering wheel sweats under my hands in spite of the A/C. Unless Grandpa's driven right into a lagoon or had a horrific crash, I'll find him. I'm certain. The newly minted compass rose on my back aches. I sit forward so that the gauze protecting the tattoo doesn't press against the back of the seat. I imagine an imprint of it on the cushion, with its sixteen sharp points, the North marker a bit larger than the rest, pointing towards heaven.

I turn north on Hwy. 51 and try not to slow traffic too dreadfully as I peer between each building and glance down the side streets. The other drivers, swerve around me, probably thinking I'm another disoriented senior. One man gives me the finger as he floors his sleek Caddy past my ancient Chevy Nova. I pat my car's dashboard reassuringly while I scan both sides of the highway. No offense taken.

Long shadows crisscross the shoulder of the road when I finally spot what I'm looking for – an empty golf cart sitting haphazardly at the edge of a parking lot at a gentlemen's club. I pull into the lot and kill the engine. For a moment I sit with my head on the steering wheel. I can barely stand to walk into this kind of place. When grandpa lived with us, Mom used to send me into bars to make him come home. I hated it, but I couldn't argue with Mom. It was an errand that my mother used to do when she was a little girl and she couldn't do it anymore. I imagine a long line of little girls, stretching back to some pre-Dickensian era, sent into bars to retrieve stray men.

When I went into those dives, they smelled like urine and liquor, as if the men still pissed into a trough underneath the bar so they could continue to drink without missing a beat the way they used to a century earlier. I'd find him and he would be seated at the bar, the center of attention, proclaiming this and that with authority, waving a gold-ringed hand in the air. Never with his arm around a woman, although he'd have some held in rapt attention listening to his tales. Gramps wanted to be king, or emperor, the biggest man south of the Mason-Dixon line. He was sure he had royal blood, hidden somewhere in a forgotten family archive when actually we were as plain as dirt. Probably some great-great grandparent came over in steerage from one of those villages that are referred to variously as being in the Austro-Hungarian Empire, Poland, the Russian Empire, or Slovakia - some little Podunk place in Eastern Europe.

I shake my head and steel myself, remembering that I am in the here and now, not the way back then. I'm not a little girl, or even a girl, but a longtime grown up woman. I imagine my mother in heaven looking down and I sigh. "Here it goes, Ma – rounding up the stray doggy." I should have gotten my masters degree in Art History and Elder Care combined - two creative fields.

I walk slowly towards the unopened door. It's a private club. They can refuse admission to whomsoever they chose. A man, a large lumbering beefy sort of fellow, steps out and blocks my path.

"Gentlemen's club, ma'am. Don't think you be wanting to go on in there. I can redirect you up the road a piece, if you like, to a good place for ladies." His huge form keeps me from seeing inside the establishment. I calculate quickly, which to use, charm or authority. I decide to split the difference.

"Family emergency, sir. My grandpa's needed back home. Mom's in bad straits. Needs him to come quickly." I'm sure my Mom would be in bad straits too, if she could see this scene. I tilt my head and stifle a choking sob.

He frowns. I know that his job description is to turn me away, empty handed. But he's Southern. Can't resist a lady in distress. He thrusts his chin forward as he thinks. Slowly. I try to look teary-eyed and helpless. Most of my tattoos aren't visible. They wouldn't help with this charade. The bouncer's face softens a degree or two. I know I've won.

"Suppose I could deliver some such message, if you be looking for this la-de-da white haired gentleman, dressed up pretty fine. Been here some time now, most of the day in fact. Rode in on that there cart that's sitting crooked, parked over that-a-way."

I fumble in my purse for a pen and write a quick cryptic note on a crumpled scrap of paper, signing it Suzy-Q. I tell the bouncer that I'll wait in my car if he'd be kind enough to escort Grandpa out.

The temperature is cooling as twilight sets in and from miles and miles away a salty breeze blows, suggesting the promise of water. When I smell that ocean air, I feel the motion of its waves and the tide. Something alive that never sleeps. A constant. It's what keeps me here, in Florida, floating in amniotic fluids.

A few minutes later, the door opens. A woman walks out tugging at a trench coat wrapped around herself. She yanks at a belt, cinching it, and frowning. Her plucked eyebrows form pleats above her nose as she squints and looks about the parking lot. She spots me, clenches her fists, and heads across the gravel toward my car teetering on her high-heeled shoes. Her ankle turns. She stumbles, dropping to the ground, howling.

I jump out of the car to help her. The ankle is already swelling when I reach her. The cheap plastic heel has snapped off of one shoe. "Damn, damn, damn," she curses rocking back and forth, sobbing. Mascara cascades down her cheek.

The woman's coat is gaping opened and I realize that she is close to naked underneath it. Just then the bouncer arrives with Grandpa in tow.

Grandpa startles when he sees me. "Frances," he says. "What are you doing here?" He takes a step backwards. I try not to look confused and touch my face to assure myself of my identity.

"My wife," he explains to the bouncer.

"Whore!" the trench coat woman hisses at me. Her teeth are lipstick stained. Her eyes are red from crying. The whole scene comes into focus. There's only one graceful way out of this one.

"Harold," I cry and fling myself at Gramps. I've never called him by his first name before now. "Harold, I've been waiting all day for you, darling.

Come home now." I turn to the bouncer who is staring at me. He's spotted the tattoo winding up my exposed leg. Let him stare. "I'm so sorry to have bothered you. You've been a peach, my husband and I are ever so grateful. We'll get the cart later." I hand him a folded twenty. He shoves it into his pocket without looking at the denomination.

He jerks the injured woman to her feet and herds her back, towards the club. She limps along still sniffling.

I take Gramps by the arm and lead him to my car. I open the door, bow slightly, and gesture for him to enter. He kisses my cheek with boozy breath, slides into the car and shuts his eyes. Already lost in a dream. I leave my hand a moment on his shoulder and see a young man sitting there with a broken heart, a young man with thick brown wavy hair, bowing his head. His chest aches and he is clenching it to hide the wound, to close up the spot where people can see in. My own chest flutters and aches.

"I love you, Harold," I tell him, meaning every word.

"I love you too, Frances," he says softly, opening his eyes for one moment.

JEANNE SIROTKIN splits her time between the Detroit Area and Traverse City. A Motor City native, she lived in San Francisco, Colorado, and Texas before returning to Michigan. Her work has appeared in the *Cimarron Review, Chattahoochee Review, Arcade, The Northville Review, This is Women's Work, 14 Voices – Other Voices Press, Freeze Frame Annual, Tule Review*, and *Wordworks*. She also has a chapbook *An Unzipped Dress* from Golden Mountain Press.

www.ingramcontent.com/pod-product-compliance
Lightning Source LLC
Chambersburg PA
CBHW030637120726
47904CB00006B/2181